Dead'er

Roger R. Blenman

Hamilton Books

An Imprint of
Rowman & Littlefield
Lanham • Boulder • New York • Toronto • Plymouth, UK

Copyright © 2015 by Hamilton Books
4501 Forbes Boulevard, Suite 200, Lanham, Maryland 20706
Hamilton Books Aquisitions Department (301) 459-3366

Unit A, Whitacre Mews, 26-34 Stannary Street,
London SE11 4AB, United Kingdom

Library of Congress Control Number: 2014949725
ISBN: 978-0-7618-6482-0 (paper : alk. paper)—ISBN: 978-0-7618-6483-7 (electronic)

∞™ The paper used in this publication meets the minimum requirements of American National Standard for Information Sciences Permanence of Paper for Printed Library Materials, ANSI/NISO Z39.48-1992.

Lye'ver: The usual state of a human person, male or female. Someone able to eat, or grow, or feel a touch on their skin. Say it like you would say alive. Alive-er. —N.P.H.

Dead'er: A strange situation to find oneself in. —N.P.H.

What happens to
an abandoned library?

E.B. White said,
"a book is a garden, an orchard,
a storehouse, a party,
a company by the way, a counsellor,
a multitude of counsellors."

What happens then to
to books abandoned?

Surely those stories still long
to be shared.
Do books long for a new owner?
Seeking one by happenstance
or serendipity?

Just such a case has brought
this book to you.
This book was once one of thousands
in a collection owned by one Irene P.

Who she was is a story yet to be written.
This volume from her abandoned library
now belongs to you.
May it inspire,
entertain and astound,
but most of all, may it rest well,
cherished in your library.

Delta Literary Arts Society 2023

Contents

Chapter One

A "Vacation without Regret"

A BEACH IN MEXICO, NOVEMBER 2008

It was the second last day of his vacation before Sean was sure what he was seeing. It was so plain this time that Sean wondered how he had ever doubted that they were messages. But there it was, in the detritus just at the high water mark. In bits of driftwood, scraps of a few types of seaweed—mostly stems and fronds, and odd bits of rope made from some sort of fibre—a word was spelt out: HASTING.

His memory was not to be trusted. When he got back to the hotel he tore off a piece of stationary from the little pad on the desk. The paper was watermarked with the name of the hotel and some poorly worded slogan rhyming fun and sun. When the pen did not write at first, he was scared that he would forget the words, especially now that he was determined to uncover their meaning. He alternately shook the pen and scratched its tip in circles on the note pad. In a few moments it started to leave blue ink on the paper.

He put down all the words in order: NOBLE—from his first morning on the beach. He had been shaking off a tiny bit of jetlag and the fatigue of the cramped flight from Vancouver, walking aimlessly up the still deserted strip of sand in front of the low rise of the hotel building. He saw the word but had not believed it. Who would bother to spell out a word in sand? Children? A pair of lovers?—possibly: he had seen couples in the lobby while he checked in, and later in the dining room while he had worked through a meal of some kind of fish and rice. It could be someone's name—just the sort of thing a lover would do: spell out a paramour's name on the sand. But what kind of name was Noble? And there was no heart encircling it. No, "together forever" written underneath. He was upset for a moment because no one had ever written anything like that about him, in the sand or otherwise. Maybe he was even more upset that he had no one to write about and no one who would have been pleased to see it. Then he remembered that this was to be the "Vacation without Regret." He was not to regret a minute of it, even if he met no one at the bar or the pool. It was good not to have expectations, he figured, even if the travel catalogue had been filled with pictures of smiling, youngish women in scanty swimwear.

On his first evening at the resort, Sean went to the Welcome Party. The walls were decorated with palm trees made of shiny green foil. Inflated flamingos swung from several of the light fixtures. A few had lost their air and hung like pink ribbons. Hostesses in long colourful skits and bare mid-riffs walked through the crowd offering complimentary drinks in tiny plastic cups shaped like cut open coconut shells. Sean spotted a couple of girls whose wristbands were the same colour as his.

"So you guys are here on the all-inclusive package too!" Sean hoped that he had not sounded over eager.

One of the girls looked at Sean and nodded hello, then she turned back to her friend. Sean smiled at the back of her head for a moment before moving on.

He tried speaking to other girls but the only ones who responded were carrying trays of tiny cups.

"These are really fruity," Sean grinned at one of the coconut drink carrying girls, "I wonder what's in them?"

The girl smiled and offered Sean another half shell.

Sean decided that he liked coconut, and whatever else was in the drink. "Maybe it's pineapple." Sean approached another of the coconut drink carrying girls. "Is this pineapple?" Sean pointed into the tiny cup. The bar was noisy and Sean hoped that he was not shouting but he could not be sure.

When Sean woke up there was a drill pressing into each of his ears, and a knot that felt like a tumour growing in the middle of his head: something pressing out his eyes from the inside. He was dizzy on the way to the bathroom. After urinating—he was sure most of it hit the bowl—he lay down again, and slept until it was time to head down for the dinner buffet.

PARCH—from the third morning. He was up and out early trying to pick the best of the beach chairs for himself. Each chair had an attached umbrella and a place in both armrests for drinks. He wanted to get a chair that would allow him to watch both the pool and the ocean—there was no telling which would have the better view later in the morning, when the rest of the hotel guests, including the women, came out for the day's tanning.

He did not believe that Parch at first, not even being sure that it was a word. The P caught his eye and he might have thought it only an interesting arrangement of seaweed if it were not for the r that he saw a little further on, made of what might have been broken bits of shells and driftwood. Then he teased out the form of an angular h in a half dozen more pieces of driftwood that were nearly buried under a mess of seaweed and wet sand. From that point it was only a few minutes until he deciphered what could only be the round stokes of a script a and then the shallow curve of a c, one between each of the first three letters he had found. He wrote the letters over, carving their simple shapes into the sand with a piece of driftwood that did not seem to be part of the word. It was sometime before he recognized Parch. He was thinking at last of the process of writing fancy words on fancy paper when the word parchment came to him. He looked at the letters again, wondering if the -ment was hidden in the beach litter to the right of the letters he had already deciphered—the very pile of material from which he had drawn the driftwood to rewrite P-a-r-c-h in the clean sand high above the water mark. Suppose he had destroyed the -ment in that careless moment. Maybe the -ment was meant to be part of the word. Maybe there was no word at all.

The next morning Sean took the special bus tour, "included" in his vacation package. He left the hotel early, marshalled out of the lobby and onto the bus by an efficient hotel tour guide in a bright blouse of local design. Despite the promise of her clothing, once the tour got underway he was disappointed to realize that her accent was American and that her commentary was being read off the clipboard she held like a barrier between herself and the young man in the front seat. Himself.

The tour bus also had about a dozen couples, of various ages, including a male couple who held hands only while on the bus, and who wore matching T-shirts, of a design he had seen in the hotel gift shop. There was also a gaggle of seniors, most of whom sat at the back of the bus, slouched like teenagers. Whenever the group disembarked, at a market or historic site, they complained loudly that the country was simply too hot. Then back on the bus they complained again: the air conditioning was set too cold. Sean found the trip interesting however, particularly an imposing church and its adjoining mission complex, both historically and architecturally significant according to the American guide in her vivid blouse. The passengers were allowed off the bus to explore the area around the brilliant whitewashed buildings. Sean was glad he had bothered to wake up early enough to take the tour.

The following morning was when he found Hasting. He thought at first that the word might have been Haste but the bright bit of coiled fibre rope he spotted a little distance above the jumble of detritus seemed like nothing other than the dot of an i. Perhaps the dot of a j but he knew that there were no words spelt H-a-s-t-j-. Similarly what he took for a t might, given the way the piece of seaweed lay across the driftwood, have been an x. But he was not going to let ambiguous lettering get in the way of the obvious: he was receiving a message, one word at a time, and this day's word was Hasting. This was the day he wrote the three words down on the complimentary hotel stationery and puzzled over them as he lay on the beach. Several times that day he took the paper out of the tiny pocket in the waist band of his swim trunks, unfolded it and tried to rearrange the words into something that made sense. Noble Haste-ing? Parch(ed) Noble. Noble Parch(ment). Haste, Noble (find the) Parch(ment)! Sean wondered if he himself was the noble referred to.

A break might help, he thought, to clear his mind. He thought of splashing out into the ocean, maybe going far enough to let the water reach his neck, but he resisted, not wanting to wash off the sun-blocking lotion and have to go into his hotel room to reapply. If he did so he would lose this perfectly located beach chair that he had come out early in the morning to claim.

On his last full day at the resort Sean did not go out to the beach until the morning was well underway. All the chairs on the stretch of sand between the pool and ocean were taken. There were, fortunately, a few empty chairs left further up the beach. These, although not in the first rows closest to the water, had a good view of the ocean. Sean thought to himself, that, given the events of the morning, it was good thing that he could not see, or be seen, from the poolside hotel entrance. It's all worked out ok, Sean reasoned after he calmed down. This was to be the "Vacation without Regret," and it was going to be, he determined. The messages in the sand were a bonus. Sean suddenly realized that in the excitement of the morning he had not looked on the beach for the day's word. It was too late now to do so now. The stretch of sand in front of the hotel had already been churned over by dozens of feet. Any driftwood thrown onto the shore in the night, even if it had once been arranged by unknown forces into a message for him, was now reinforcing the walls of some sand castle or providing a convenient drawbridge to lay across a sand-lined moat.

It was too hot a day to think. It was a day to lie back in the beach chair, maybe brave a bit more sun than he had all week, pass his final afternoon in Mexico before heading home to Vancouver the following morning.

Noble:

I haven't been rolled up in years. Rolling up was what kept us Dead'ers going—without getting rolled up every once in a while we fade down. To fade down is to get weaker and weaker. What's worse, is that when you fade down your haunt gets smaller. I remembered when I could wander miles across the city. Now my haunt was down to one building.

There was nothing I could do about it really—just wait and hope for a Stringer to come along and roll me up. I had been waiting for years when

Sean moved into my haunt. Sean didn't seem to have any idea what he could do, but I needed him to know. He was a Stringer, and a good one. And by good, I meant strong.

Sean wasn't my first Stinger. Years ago, each morning for weeks I stuck leaves against the bedroom window of one Stringer who lived in a house in my haunt. Every morning when he got up, the first thing he did was look out his bedroom window, before peeing or wiping the sleep-foam out of the edges of his eyes. And there on the window every morning, was a letter I had left, as plain as when you make a dog bark by screeching in his ears. And he never once spelled anything out. I wrote out my whole name a letter every day. Nothing. Then I tried his name, a letter at a time, figuring he'd recognize that at least, and we would get the whole process of messaging started. Nothing. Then I hit a payload of an idea. I squeezed his initials on the window, written out in dead leaves, figuring that even the densest Stringer ought to be able to pick that out of the ordinary. It took me all night to get both letters fitted in. I jumped in and out of the house to make sure it looked right from the inside of his bedroom, which is of course the direction from where he would see it in the morning. It worked. It really worked. He read the letters aloud and even laughed a bit to himself. The next morning I started in on my name. N-O. That was a far as I got. I ran out of leaves. It was only November so there should have been lots of leaves around still. But there weren't any I could find in my haunt, just one or two that the rakers and street sweepers had missed, not enough for a Purging letter. I was snickered for anything moveable that I could work up off the ground to spell out a message. I can only move dead things—things like me, leaves, and if I was stronger, bits of wood too.

That Stringer was gone before the next fall. He turned off or moved or something. And I started ghosting for a few years, fading down and down the whole time. Then Sean moved into my haunt. Knocking!

When Sean got back from his vacation I'll admit I was a little bit impatient to see how much of the message he got. You wouldn't believe what I had to promise to do get Pedro to put all that driftwood and seaweed into the shapes of letters. The seaweed was the easy part he told me. It's newly dead itself and so doesn't mind so much being bent to the will of something other than the waves and the winds. It must be like the leaves here in Vancouver then, in the fall at least. I figured that if I wanted to, I could spell out entire sentences with them. Not that anyone would have noticed. No matter how fresh you were, you could only move a few at a time, and then the wind could still pick them up again once you've put them down, all nice and neat in letters. There were always hundreds more leaves that could fall on top of, or in between the ones you've laid out, so it's nearly hopeless trying to get a message to anyone that way.

Sean slept the first day back from his vacation. He just curled up and lay in the bed the whole day. I almost envied him a bit. The way he could just zone everything out and sleep like—well, a Lye'ver would say—like a baby. Lye'vers ought to know better than to say that. Even they can see that a baby almost never sleeps at peace. He's always full of thoughts of hunger, or fear, or loneliness, or the need to crap. And he has no idea what's going on. He doesn't know what he's lonely for, or that loneliness is the bad feeling that goes away when he sucks on his mother's teat—because his hunger and boredom go away at exactly the same time. And taking a crap hurts a bit. You can see it on his face. I'm guessing at all this. It's not like we Dead'ers have insight into what a baby thinks. We have to read it off his face just like we have to do with any Lye'ver, or any Stringer for that matter.

That evening Sean got up, went to the bathroom, and then microwaved something out of the freezer. He ate it and then played with himself a bit. He did that lots while watching that woman detective on TV.

I got sick of waiting. I reached out to Pedro. It wasn't as hard to do as it might have been. He was probably reaching out to me at the same time. Or he was getting stronger. He must have a really good Stringer. Purging lucky ghost.

"¡Hola!"

"Hola, yourself gringo." Pedro's English was pretty good even if his accent was nearly impenetrable at times. He got to listen to lots of tourists. I got any Spanish I knew ghosting over people's shoulders at textbooks or peeping in while they watched foreign movies. Neither opportunity was very common in my haunting.

"¿Coma-est-ta?" I tried.

"Bueno," Pedro replied. "And knock it off. You know about as much Spanish as your Stringer. And he got his face slapped on his last day here."

"What happened?" I liked my Stringer but sometimes Sean did some things that made me wonder if he hadn't been dropped on his head as a baby.

"Look, I haven't got much time. My Stringer is going to leave my haunt and head home for Christmas. I'm trying to get her to roll me up a bit before she goes."

I shivered at the way Pedro could roll an r. I wished for a moment that my Stringer were Spanish.

"Why don't you go with her?"

"Mi amigo. Nobody is that strong. You'd need a busload of Stringers to tag along—everyone chanting your name. And who gets that anymore?"

Pedro was funny, the way he talked sometimes like he knew so much. I had to tell him most of what he knows about being a Dead'er. He was stronger when he was fresh—newly dead, but stupid, or naïve really. Not stupid. He figured out pretty quickly not to go too far out of his haunt, or that not all Stringers can be trusted. Or all Dead'ers either. Some Dead'ers are Purging ghosts.

Pedro got to the point, "I got him to say it!"

"Knockers! You did? What did he say? What?"

"Slow down Noble. You sound like an Irishman when you're excited. What do you think I got him to say?"

"My name?"

"Noble Hasting." When Pedro said my name the vowels went south for the winter and the h disappeared altogether.

"But that's not my full name."

"¡Dios! It's close enough," said Pedro.

"You think it is?"

"Did you feel like you rolled up at all this week?"

The thing every ghost wants is to roll up. It makes you stronger, better able to move things, and best of all, it makes you feel like a real person—for a while.

"I don't know," I said. "Do you think it works outside of my haunting?"

"You're asking me? You're the one who talks to all those old Dead'ers. Not me. I don't want anything to do with them. Most of them are creepy."

Pedro was right; many of the old Dead'ers seemed to want to spend their time frightening Stringers half to death. It seemed pointless to me, except that it probably kept the old Dead'ers rolled up. Half to death: ha ha ha! It would serve them right, killing off a Stringer and then having to share a haunt with him.

"Listen Noble," said Pedro, "I have to go. Your Stringer has your name on a little piece of paper. Well maybe not your full name. He missed your middle name altogether the first time I wrote it, and he got the letters all wrong the second time. I wrote Petros but he got something else."

"It's Peter, not Petros!" I almost shouted at Pedro.

"¡Dios! Close enough! And he didn't get either. When I wrote your last name he pulled apart de esss before he read it. But it's close enough, yes?" Pedro was sounding fainter. Maybe the reaching out was costing him strength he'd rather spend some other way.

"Thanks Pedro. I should let you go."

"Yes. It's about time. One more thing about the paper with your name on it: he kept it in his pocket when he was here."

"That's great news!"

"So it is: until he does his laundry."

Pedro was very practical. That was one of the things I liked about him.

"Goodbye. Thank you again."

"Adiós amigo." He said his goodbye in the sort of accent you'd have if you didn't really know any Spanish. He knew he was being cliché but it was funny despite that, or because of that. I'm not sure which.

I've never seen Pedro of course; our haunts are too far apart. He's been haunting the beach resort for years. In many ways he must have still been the teenager he was when he drowned there. When I pictured him I saw shaggy dark hair and big brown eyes—intelligent but sensitive eyes. I thought he would be broad shouldered but not too muscular, more like a soccer player than a football player. He definitely didn't have a swimmer's build. I knew that that was a bad joke but I loved grave humour. I got the feeling that I shouldn't make a joke like that with Pedro. He still wasn't ready for it. Not even after years. I knew he missed his parents. And that's one of the reasons why he kept trying to roll up and one of the reasons that he was always so willing to help anyone out. I don't think what he had planned was a good idea. He could not know if his parents were Stringers or not. And even if they were Stringers and could hear him what did he plan to say to them? And what would they want to say to him: we missed you son? Of course they did. What would he bring them besides fresh pain?

Chapter Two

Trouble Is Sure to Find Those Who Run from It

Lucky Numbers 45, 62, 21, 11, 15

Sean disliked his building's laundry. It stank of mould. Once Sean found what he was sure were rat feces in a dryer lint trap. He scooped them out with some sheets of fabric softener—a waste of a couple perfectly good sheets. Sean complained, but the fat oaf of a building manager just shrugged, "Probably just bits of dirt!" he laughed. Then he scratched at his underarm. "Or more likely, chocolate."

Sean wished he had saved some of the droppings. He pictured himself shaking out the sheet of fabric softener over a warm bowl of oatmeal and then offering the steaming bowl to the manager. "There you go, breakfast," Sean smiled, "with chocolate sprinkles!"

Narrow and poorly ventilated, the laundry room was an afterthought, installed long after the building was constructed. The building itself was old. Sean was not sure how old but he knew that it had started out as something else and had been converted to apartments in the fifties, or sixties, or some decade like that. The rooms were odd shapes and sizes. The door to his suite led into his one real room, a combination living room/bedroom. He had a couch with a foldout bed but he seldom put the bed away—only when he had company and those occasions were infrequent. Sean also owned a chair, a small bookshelf, a low table, and a TV. From the main room, a doorway to the right led to the narrow, windowless, kitchen/eating area. On the far side of that room was the door to the peculiarly oversized bathroom. The bathroom, however, had only a tiny window and this window was stuck part way open because someone had painted over the window, its frame, and the walls with a thick coat of glossy pink. Where the paint was chipped, a plain white showed underneath.

Sunday mornings Sean liked to strap on his digital watch. In addition to the chronograph (Sean preferred the fancier term for stopwatch), date, and time features, the watch also had a countdown function. Practice had brought Sean to his most efficient laundry day routine: ten minutes to find and pack up his dirty clothes. If he were more than a few seconds over this mark, he scolded himself for having thrown his clothes too carelessly on the floor. Two minutes to lift the suitcase of dirty clothes down the stairs and out to the square of sidewalk in front of his building. Eight minutes walk from there to the Laundromat. Plus one minute allowed if safely crossing the street required that he wait for the light to change. One minute, firm, to load the washing machine. Twenty minutes wash. Three minutes for the transfer to the dryer. Only fifty-nine minutes to wait while his clothes remained in the dryer. (The display claimed sixty minutes but he had timed it himself with the chronograph.) Two minutes to empty the dryer, and repack the suitcase. Seven minutes walk back to the apartment. (Why it was shorter going home was a mystery to Sean.) Three minutes back up to the apartment. On a good day the whole thing was accomplished in less than two hours. Sean would empty the clothes onto his bed and spend another hour or so, putting only a little of his attention to folding his clothes and much more to watching TV.

Sunday morning after his return from Mexico, Sean gathered his laundry. There were some good memories from the trip, he decided. There was sand in his swimming trucks. He held them up and started to flick them. As he did so a slip of paper fell out and floated, like leaf, towards the ground. It looked for a moment as if its flight would take it under the bed, but just before landing, the slip changed direction. It flew up again, as if caught in a breeze. The paper floated out into the middle of the room, hovered for a moment, and then dropped directly onto the low table. Sean noticed none of this.

Wednesday, Sean had Chinese food: take out. At 7 pm he took his feet off the table and placed the half empty food containers in their place.

"Where's the remote?" He rummaged in the chair he was sitting in. Then the bed. Then he saw the remote on top of the TV. He fetched it and sat back down, clicking away from the news till the TV was on the channel that broadcast *her* show.

And there she was.

She did not look very pretty in the opening sequence. The first time she appeared she had her blonde hair tied back in something like a ponytail. The camera lingered on her profile for only a moment as she held up a microscope slide or something to the light and peered at it through safety glasses. Then the scene cut away to the others: her partner, a taller, handsome, but tough-looking man; their boss, a slightly older woman, nicely built, but who always wore a business suit—so one ever got a good look at her assets; and their research guy, an awkward young man whose ears stuck out and who always had on a lab coat. Then the camera returned to her. This time she had her hair down. This time she was beautiful. Her hair brushed her shoulders gently, like slow motion waves of silk thread, like gossamer sheets of spun gold, like a soft rain of precious yellow petals—as she whipped a snub-barrelled gun from behind her back and yelled: V.P.D! Freeze douche bag!

The TV cut to a commercial.

Sean searched the takeout containers for the fortune cookie. "Best part of the whole frigging meal," he mouthed to himself. His stomach felt uneasy. Sean found the cookie in the container that had held the spring rolls. He belched. He picked up the fortune cookie with two fingers. There was moisture inside its cellophane wrapping. Some soya sauce had seeped in through a tear. Sean pulled the wrapping apart. Half the biscuit was soggy.

"Egh, good enough," Sean mumbled and pulled open the biscuit. There were two pieces of paper inside. The first one read: Trouble is sure to find those who run from it. On the back of the rectangular slip of paper was a sequence of numbers, 45 62 21 11 15. Sean was not sure about the last two numbers since the ink had smudged. The last two numbers might have just as easily been 10 and 12, or 12 and 16. Sean crumpled the paper.

The commercials ended and the TV program restarted: she was on, kick boxing in some sort of gymnasium, a delicate ring of sweat along the low cut neck of a tight fitting top. But Sean saw none of it. The second piece of paper held three words: Noble Parch Hasting.

"Whoa!" Sean took his left hand out of his waistband and used both hands to carefully spread the paper out. "It's the frigging message again. From a frigging fortune cookie this time. Farts in a cup! I had forgotten about it." Sean suddenly realized that he had been blurting his thoughts aloud. The walls were thin in this building. If the neighbours heard him talking to himself again, they might think he was crazy. He turned the volume up on the TV.

Sean puzzled over the message. He grabbed his phone and did a quick Internet search. Nothing on "Noble Parch Hasting," nothing on "Noble Parch," but plenty on nobles signing a parchment. Sean did not think that that was it. Plenty of hits on "Hastings": Battle of Hastings 1066; Hastings Street, Vancouver. Plenty of hits on people named Hastings. Maybe Parch Hasting was a name. Sean said it over to himself a few times. "Parch Hasting. Parch Hasting." It was not anybody's name according to his search engine. What about "Noble Hasting." Sean said it over a few times. "Noble Hasting. Noble Hasting. Noble Hasting." It felt weird. No, it sounded weird. "What kind of dork-a-ding-dong name is Noble?" What would your mother call you when you were a baby? Nobly-woboly? Woboly-Nobly? Sean laughed out loud. It seemed cold in the room for a second or two.

Sean thought that he might go to the library on the weekend. That was where they went in the detective show when they wanted to figure something out; either that or they went to see the geeky guy in the lab, or the nerdy guy who spent all his time with computers. Sean thought and thought and came to the conclusion that he did not know anyone who fit either description. There was, however, Mandy in 3B.

Mandy looked smart. Not smart like the detective researcher on TV, but smart like, well, Sean was not sure how smart she was but he had noticed that she usually had a book or two with her with she came or left her apartment. He got this knowledge from occasionally, by chance, running into her as she walked up or down the stairs to or from her floor. These random meetings had taken place in the three months since she had moved into his building. Sean also knew her name from having accidentally taken her mail from the box next to his. It was an honest mistake of course. The lock on her mailbox had come open when he stuck his key in and wiggled it back and forth. The little door had swung open and the mail was in his hand almost before he realized that it was hers. He was truly sorry, so immediately after reading her name on an envelope he placed the mail back into the box, arranging the envelopes as if they had not been disturbed.

If the letter carrier should place her mail in among his, Sean thought, it would provide an opportunity for him to deliver them to her in person. But, Sean realized, knocking on her door might require more a bit more nerve that he had been able to gather so far.

By the time Sean had finished thinking about the message, and about Mandy, the detective show was long over. There was nothing good on the TV for the rest of the evening before Sean's bedtime. Regardless, he watched a couple of episodes, back to back, of a sitcom with a laugh track. It was about a family with a boatload of kids. The show was set in the family's living room, which was somehow where all the important conversations took place—never in the kitchen or the bedroom. The show was very unrealistic, thought Sean. In his own family all the important conversations had taken place in the kitchen: "Why is your report card so bad?" "Why don't you pick better friends?" "What are you going to do with your life?" And the really important arguments had taken place in his parent's bedroom. And he wished that there had been a laugh track. It might have helped.

Sean turned off the TV just after 10 pm. He did not like watching the news. Sean dropped his street clothes on the chair and picked up his pajamas off the bed. He put them on and marched through the kitchen to the bathroom. Halfway through brushing his teeth, Sean paused. There was something that the detectives did that he could do as well. To help solve a crime, they put everything up on a board: pictures, diagrams, notes, hunches: A Case-Solving Chart. Then they drew lines between things that might be connected, added in bits of evidence, circled key bits of information, facts.

Eventually someone, staring at the material on the chart, would have an insight that would "crack" the case. In a hurry all of a sudden, the team would scurry off to make an arrest: a "bust." Funny name for an arrest taking into account the assets of the female members of the team.

Sean pictured himself making such an elaborate diagram. He would draw a mesh of lines connecting shreds of evidence into some coherent scheme. Thoughtful analysis of the web of information would lead him to a sudden sharp insight. The message would lay plain. Deciphered. Obvious now once all the heavy thinking had been done.

Sean, toothbrush still in his mouth, looked around his apartment for a suitable place to start his Case-Solving chart. He needed a flat, uncluttered, well-lit surface. He dared not draw on the walls. The building manager had been clear about what was, and what was not allowed. The oaf had told Sean that he to ask permission to put pictures, posters, or anything on the walls at all. The fridge door was too small for what Sean had in mind. Discouraged, Sean returned to the bathroom to spit out the mouthful of toothpaste and saliva. He looked up from the sink. The bathroom mirror. Of course. The perfect spot. Sean pictured the elaborate diagram he would draw. Lines and circles around information, and arrows, and lists, and pictures, and, and, … in the end Sean had only two things to put on the bathroom mirror: the scrap of paper from the hotel on which he had written the words: Noble Parch Hasting; and the slip of paper from inside the fortune cookie with its half-smudged proverb: Trouble is sure to find those who run from it.

Sean peeled away the tape that held together the edges of a takeout food container and used it to stick the two slips of paper to the mirror. The rest of the container and the plastic bag he had carried it home in, he put in the recycling bin.

For the next three days, every time Sean looked in the bathroom mirror, he mouthed the words to himself. Sometimes he said them one after another. Sometimes he mixed the order up. Sometimes in frustration, the meaning of the words continuing to elude him, he half shouted them at the bathroom mirror. Sometimes after work he sat in his room in his underwear watching TV and, during commercial breaks, said the words aloud. Sometimes he mumbled the words between mouthfuls of takeout Chinese or Thai food. Once getting up in the middle of the night to pee he wrote the words as he said them, flicking the yellow stream back and forth to make the shapes of the letters in the toilet bowl.

Saturday after work, a few of the guys at the dealership were going to go for drinks at a pub in the east end of the city. For once Sean had been invited. Since most of the guys drove, Sean needed to move quickly if he were to arrive while the evening were still fresh. He got a ride home with one of his coworkers, said good-bye at the curb and bolted into his apartment. He had to get out of his work clothes, shower, and then jump on the bus heading east out of downtown.

Racing up the steps, Sean kept repeating the address to himself: Clarke Street and Hastings Street, northeast corner. Clarke and Hastings, northeast corner.

On the way up to his second floor apartment Sean passed Mandy from 3B who was heading down the stairs with a basket of laundry. Without pausing to think, he called out to her. "I wouldn't use the machines in the basement if I were you, Mandy—I found rat droppings in one of them a couple months ago—and the building manager is a fat oaf and won't do anything about it— but if you can hang on to your dirty panties till Sunday I can show you where there's great Laundromat not too far from here—and it only takes me one hour and fifty-five minutes, including travel time, as long as I fold my clothes back here on my bed, instead of there, because the tables there are so small."

"What?" asked Mandy.

"Laundromat—Sunday—with me!" said Sean. He was already well past her. "Oh it would probably take you ten minutes less since you already have your clothes stuffed into that little basket thing that you're carrying." He flung the words over his shoulder and disappeared through the door to the second floor hallway.

"When?" asked Mandy.

Sean's head reappeared briefly in the stairwell above her. "Anytime on Sunday," he said. "I'm in apartment 2D. It's almost directly below you but over one to the left." He disappeared.

"Where?" asked Mandy but Sean did not reappear.

Mandy continued down to the basement and then along the dimly lit hallway to the laundry room.

She decided that she would talk to the building manager. She did not like being harassed, or maybe even stalked, by one of neighbours, even if he were good-looking in an awkward sort of way.

Neither the basement hallway nor the laundry room were well lit. Mandy placed her basket down on top of a machine. Now that that guy on the stairs had mentioned it, the room did seem very poorly kept. It was worse than she remembered. Mandy could see cobwebs dangling from the ceiling in one of the corners. The room smelt of mould. A sudden cold seemed to flow by her face. Mandy shivered but in an instant the feeling had passed. She pulled open a dryer door and peered into its lint trap. The container was empty except for a few innocuous-looking tuffs of grey lint. Again, something cold seemed to brush by. Mandy's left ear was chilled briefly. Instantly, she thought of spiders and ran her fingers quickly through the hair on that side of her head.

"Creepy place," she said to herself, and began to swing dryer door shut. But now, scattered in the lint trap, were a half dozen dark pellets, each about the size of a grain of rice. Mandy slammed shut the dryer door. "EWWW!"

Sean floated into his apartment. The race up the two flights of stairs, and talking, actually talking, to Mandy from 3B had him flushed. Anything was possible. This was his night. He was the man. All hormones and adrenalin. Nothing to stop him from taking the pub by storm tonight. Wit, sex appeal, he had it all. He hoped that there would be women to flirt with once he got there.

Sean pushed the apartment door closed behind him and stripped on the way to the bathroom, dropping his work pants and shirt on the kitchen floor. "No time to waste," he thought.

Once in the shower he took his time soaping his underarms and then his feet, the two places that seemed to accumulate the worst odour while he worked.

"Clarke and Hastings here I come…"

It hit him. The revelation. The insight. The case-cracking break he had been waiting for since spelling out the words in the sand on the beach in front of the resort in Mexico. The message was a name. He had suspected that it was somebody's name but he had not got it right at all. The last word was not Hasting. It was Hastings, with an s. It was completely obvious now. The message was the name. There were plenty of guys named Noble. The Internet had told him that. What he had to do now was find out who this Noble Hastings was. Parch must Noble Hastings' middle name. That would probably be the key to finding the right Noble Hastings from the thousands out here. There were probably not very many Noble Parch Hastings in the world. Maybe only one. Sean felt a sudden chill. He turned the hot water up. "Noble Parch Hastings," he said again out loud and began to wash the soap out of his armpits.

"Unless," Sean suddenly shouted, "I got the middle name wrong too."

"Parches. Parted. Larch. Harch. Farch. Starch. No. Stick with P. Parch. Parcel. Purcel. Purl. Pearl. Parl. Paul. I got it. Noble Paul Hastings! That has to be the name. Now, what about the proverb from the fortune cookie?" Sean hummed to himself. "Trouble finds those … no that's not it." Sean stuck his head out of the shower and peered at the mirror. "No that wasn't it at all." He read the slip of paper carefully. "Trouble is sure to find those who run from it." Sean pulled his head back into the shower. "But I'm not running from trouble baby," he said. "No way. Not even if Noble Paul Hastings turns out to be … be what? What could be so special about Noble Paul Hastings," he asked himself. Sean lifted up a leg and began to rub the soap off his foot. Maybe the numbers on the back of the slip of paper from the fortune cookie held more answers. Sean leaned out of the shower. He did not want to put his freshly rinsed foot back down in the soapy water in the bottom of the bathtub. He looked at the distance to the slip of paper on the mirror and placed one hand on the edge of the smooth porcelain sink to steady himself. Reaching out with his left hand he just managed to grasp the fortune cookie proverb between two fingers. He pulled and the slip of paper came free from the bit of tape holding it the mirror.

Sean looked at the numbers and then turned the paper over and reread the fortune. He giggled, "Sometimes trouble is exactly what I want." He raised an eyebrow at his reflection in the mirror. He frowned. The mirror was fogged by the condensation from his shower. "The ladies deserve a better view; don't they?" Sean cleared a section of the mirror with his fist.

"Trouble with a T, ladies, is coming your way. T, T." Sean paused. "T … not Parch but Patch. Noble Patch Hastings. But Patch isn't a name. Patch … Pitch. Pinch. Patcher. Pitcher. Pit-cher. Peet-cher. Peet-er. Peter! What if the guy's name is Peter not Paul?" Sean tried it out for sound, "Noble Peter Hastings."

"Yikes it's cold in here." Sean looked in the mirror again. A face appeared beside his.

"What the…" Sean spun around to look behind him. His hand slipped off the edge of the sink and he plummeted forward. "Who are…" Sean never finished the sentence. His forehead struck the sink on his way down and everything went black.

Chapter Three

Purging Hope

Noble:

If I wanted to try and tell you what it was like to roll up a whole long way all at once…

Try this: imagine that you never got a present in your whole life. Nothing. You never got a present for Christmas: any Christmas. And you never got nothing for your birthdays—back to when you were born. And even nothing for your confirmation. Just nothing. Then on top of all that bad feeling, you figured out that you are growing up. And growing up means that toys and such shouldn't mean as much to you—but inside you it did mean something. Inside you was some hope. But it was a stupid hope because you weren't a child anymore. Nobody gives you toy when you're supposed to be growing up into a man.

So all this sadness was sitting on you like something that fell on you. Something heavy that you couldn't pick up. And you lived like this for a long, long time.

Then when you were sure that there was nothing for you, somebody put a whole set of presents in your lap. It was all the fancy things you never got. All the toys that could have been every birthday that you ever had, and all the presents from all the birthdays that you were going to have even if you lived a hundred years. All of that, all at once. And it was yours, no lie. What you felt then is maybe half of what rolling up is like.

When you roll up like I did, when your Stringer finally calls your name out loud, you realize that you had absolutely no idea what a Dead'er was or what a Dead'er could do.

What did I do? I did this:

First I stopped Sean from completely knocking his brains out on the sink by pulling the towel off the rack and putting it between his thick skull and the porcelain while he was falling. Yes. Rolled up I am that fast. And the towel was 100% cotton and dry so it wasn't too difficult to pull down since I was moving it in the direction that it wanted to fall anyway.

Then I called out to Pedro but he was out of his haunt so he didn't say much back to me. I told him "Gracias" about fifty, score, dozen, hundred times. I think I heard him reply "¡De nada!"

Then I went into Sean's kitchen and scanned the floor under his stove till I found some chocolate flakes among the rest of the dirt under there where he never cleans. Sean loves chocolate and he's a messy eater. I pushed the flakes across the room and let them fall down the heating duct right to the basement. Then I slid down the heating duct too. There were only a few ways to move through Sean's building because of all the wood in the walls and floor. Then came the hard part, working up the flakes off the basement floor into the dryer lint trap just when Mandy had the door open. I knew that she fell for it when she came back up the stairs without doing her laundry. Knockers. I'm good.

I passed out a window and headed north. I knew the direction without looking. The place I was going seemed like part of me. I passed the edge of my haunt and of course I faded down a bit but I still felt the strength the Stringer's naming had given me. This time I was strong enough to keep going. I glided past streets and alleys and buildings that hadn't been there the last time I made the trip. A lot had changed. There was a park where there used to be a big old apartment building. Then, in another place, there was parking lot where there had once been a park. Here and there new buildings, stores, offices and gas stations, stood where before there had only been houses. Plenty of the old houses were left however, but I could tell that they had been painted or added to over the years, new decks, porches, new roofs, a new room or two on some of them.

I travelled to a place I had not been in years. It had never been anything more than a plot of ground—a plot where all my hopes were buried.

When I arrived I was silent for a minute. I just stood still. I felt and listened. Then I hovered over the plot. It was still part of a garden, the way it had been decades ago but I saw that the property line had changed. Someone had built a wooden fence across the plot, cutting off maybe a quarter of it. Part of it now lay in a garden that belonged to the house to the west. I lay on plot as best I could but the fence was in the way. And then I called out to him. I called and called. I called with everything I had. And I could feel myself fading down with the effort, but I didn't care because this was the closest I'd been to him in decades.

I stayed there all night, calling and listening. When the sky was lightening a jogger went by. He shouldn't have been able to see me, especially with daytime coming on, but maybe he was some sort of Stringer. He looked twice in my direction. I was curled up on the ground. I wondered how I looked to him. Maybe he saw some pale over-sized pumpkin or some nearly translucent white vegetable, forgotten by the harvester, among the trash of a mid-November garden.

Sean did not have many good dreams. Some nights his dreams were merely sad. Other times they left him surly, depressed, and even frightened. The worst dreams were the ones that seemed the most real. In them he was a boy again. He was in his bedroom but he could hear his parents arguing through the adjoining wall. They would yell and yell at each other. Then the yells became shouts, and the shouts became screams. There were vicious accusations and the answers were swear words. Impossible challenges were hurled. Things would be thrown. He would hear a brush hit the wall. The tinkle of glass from a hand-held mirror. Then a sudden sharp silence. Then crying. Sobs. Sean's dreams usually ended there. He would bolt awake panicked, disoriented, his breathing painfully rapid and shallow. It would take him minutes to calm himself, to recognize that he was in his own apartment, to be reassured by the blinking red light on his stereo, the faint glint of the street light off the dark TV screen, the intermittent drip from the tap in the kitchen that he could never close all the way. And finally the sound of his own breathing, slowly calming, slowly returning to normal.

When he had been a boy, there had been no way to wake up from the nightmare; there had been no dream. The sobbing he heard through the wall would stop sometime in the night. The next morning at breakfast, his mother would be red-eyed and his father shame-faced but they would act as if nothing had taken place, as if their son had not also lain awake half the night sobbing from terror.

But Sean had good dreams too. And this was one of the best. He was naked in bed with Mandy from 3B. It was just like in the movies where no one wears pajamas. It made sense to Sean since pajamas, even though they were warm, were definitely unsexy. "I suppose" Sean mumbled in his dream, "the guy and girl keep each other warm. Who needs pajamas?"

"Apparently you do," said the dream Mandy from 3B.

Somehow she was dressed. This made no sense. The girl never needs clothes. It was the guy who sometimes kept on his boxers. Perhaps she had thrown on something to go to the bathroom.

"You won't need anything on in here, baby!" Sean lifted the edge of the covers to invite her into bed. She looked amused didn't move from her position.

"I'm glad to see that you're conscious. And it looks like your blood pressure is back up to normal too." Dream Mandy from 3B said, her eyes glancing down for a moment.

Sean remembered to lower his voice. "Sure is baby. Sure is. Why don't you crawl back into the love nest..." He rolled onto his side and moved to prop himself up on one elbow. Something wet and cold fell off his forehead and onto the pillow in front of him.

Mandy from 3B picked up the cold thing and pressed it back against his forehead. "If you're going to move around you'll have to hold this in place yourself." The thing was an ice pack wrapped in a towel.

Sean suddenly remembered the slipping and the falling. "I slipped and fell in the shower. But Mandy from 3B found me—I had been showering that explains why I'm na—" Sean grabbed the sheets madly and tucked them in around his waist. He felt his face flush. There was no dream.

"A bit late for all this modesty, isn't it?" Mandy from 3B was laughing at him.

"But-, but-..." Sean stammered. He realized that as far as his modesty went, the situation had not improved. He grabbed a pillow and placed it over his lap.

"Don't worry. I'm a nurse. I've seen worse. Or better … I'm not sure which applies in this situation." She was laughing at him again.

Sean tried to relax. He thought that changing the subject might help. "How did I get into bed anyway? Were there paramedics?" The thought of even more people having seen him with all his parts on display brought back his stammer. "Ha-, ha-, ha-, how did…"

"I told you I'm a nurse. Well a nursing student actually. Moving bodies is part of my training. It wasn't so difficult. You don't weigh very much." She looked at his face, "Sorry. I'm just being matter of fact."

Sean had one hand on the ice pack and the other on the pillow in his lap.

"And you need not worry about the other stuff. I grew up with a three brothers, two older, one younger. I used to baby sit the younger one. There's nothing about boys that I've not seen before. Even that."

"But I bet they never put on a show for you." Sean's face flushed again.

"Probably the less said about that the better."

Sean nodded in agreement. His head hurt when he moved it.

"You'll probably be sore for a while. When you feel recovered enough to walk we should get you checked out for a concussion."

Sean nodded again, but more slowly this time.

"I'm wondering how the accident happened. Do you remember it? Many people get retrograde amnesia after being knocked unconscious like you were. I'm pretty sure you hit your head when you fell and that bump on your forehead is not the cause of your fall. There must have been something else. What do you remember?"

Sean searched his memory. "I was taking a shower…"

"Did you slip in the tub maybe? That happens to quite a few people, but usually they are older than you. Seniors mostly. For them the accident can be fatal, usually not from the fall itself but from complications, like a broken hip, arm, or wrist bone. Do you know that if a senior has significant bone loss that she can snap the bones in her forearm just by putting out a hand to break her fall?"

Sean decided that Mandy from 3B had a nice voice.

"I don't think I slipped in the shower," Sean said, "Something else happened that fright—that startled me." For some reason he didn't want Mandy from 3B to think he had been scared. It felt strange to have a feeling of having been frightened and to have no clear recollection of what he had seen. Sean swallowed. "I remembered being surprised by something … something that made me turn to look."

Mandy leaned forward. "Really? What?"

Sean studied Mandy for a moment. It was the closest he had ever been to her. She had her lips pressed together, concerned, questioning. Such nice lips. She was really pretty, thought Sean. And her eyes, he mused, they were really kind, but maybe a trifle mature for her face. Maybe she was tired. You could tell a great deal about someone by their face—there's plenty in any face for you to learn from, even a face you're seeing up close for the first time.

Suddenly Sean remembered exactly what it was that had frightened him. An instant later he decided that he would not tell Mandy from 3B what it was. He did not know what she thought of him. She was being nice even though he had thoroughly embarrassed himself in front of her in a way that would have made any normal girl run screaming from his apartment. Maybe Mandy from 3B was not normal. Maybe she liked him. Or maybe, he thought with sadness, Mandy Simms was just being a good nurse. Either way he was not going to tell her about the disembodied face that had appeared behind him in the mirror. He was already going to have enough trouble convincing her that he was sane.

Mandy saw he was troubled by something. "What was it? You can tell me. You should realize that I'm not easily embarrassed." She smiled into his eyes. "So there is no reason for you to be embarrassed either."

Sean adjusted the ice pack on his forehead, and used the movement as an excuse to look away from Mandy's eyes.

"No, I don't remember what it was. I think I just slipped in the bathtub. Maybe I had that retro—"

"Retrograde amnesia."

"Yah maybe I had that. Does it make you black out?"

"No." Mandy leaned back, but she continued to regard Sean with a quizzical look. "Retrograde amnesia starts after the accident so it can't cause an accident. Something else did occur to me however. When I came into your apartment the shower was still on and hot. Maybe you were taking such a long hot shower that you had extended vasodilatation in your extremities, and as a result your blood pressure dropped sharply, and you fainted. You might have recovered quickly on your own except for compounding the problem by banging your head on the way down. That would explain the extended period of unconsciousness."

"Nice diagnosis, Nurse Simms. I'm impressed." Sean suddenly sat upright. "Extended period of unconsciousness? That means I was out for a while, doesn't it?"

"Well I don't know how long you had been out when I found you but…"

"What time is it? I have to get to the pub! Clarke and Hastings, northeast corner. Damn I'm going miss everything."

Mandy smiled but her tone was firm. "Young man you're not going anywhere." She picked up the towel with the ice pack inside. "I'm going to head into the kitchen and change this. The ice is nearly all melted."

Mandy's expression had changed; the concern was replaced by a look that matched her energetic, efficient movements. Sean sighed inside, but just before turning to the kitchen Mandy reached out a hand and pushed Sean back down into the bed.

Sean smiled once she had turned away. There was a warm spot on his chest where Mandy from 3B had touched him.

"Hey," Sean called out, "When you come back you can explain how and why you came to be in my apartment." Sean grinned. That should take the edge off of her smugness, he thought.

"For starters the door was open." She answered Sean over her shoulder but then continued talking even though she disappeared into the kitchen. "I was going to thank you for the tip about the dryer but when I tried to knock on your door it just opened. I yelled 'hello' but no one answered. So I came in to investigate. Long story short, there you were on the bathroom floor: naked as a newborn. I thought you were dead at first but of course I checked your pulse—Hey, don't you have anything to eat in your apartment?"

Sean's smile turned into a grin. She was going to stay for a while. His night was turning out better than he could have dreamed.

Sean heard more of his cupboard doors opening and closing then Mandy reappeared in the kitchen doorway.

"I'm going to pop up to my apartment and heat you up some soup. You should eat something. I'll only be a couple minutes. I've got more ice up there too."

Sean met her eyes. Once again there was a smile in them even though her tone was firm.

"And while I'm gone you can figure out how to explain how come you know my name." She fixed him in pointed stare and then left the apartment.

The grin faded from Sean's face. He searched under the covers till he found his pajamas and then, without leaving the bed, began to pull them on.

Noble:

I don't know what I was thinking. I used to think that there was nothing but hope. Hope was something you could count on when you didn't have anything else: "Oh it doesn't matter that you don't have a body, Noble, you have hope." Or, "Noble although you've been dead for a hundred years, you won't let yourself fade down, you have hope." "Don't worry if you don't have a single Stringer in your shrinking Purging haunt for three decades Noble, it doesn't matter, you have hope." Purging hope.

Well I don't have hope. I bled everything I had into that plot. Everything. I didn't have enough left to crawl back to my haunt on a Tsunami of fresh ashes going the same way. Everything. I faded down right there because that plot was the only reason I was hanging on all these decades.

I don't know what I was thinking. Stringers are pretty hard to come by. And getting them to help you roll up is pretty much impossible most of the time. You have to really work your butt off. And then when they roll you up they're able to see you. And that's strangely hard to take since you are probably used to not having a body at that point even though not having one used to make you Purging sick. So the whole thing's a desperate lost cause. Unless of course you're distilled evil like Mary, or distilled, concentrated evil like Hearst, and you don't mind stealing a Stringer from some other Dead'er's haunt, or if you don't mind if a Dead'er or two fades down all the way and then you take their Stringer and stretch out your own haunt.

I should have known that Gavin would not have made it through. He was shier than I was. I think all your worst traits get amplified somehow when you become a Dead'er. So I'm shy, and careless, and forgetful, and boastful because that's all I ever was. I would be a thief too but what would a Dead'er want to steal? And Gavin was none of those things except maybe shier than me. He was good, and truthful, and honest, and perfect in every way, except for one fault. He loved me. And I say that that was his only fault because he was a good person and to love an unscrupulous, petty-thieving urchin, was a pretty far come down for him. And the reverse is true too. I was reaching pretty high above myself to love him, morally speaking only of course, because neither of us ever had two pennies between the two of us. So the best part of me was loving him.

But none of it matters now. And I've got no qualms about fading down because I even paid my debt to my Stringer. And Mary could Purging rot for all I care since she stole my Stringer years ago. And I only hope that she doesn't get ahold of Sean because I like him and I would hate to see what Mary might ask him to do. And all my debts are paid, except maybe to Pedro but I've got no strength left anyway. So sorry. Pedro. I'm just going to lie here and watch the sun go by for as long as I can.

Chapter Four

Summon Me Mary

For exactly three days Sean remained convinced that the fall in his bath-room was the best thing that ever happened to him. He had met Mandy and she seemed to like him, even more than just as a patient. After consulting on the phone with someone at the hospital, Mandy had decided to spend that night in his apartment: unfortunately it was only to nurse him. She sat up in a chair and woke Sean every few hours, checking his pupils and asking him if he had a headache. In the morning she patted his hand and said, "You'll be ok," and left.

Sean left flowers for Mandy on Monday. Tuesday she left him a first aid kit. Wednesday he picked up enough courage to knock on her door.

She answered the door fairly quickly and smiled when she saw him.

"So," she said, "did you see a doctor?"

"Yup," answered Sean, "He said I was ok: no permanent damage done. And the bruise will go away in a while. He said I must have a very thick skull."

Mandy continued to smile but did not join him in the laugh.

"That's good to hear," she said after a short silence.

"Yes it's good to hear." Sean felt stupid for repeating her, and then wondered how he might bring the conversation around to asking her out.

"Well," Mandy said, and made a slight motion as if she were about to close the door.

"I, umm, I didn't get a chance to thank you properly…" Sean hoped that his face was not beginning to flush.

"Yes you did," Mandy stepped to one side so that Sean could see into her apartment. The roses he had given her were in a clear glass vase set on a sturdy wooden table in the middle the room. "It was very nice of you to send the flowers. Thank you."

"You're welcome," Sean said. He thought of adding, "But they pale in comparison to the blush of your cheek," but he did not. He felt his face grow warm.

"Sean," Mandy's voice had that firm tone in it. It was her no non-sense voice. Sean felt his body stiffen, as if waiting for a blow.

"I took the rat droppings to the building manager. He crushed a couple between his fingers and smelt them. Then he told me to do the same."

"And you did? Ewww," said Sean.

"I'm a nurse, remember; I've smelt worse."

Sean found that difficult to imagine.

"It didn't matter Sean, they were just flakes of chocolate."

"Oh," said Sean, puzzled.

"And you know as well as I do that chocolate melts in the heat." Mandy continued, "So…"

"So…?" repeated Sean not following her point.

"So they would have to have been planted in the dryer lint trap."

"Oh," said Sean. "But who would do something like that?"

"I don't know," said Mandy. "But there's no shortage of chocolate flakes in this world."

"I guess there isn't," Sean wondered where she was headed.

"I'm sure there's lots around," Mandy wasn't smiling. "I've been in your kitchen."

After Mandy closed the door, Sean stood in the hallway, stunned, for a moment. Then he realized that she might be watching him through the peephole. He hurried away.

"Sweet Great Pea!" said Sean as he stuck his head and arm out of the shower to reach for a towel. "My bathroom really is haunted!"

There were letters in the condensation on the bathroom mirror. Sean looked closer. Some oily substance had been used to draw the letters. The condensation had beaded along the edge of the letters and then had formed drops that had run through the characters. It was difficult to decipher the words.

"Sng mg neme
sunmnon me ej yotn vvjll
Mery IIesh
Crouuieg"

"I only wish that the ghosts or whatever would write a message that made sense," Sean thought.

Sean wrapped a towel around his waist and walked into the kitchen, looking for something with which to copy down this new message. It had been two weeks since the disembodied face in the mirror. He remembered clearly the events that led up to that moment: he had reached for the fortune cookie proverb while reading the name on the first slip of paper aloud. That was when face had appeared and it was only after that moment that he had lost his balance and fell.

He wished that he had told Mandy the truth that night. She was smart; maybe she could figure out these messages. A face in the mirror would not scare her. She would say: "I'm a nurse. I've seen worse than that … or better." Sean felt his face flush. Maybe if he told her how frightened he had been that night, and what had frightened him, she would see that he was not the kind of guy to put chocolate flakes in the dryer lint trap. But there was no way she would believe him now.

Sean grabbed the pad and pen that he used for his grocery lists. They were affixed to his fridge door by magnets. By the time he returned to the bathroom, the dripping condensation had nearly obliterated the letters. Sean took his best guess at what each of them were.

While supper simmered on the stove, Sean sat at the little kitchen table and fiddled with the letters of the message. As he worked his toe found a gain of rice on the kitchen floor. This surprised him since he had swept earlier in the day. He picked up the gain of rice and flicked it into the garbage. It would not hurt to give the floor another quick sweep after supper he thought.

Sean refocused on the message: "Perhaps 'sunmnon' was really 'summon.'" Sean wrote out the new word and compared it to the old. The switch made sense. The letters of the original message would surely have bled together. Sean continued to stare at the words on the pad. If the message had been written using an old-fashioned a, each time an a occurred he might have mistaken it for an e. Sean rewrote the message. It now read:

"Sng mg nama
summon ma aj yotn vvjll
Mary IIash
Crouuiag"

"But maybe," Sean thought, "not every e should be replaced." He tried putting back one e at a time back into the message and eventually settled on:

"Sng mg name
summon me aj yotn vvjll
Mary IIash
Crouuieg"

"I found a meaning!" shouted Sean. "name-summon-me-Mary!"

A draft of cold air stilled him. Sean looked up from the pad where he had scribbled all the different versions of the message. At the far end of the narrow kitchen, the door to bathroom was open. Sean got up, walked the length of the kitchen, closed the door and walked back to his little table. His bare feet crunched on the linoleum. "Frigging rice!" he said with annoyance. "I swept the whole kitchen this morning!" He pulled the little broom and dustpan from the spot where they hung on the wall beside the fridge. Getting down on his knees, Sean held the dustpan in his left hand and flicking the broom quickly with his right, swept the rice into the container. Following the trail of rice Sean's left hand moved up, away from him, then diagonally back towards him, then away again.

"Feels like I'm writing with my left hand," Sean said to himself. He continued to sweep. A few moments later there was enough rice in the dustpan to warrant emptying it into the trash bin. Sean stood up, dumped the wasted rice and knelt back down to finish his sweeping.

The rice on the floor spelt a word: "rowley."

"Damn!" said Sean. There had been a message in the rice and he had erased more than half of it. Sean looked with futility at the trash bin. He got up off the kitchen floor, and wrote the half word on the pad next to the previous message. Then he finished the sweeping. "What does this all mean?" Sean asked himself. He hoped this time that the result would be gentle, not frightening. He still had disturbing memories of the face that had appeared when he reached for the fortune cookie proverb. Sean made up his mind right then: no more Chinese take out!

Sometimes, as he climbed the stairs to his second floor apartment, Sean heard the door to the third floor hallway open and close above him. Sean never looked up when this happened but lingered on the landing, pretending to check his shoelaces or search his pockets, waiting for the upstairs neighbours to pass him on the stairs. It was never Mandy however. It was possible that she was avoiding him: sometimes the door above him would open and close, a footstep or two would be heard on the stair, and then the door could be heard opening and closing again. Sean forced himself never to look up at the door or stairway above him. He did not want to embarrass Mandy. Possibly, Sean thought with sick feeling in his stomach, Mandy was trying to save him from embarrassment.

A Saturday afternoon about a month after the disembodied-face, fall, and failure-with-Mandy incident, Sean wheeled his suitcase into the Laundromat about thirty minutes into his laundry routine rather than the usual twenty. From a chance remark Paula at work had made a week earlier, Sean had deduced that one was supposed to separate the light-coloured fabrics from the dark before washing. He had worn a white shirt under his coveralls. Sean had discovered that this added extra time to the sorting process, but of course none to the washing and drying times—provided enough machines were available. On entering the Laundromat Sean checked his wristwatch and then looked up, searching for an unoccupied machine. His eyes met Mandy's. Mandy smiled, but Sean immediately looked away and felt his face grow warm. He looked up again but circumspectly kept his face away from the seating area while trying to scan the rows of washing machines. There were a more than a few empty machines scattered among the four banks of washers and dryers in the large room. Keeping his eyes straight ahead, Sean headed toward a pair of empty washing machines that sat side by side. He opened his suitcase and loaded the two machines, lights in one and the darks in the other. He added detergent, pushed in some coins, and set their wash cycles in motion. Sean checked his watch. Five minutes. It should have only taken him two minutes, three at the most, allowing extra time for the novelty and difficulty of loading two washing machines while avoiding looking over his left shoulder. Sean looked up from his watch toward the wall clock above the coin-operated dispensers of detergent, fabric softener, and novelty toys. Being directly opposite the seating area, it should have been a safe place to look, but sometimes nowhere is safe. Mandy was standing directly in front of him.

"Hello Sean," she said. Her smile was genuine this time, unforced, unsurprised. Her voice was like water splashing over rocks in a mountain stream. Or maybe that was because she had to half shout to be heard above the water pouring and sloshing in the washing machines all around them.

"Hello!" Sean was surprised that his voice did not sound at all panicked.

"How have you been?" There was a slight incline to her head.

Something inside Sean screamed, "She really wants to know! She really wants to know!"

"Oh, I'm ok." Sean said. Again, to his surprise, his voice was without panic.

"The bruise seems to have cleared up nicely." She made a move as if she would touch his forehead but stopped herself and let her hand fall back to her side.

Sean, seeing the movement, barely resisted an urge rush his forehead toward her fingertips. He found himself, instead, bringing his hand to his own forehead. It was damp with sweat.

"Could you, umm, excuse me for a minute?" Sean asked.

"Sure," Mandy said, and gave Sean a different sort of smile. "I'll be over there for a while." She pointed toward the seating area. "I had just started the dryer cycle when you walked in."

In the bathroom Sean splashed water on his face and then dried it with a wad of toilet paper. He looked at himself in the mirror. "You're not a bad-looking guy," he said. He had not bothered to shave that morning. "With a good haircut and a fresh shave you'd be pretty, fetching slick." Sean winked at his reflection. He flushed the wad of toilet paper and then sauntered out of the bathroom. The sound of the flush followed him into the waiting area. A woman in a beige cardigan frowned at him over her glossy magazine. Sean realized that she must have heard the noise of the flush without the following sound of hand washing at the sink.

Mandy had a textbook on her lap. She closed it when Sean approached. He took the seat next to her.

"I don't want to keep you from your studies." Sean congratulated himself for not saying any completely moronic.

"Don't be silly," Mandy replied. "I welcome a little break."

Sean looked at the book in her lap. There was a picture on the cover showing the outline of a human figure. The figure was filled with tiny lines running from the center of the chest down the legs and arms. Sean thought that the lines might be veins although they were not red.

Mandy saw him looking at the book. "It's my anatomy text book. It's quite interesting." She made a move to open the book but Sean looked away quickly.

"Maybe another time," Sean mumbled. He looked at his hands and then pressed them together. He hoped that Mandy could not see that they were damp.

"I found this Laundromat on my own. You promised to show me but you never did follow through."

Sean looked to see if she was teasing him but he could not tell. She was not smiling as she had before.

"Don't worry, I'm not angry at you anymore." Her smile came back but Sean could tell that she did not fully trust him. "I'm not sure I've forgiven you for looking at my mail but you were right about the dryers in the basement. I did find rat droppings in them. I took them to the building manager but he didn't pay any attention to me. He said that they were probably more chocolate."

"How did you know that it wasn't more chocolate?"

"Oh, they didn't taste all like chocolate!" She held his eyes with a steady stare for several seconds but then started giggling. "I didn't actually taste them silly," she said at last.

"It wouldn't have surprised me one bit," he said. "You're a nurse. I'm sure you've tasted worse." Mandy burst out laughing. It was like sunshine. Sean felt his face grow warm again.

Mandy's laundry was done before Sean was even halfway through his dryer cycle. She collected her clothes quickly and returned to where Sean was seated.

"You're too right about the tables here being too small to get any folding done. I'd wait for you and we could walk back to our infested building together, but I'll have fewer wrinkles to contend with if I can get these things on hangers quickly. And I've got more studying to do. I've got a rotation coming up in…"

"Infested building?" said Sean.

"You mean they haven't been in your apartment? You're lucky! They've been all over my kitchen twice! Kurt right across from you and Mrs. Endicott in 2B, told me that they had the same thing happen in their apartments?"

"You mean that they saw the boy's face in the mirror too?"

"What boy? I'm talking about the rice all over the kitchen floor. Hasn't it happened in your apartment? I know it must be the rats because I would have noticed if I had spilled that much rice—and all over the kitchen floor! Funny because I thought that the rats would eat the rice not spread it everywhere. I almost think our building's haunted by rat-ghosts because we never see any of them, just their droppings in the basement, and now the rice everywhere."

"I had the rice too!" said Sean. "What did your rice spell?"

"Spell?" Mandy raised her eyebrows, "What did *your* rice spell?" She held Sean's eyes with a steady stare. Sean hesitated. Mandy started giggling. "Sweep me up?"

"No. Nothing." Sean realized that he had been holding his breath.

"Kurt says that he is going to file a complaint with the Heath Department or with the Government Rent Control Office or something like that. I told him I'd sign the petition. I imagine the manager will try to say that it's candy sprinkles or something like that!"

"That's funny." Sean forced a laugh.

"But I hope they make him do something. I really don't want to be living with rats but I can't afford to move or anything right now."

"Maybe it's not rats," said Sean.

"I've been thinking that. Maybe it's just mice! Somehow that doesn't sound as bad as rats."

Mandy gathered her books and her laundry bag. "See you around our sweet infested halls!" Mandy ambled out of the Laundromat, the over-loaded bag swinging at her legs.

Sean watched her through the glass doors. She turned the corner towards their apartment and slipped of sight. Sean sighed; not once did she look back.

Chapter Five

"Plenty of Guts for a Skinny Boy"

When Sean applied for the job at the car dealership he did not think that his expectations were too high. He pictured what his working outfit would be: a snappy-looking blazer, slacks ironed to a razor crease, high-quality leather shoes—leather right to the soles, and maybe even a tie too. Sean was not sure about the tie. He disliked the feeling of constriction at the neck and thought that maybe salesmen might be more effective if they looked and felt relaxed.

Just to be safe, however, he wore a tie to the interview.

The manager nodded encouragingly as Sean answered the first few questions.

"Yes, I've held down a few jobs," Sean nodded back at the older man. "I used to do all the gardening for my neighbour. She had a huge lot!"

"Gardening?" the manager scrunched his brows and picked up Sean's resume from where it lay on the table. "What about sales experience?"

"Well a little, not much, exactly." Sean pulled at his tie.

The manager looked up from the resume with a raised eyebrow. "There's none listed here…"

"Well no actual formal experience," stammered Sean.

"I see." The furrow in the manager's brow deepened.

Along with the wardrobe Sean had also pictured his working conditions: some sort of office: a large desk across which he could reach to shake hands with satisfied buyers, sealing the deals that brought him ample commission cheques. He had even imagined a secretary: an attractive woman, perhaps a bit older than himself—she would be very professional and efficient with her work, but also she would be endowed with ample assets. Sean had a vivid image of his secretary entering his office, "Here's your coffee Mr. Hughes."

She put the cup down and then leaned over his desk, "and here's the letter you wanted typed," She smiled at him. "Nice tie."

"It says here," the manager continued, "that you washed cars."

"Yes," replied Sean, "for the neighbour I used to garden for. She said I was good at it. I did hers every week and she told some people and I ended up doing theirs as well."

"That's good," the manager said tentatively.

"I learned a lot about cars," added Sean hopefully.

"Then I've got just the thing for you; we need a lot boy."

"Lot boy?" echoed Sean.

"You'll wash cars, move cars around the lot, do odd jobs at the dealership."

"Not sales?" said Sean. His visions of the office, the secretary, and even the sharp-looking blazer and creased pants began to dissipate.

The manager shook his head, "I don't think you're ready for sales. Lot boy on the other hand, I think you can handle. I'll even bet that you have fun at it." The man read Sean's expression. "Consider it an entry-level position," he added, smiling.

The manager was right. Sean grew to enjoy cleaning cars. Most days the work was easy: newly delivered cars were already spotless on the inside. Road dust or rain spots on the exterior could be quickly eliminated with a rinse and a wipe with a chamois. Eventually Sean was trusted the drive new arrivals off the truck and into the lot. Sometimes, if all the regular drivers were busy, Sean could be asked to drive a car up the narrow ramp and through the sliding glass doors into the showroom.

Customer delivery gave Sean a sense of pride. Once a purchase was complete it was Sean that the salesmen called on to wash the test-drive dust or mud out of the wheel wells, double check the interior, and drive the car to the dealership's front entrance. Sean last act was to place a paper mat, bearing the dealership's name and logo, on the floor in front of the driver's seat.

Midsummer, the manager appeared as Sean was hosing down a car that had only been test-driven once.

"It's the slow season for sales, eh?"

Sean nodded.

"That's why it's time to let you go," the man laughed, "No need for that face: you're not being fired; you're being given a re-motion."

"Re-motion?"

"It ain't a promotion; it ain't a demotion."

"What is it?" asked Sean.

"It's get yourself into one of those coveralls. From now on you're with the used car lot."

Along with the usual trade-ins the dealership's used car lot held vehicles that had never been sold but that were also no longer current model. Sean found detailing, the painstaking cleaning of a used car, tiresome. The removal of bird crap and backseat upholstery stains were particularly challenging. Sean was now also expected to assist the mechanics. He brought cars in and out of the shop for them and if there were no cars to be moved or cleaned, and if the shop had been swept, Sean would stand among the mechanics while they worked, ready to fetch tools or help move heavy objects.

His first time in the mechanics' lunch room Sean sat at the table between a man whose coverall read, "Mechanical Technician," and another whose read, "Engine Repair Specialist." Sean's coverall was plain.

Sports came up first. Around the table a handful of men broadcast their predictions to the whole group. After a few minutes the talk split into several conversations. The sports talk continued for some, while other groups moved on to news events, movies, vacations, planned or already taken. The men on either side of Sean turned away from him to face others. Sean heard bits of conversations: discussion of a war going on somewhere, someone's daughter and her violin, complaints about a wife. Sean turned to focus on the group to his right: Movies! Sean thought, they're talking about movies—and now it's about one I've seen! Sean cleared his throat. He began, "I've seen it; it was really good except for the part where—."

For a moment Sean knew exactly what it was like to be invisible. No, not invisible, he thought, to be—outside: outside of everything. To be able to see and hear, and still not be seen nor heard. Sean turned away from the group and ate his lunch quickly.

The mechanics ate at noon. Sean began to eat his lunch at one.

Two months after his transfer to the used-car lot Sean was well settled into his routine. It was surprising therefore when the door to the mechanics' lunchroom swung open and a woman entered.

"See! I told you he'd be here! He's a growing boy and needs his food. Not like you. Maybe for a year you should skip lunches. Look at your belly!" The speaker was Paula, a tall, heavy-chested woman who worked as a receptionist, office manager, and even part-time sales lady when things were very busy. She favoured large, shiny, dangling earrings, and numerous necklaces wound like ropes across her chest. The heavy jewellery suited her however; it matched the voluminous hair, brassy voice, and striking eyebrows. She wore high heels that looked impractical for a woman her size, yet she moved about the office or car lot with the smoothness and delicacy of a figure skater.

A male voice came from behind the woman. Sean could not see the man but recognized him from the wide shoes and thick ankles. "But my wife she pack my lunch every day! You want she should find out I don't eat the lunch she make? She'll say 'Why you no eat my food?—You no love me?' Then she cry! Is that what you want?"

"Nonsense," said the woman. She stepped into the room and then to one side so that Sean could see both her and her companion. She turned to the much shorter man and put her fingers to her lips. "Hush, Antonio, the boy doesn't need to hear about your marital problems."

The thick-bodied, wide-shouldered man was the dealership's driver, Tony Andretti. He was nominally part time but seemed to be at the dealership as often as almost any of the other staff. He was responsible for, among other tasks that Sean found less interesting, moving cars on and off the delivery trucks, and into and out of the show rooms. When the regular service driver was already busy, Tony would also fetch automobile parts from suppliers. From Sean's point of view however, the most interesting of Tony's duties was test-driving new cars before delivery to customers.

The olive-skinned, fleshy-faced, Tony, even in middle age, was a handsome man. He had lost most of his hair but had the sort of head that seemed to prefer less hair. He arrived at work each day freshly shaven, although, within a few hours, a salt and pepper shadow beard would march from his below his lips, down to his chin, and having conquered that dimpled surface, up his cheeks.

Even if you were the butt of his joke, you felt like laughing along with Tony. This power of his was as much in his eyes as it was in his manner, or voice. His eyes were round, dark, and lively, set deeply in a guileless face. They drew you into him. You felt like you were talking to a soul that had somehow resulted from a merger of a trusted family friend and your own grandfather. The manager tried periodically to convince Tony to sell cars for the dealership but the Tony always replied, "What for I sell cars? With a name like mine I was born to drive." Then he would add something to lighten the mood. "Maybe I no drive fast enough for you?" The manager would walk away from the grinning driver with a bit of nervous laughter as if his worst fear were potential losses to his inventory.

From time to time, Tony, in handing keys over to a potential customer, would say something like "She's a good car," or "This could be the car for you." Invariably the customer purchased the car in question. Once when a couple was about to take a sporty coupe out for a test-drive, Tony handed the man the keys to the small car but looked at the woman and said, "Over there is a car more for you two," and pointed to a used but study-looking four-door sedan. The man came back from the test-drive, thanked the salesman and left the dealership. The salesman glared at Tony of the rest of the day but the next afternoon the man reappeared with a check for the sedan.

As far as the dealership's manager was concerned, Tony made those sort of comments much too infrequently. Most often, if asked directly about a car, Tony would just shrug. This annoyed the manager who, like the sales staff, was paid on a commission basis. Tony, of course, would have been a disaster as a car salesman; he was honest.

The first thing that Tony said to Sean was "Sorry to bother your lunch, but I need another driver, pronto." Sean packed up his half-eaten lunch and followed Tony out to the car lot. Tony waved Sean toward the passenger side of a car parked outside the backdoor of the dealership. Its engine was already running. They drove to a dealership of the same franchise across the city where they collected a new car to bring back to their own lot. On the way home Tony let Sean drive the new car.

Every few days Tony, Paula, or both would appear during Sean's lunch hour. He grew to love their company.

"Don't let him fool you with his hard luck story," said Paula. "He made his fortune somewhere else—mafia for all I know. He's only here because his wife won't let him stay in the house during the day."

"Is that true?" asked Sean.

"Yes unfortunately. My sweet Claudetta prefers to have the house quiet. She likes to read the romance novel all day. So I ask her. Am I not enough romance for you? And she says you are too much of everything. Go to work and leave me alone."

"No, I mean the part about the mafia. Is that true?"

"This Paulette, she love to talk too much. If I was Mafioso I order a hit man. I say: look for big woman who talk too much. Hit man walk in here. He could make no mistake. Just use ears."

For Sean, a good day at work was one in which Tony needed him to come along on a car drop. The Monday after Sean met Mandy at the Laundromat was a very good day.

"Plenty cars today," said Tony.

Sean grinned.

"You no need this," Tony indicated Sean's coverall. "Today you drive plenty."

Their first delivery took them to a dealership in the suburbs. Tony drove the new car. Sean followed in one of the dealership's older vehicles. When they arrived Tony was greeted by a man who seemed to want to be recognized as a salesman stereotype. The man wore a loud blazer paired with a mismatched tie and slacks. A tall, gaunt youth in a coverall emerged from the building and took the keys from Tony. Tony slapped the youth on the back before walking to car where Sean was waiting. Tony indicated that Sean should move out of the driver's seat.

To Sean, Tony always seemed an exceptionally cautious driver. He kept both his hands on the wheel, unless reaching to work a manual transmission. This day, although he drove as carefully as was his habit, he seemed distracted. From time to time took his eyes off the road as if appraising Sean.

"Time to see cardiac surgeon!" said Tony at last. He thumped his own chest then put his hand back on the steering wheel.

"Oh!" remarked Sean. "Are you sick? Do you need an operation? My uncle had to have heart surgery. We were all scared but afterwards he was ok. He even could ride a bike."

"Oh, is that so?" said Tony, his accent thicker than usual.

"Yeah really!" said Sean. "They are pretty good at that stuff now. You don't have to be scared of heart surgery—even if you're old."

"Oh, I'm an old man now?" murmured Tony.

Tony drew in his shoulders and sank lower into the car seat. He kept the car safely in its lane but let it wobble disconcertingly, even as he continued to travel at the speed limit. It was as if the car itself were trembling with age.

"Very funny Tony. I didn't mean that you were old,"

"You know," continued Tony, "the young have more heart trouble than the old." The car was still shaking.

"Whatever you say." Sean turned to eye the car behind them. "You made your point, Ok?"

"I not make my point yet. My point," Tony extended his index finger. "You have heart trouble!" Tony tapped Sean hard on the chest, twice.

"Ouch," said Sean. "That hurt!"

"See what I mean," chuckled Tony, "you hurt right in the chest."

Sean laughed but also rubbed the spot over his sternum where Tony's thick finger had landed.

"It's not the outside that hurts. It's inside. It's all over your face. And what is it, girl? Boy?—who knows these days,—it hurts you."

Sean looked down at his hands. He scratched his forearms. Then he glanced out at the stores and homes they were passing. They were in the north end of the city. Sean thought about Mandy, the way she had nursed him that night in his apartment, the way she turned away from him and closed her apartment door when he had tried to ask her out, and then her guarded friendliness at the Laundromat. Did he have reason to hope? Sean thought too about the disembodied face in the mirror. And then about the mysterious messages, Noble Peter Hastings, and 'name-summon-me-Mary.' He found himself mumbling the phrases aloud: "Noble Peter Hastings. Name summon me Mary."

"Peter *and* Mary!" Tony whistled. "You got plenty of guts for a skinny boy."

Sean looked quizzically at the older man. Tony kept his eyes on the road.

"I say to myself. He is shy boy. Maybe he like girl but he can't talk to girl. Then I think maybe he like boy but he can't talk to boy. But never, never I think: he can't talk to girl *and* boy. This is new for Tony. But it is ok."

Sean shook his head. "No, it's not like that!"

"Oh. It's ok." Tony reached over and patted Sean's knee in a fatherly way. "Once, you know, long time ago, Tony Andretti could not talk to a girl. Yes he was handsome man. No, you would not believe to look at him now." Tony patted his own stomach. "Then I did not sit and drive all day. Then, every day, football! I was beautiful. And such a head full of hair. Like a woman, my hair. Maybe even you would like. Such curls."

"No, really," said Sean.

"But I could not talk to a girl. She too beautiful. Like Sophia Loren, beautiful. I could not talk to her. I could not look at her. Then I met my wife. I could talk to her. Then I talk to my wife. Then I look at her. She beautiful. I marry her."

"Your wife is beautiful?" asked Sean.

"Not now so much," mused Tony. "She a little fat, a little old." Tony made a noise in his throat, "but me too. No?"

"No," repeated Sean.

"No? You no think me old and fat? You like old man too?"

"No, no, no I mean…" Sean stammered.

Tony laughed so hard his belly shook. "Look at you. I tell you the truth. You no talk to a girl. She not for you. I don't know much, boy like boy, but same thing. You no talk; you no fall in love."

Sean looked out window again. They were passing through one of the oldest sections of the city. The houses were larger here and many of them had gardens.

Tony continued. "This boy you like. He beautiful, yes? You talk to him?"

"It's not like that. It's a name I found on a piece of paper in a fortune cookie which was the same name that I saw written in sand and driftwood on the beach when I went to Mexico last month."

Tony was suddenly serious, "A name?"

"Noble Peter Hastings. That's what I think it was. I found a different piece of it every morning when…"

Tony cut Sean off, his accent suddenly gone, "Sometimes names bring strange things. You should be careful."

"Well I don't know for sure it's a name. Noble? That's not a common name. Peter however is…"

"Look. You a nice boy. I like take you to drive with me. But if you call names I no drive with you no more. Understand?"

Sean nodded tentatively. He had never seen Tony so much out of humour. "It's just a name," Sean continued.

"You tell me nothing happen when you say a name you find written on beach?"

Suddenly things snapped into place for Sean. "Wait. Last time I said the name, that was when the face came in the mirror—I said, Noble Peter Hastings, and then the face came in the mirror and I fell and hit my head and that's when Mandy…"

"So you see il fantasma, this ghost, when you say name and now you say it again in the car with me? You stupid, no?"

Sean felt his face flush, then he felt a sudden chill, like someone had briefly opened the car window to the December air.

"Boy, have I been stupid," thought Sean, "All I had to do was say the name and show Mandy the face. She wouldn't think I was crazy if she saw it for herself. Maybe she would even think I was brave for summoning the ghostly face."

"Sorry." Sean looked at Tony. "I didn't think…"

"No, you no think. But you have good heart. You no think bad things. I tell you two bad things now. No one else see ghost; only you. Everyone think you stupid or crazy." Tony shrugged, "You want to be the crazy man? Is no good. You leave family. You leave home. You leave good business. You come to new country and drive car. Only wife no call you crazy because she love you. So maybe she crazy too."

"You saw a ghost too?" Sean found himself trembling.

"No. I no see ghost. Only a crazy man see ghost."

Sean tried to look at Tony's face but the older man was staring straight ahead. His lower lip was trembling.

"But you did see a ghost, didn't you? You have to tell me."

"I no have to do nothing," said Tony, "only drive this car. But you," Tony continued after a pause, "you have to do something."

"What?" asked Sean.

"Shut-up!" said Tony, but his voice was without anger.

"Oh." Sean settled back into the car seat and looked down at his hands. They rode in silence for a time. Sean found himself reaching for the car radio button but he stopped himself. It was what he had done when there had been tense silences between his parents in the car. Sean promised himself he would try to forget that time of his life. When Sean looked out of the car window again they had left the north end of the city and were just a short distance from the dealership. In this newer part of town there was ample space between the mid-rise apartment buildings and the low sprawling light industrial buildings that now occupied what once had been farmland.

Tony waited till they had turned off the thoroughfare and into the car dealership's back lot before breaking the silence.

"One good thing."

"What?" asked Sean.

"The ghost no follow you. You no say name. Ghost no follow."

"Follow?"

"No more," said Tony. He sounded like himself again. "We no talk about this no more. Ok?"

"Maybe," answered Sean, puzzled at the changes in Tony.

"We won't talk about ghosts anymore!" commanded Tony, his accent imperceptible again. Then, as if to correct himself he added, "No talk of il fantasma, yes?"

"Ok," said Sean, wondering how Tony was able to make his accent come and go at will.

"Now we go talk to Pauletta," the older man continued. "You tell her I tell you to ask about girl."

"About Mandy?"

"Yes the real girl. You say to Pauletta. I ask Tony but Tony no know about girl. Now you tell me about girl."

"Ok," laughed Sean.

"And bring lunch. You ask Pauletta a question you no need talk."

Sean laughed with Tony and followed him into the office. Paula who had been busy with some papers in front of her, looked up at the pair and smiled.

"Bellissima!" Tony called out in greeting.

Chapter Six

Antonio's

Noble:

I swore I was the stupidest Dead'er out there. Stupid, dumb, Dead'er. Dumbest Dead'er alive. Ha, ha, ha. I didn't even know enough to fade down in my haunt. If I faded down in my own haunt then my Stringer could call me out, roll me up. Even if he called me out by accident I could roll up a bit and help him help me out. But no. I was way, way too stupid to do that. No. No. No. I chose to fade down so far from my haunt that my Stringer couldn't roll me up from there with a, a,—busload of Stringers chanting my name.

Busload of Stringers: that's what Pedro said. Pedro who I needed to thank for rolling me up. First thing I heard was Pedro reaching out to me, come sunset. Boy he was a strong Dead'er. As soon as the sun dipped out of sight I heard him and his crazy Mexican accent. He sounded exasperated, or even— if I didn't know any better—desperate, as if he had been trying to reach out to me for nights on end—but Pedro is full of tricks like that.

"Noble! Noble! Talk to me. Noble. Where are you? Did you find them? Noble! Noble!"

After he said Noble a few more times he let his voice trail off. I took my time answering him. "Pedro. ¡Mi amigo! Coma est ta?"

"Don't 'coma est ta' me with your butchered Spanish. You were out of contact so long that you had me so worried that I almost asked Mary to look for you. What happened to you?"

"You did what?"

"I didn't," said Pedro. "But I thought about it. That's how worried I was."

"She'd ruin everything you know—that's just the way she is."

"I know," said Pedro. "I'm not stupid."

I like the way Pedro said stupid. Stew-pid. He continued. "But you could take care of her if you put your mind to it."

I did not believe him but I didn't want to waste any energy arguing about it either. "Thanks for rolling me up." I said. "I let myself fade down way out of my haunt. It was not a terribly smart thing to do—I guess."

"You guess?" Pedro sounded agitated, "It was downright stupid."

I wondered if I could get him to say the word a few more times. He continued, "That was a selfish thing to do, Noble. I, I,…" Pedro stammered and then was silent.

"Selfish!" I thought to myself, "How dare he…"

One of the worst things about being a Dead'er is memory: lack of memory. No Dead'er had a very good memory and I must have one of the worst. My memory was already lousy when I was alive. And it got worse when I became a Dead'er. I was thinking how wrong Pedro was to accuse me of being selfish. Especially since he was only accusing me of being selfish because I had not been drifting around trying to find his parents.

Then my memory returned. "No!" The cry came from some part of me that I did not know could articulate its anguish. I remembered the rolling up. My Stringer had rolled me up good! And I had forgotten or deliberately ignored my promise to Pedro and had gone straight to Gavin's grave. I had not been there in years and I wanted to know—needed to know. Maybe there would be some trace of him. He could not have faded down completely. He had to be a Dead'er, like me. There was no way he was gone—not completely gone. Life could not be that unfair—I meant of course that death could not be that unfair. But there was nothing. I spent every bit of my energy listening for him, reaching out to him, in this one place where I thought he might be— but there had been nothing. No trace of Gavin. And that was why I had not cared if I faded down till I was completely gone too. I must have lain on Gavin's plot for weeks to have lost so much memory.

"Listen. Listen." Pedro's voice was inserted into my thoughts. "I know you have your loved ones to find, but you made a promise to me too, that's why I helped you with your Stringer. This is fair isn't it?"

Pedro was right of course. A promise was a promise. Fair was fair. I thought too about Gavin. He was the sort of fellow to do what was right— even if it hurt him some. I decided to do what I could for Pedro, and my Stringer too. But maybe I had already paid my Stringer back enough by helping with the girl he wanted to meet. If she became his girlfriend my debt to him was paid fair and straight. It would be much more difficult to be rid of my obligation to Pedro.

"I'll go look for them," I said to Pedro. I rose out of the garden and began moving toward my haunt. It felt like I was walking through mud. "Give me a hand. I'm doing this for you. I could stand to be rolled up a bit more."

"Don't be stupid. I didn't roll you up. Only a Stringer can do that—you'd better go to him. You'll need him to help you look. Have you forgotten everything you've learned?"

Pedro should have known that it irked me when he talked like that. Even if I forgot things myself from time to time, I taught Pedro much of what he knows. Pedro was about seventeen years old. He acted like that made it ok for him to boss me around. I was only fifteen. But that was only one way to add up our ages. I have been—me—much, much longer than he has been alive or dead. I was a Dead'er a hundred years before he was even born.

"Good night, Pedro," I said. "I am going to save to my energy to get back to my haunt."

I began to move toward my haunt in earnest. I remembered the way, no problem. It was slow going however, nothing like the way I had seemed to fly or float on the way out to Gavin's plot. Crossing the city I noted the large houses giving way to smaller houses, and apartment buildings. I slid through schoolyards, parks, and abandoned lots. It was nearly morning when I reached the area of the city that held the few blocks of my old haunt. Here there were a handful of commercial streets with strips of storefronts, but most of the district was residential: Tall apartment buildings, row houses, and walk up low rises, like Sean's building. I arrived an hour before Sean was due to rise for work. I thought of waking him and getting started right away but I decided to let him sleep. He would have a long busy night ahead of him tomorrow if I had my way. I watched him sleep. Most of the time there is not much to do when you're a Dead'er. Looking at Sean, I wished I were able to slip into bed too, and feel the warmth of covers pulled over me, and the comfort of another body, the sound of breathing close by.

The slip of paper with my name on it was gone from the bathroom mirror. I found it and that fortune cookie paper in the dust under Sean's sofa bed. Most of the dust I could move: it was just dead skin and hair. Some of it however, was from things that had never been alive, or dead, so I couldn't affect them: tiny flecks of paint or linoleum, minuscule fragments of broken dishes or glassware, even microscopic bits of sand and soil.

I put the paper with my name on it on the little table where he takes his meals. I left the fortune cookie paper where it was. I wasn't about to spend another evening wanting to knock Sean in the head because he mistook a fortune cookie proverb for a supernatural message.

Moving the paper out of the dust and up onto the table took some effort. I didn't fade down so much, however, that I couldn't make it up to Mandy's apartment. It took me awhile and a quite a bit of poking my head into the corners of her cupboards to figure out what I might do to get her down into Sean's apartment: make her see the spider. I didn't move the spider; it was alive. I brought the dead flies it had wrapped up to the front of the cupboard where Mandy was sure to see them when she opened the door. It was genius I think: Mandy would figure there was a spider and maybe even see it lurking in the corner above her box of teabags and jars of honey and sugar. Being female she'd scream and run down to Sean for help. I'm one smart Dead'er.

Sean was half way through cooking dinner when he heard the knock on the door. He dried his hands on a towel and hurried to the living room. It was Mandy. She did not look happy.

"Oh, I've come at a bad time!" she said. She looked Sean up and down. He was wearing an apron that read in bold red letters: Kiss The Cook. There were splotches of sauce across the chest and lap of the apron.

"Mandy, you could never arrive at a bad time." Sean was shocked at his smoothness. Mandy raised an eyebrow. Sean imagined a hint of a smile.

"I don't mean to disturb you but there's something odd in my apartment."

"Is it an emergency?" asked Sean, starting to remove the apron.

Mandy shook her head, "No, no. It isn't. It'll stay where it is till I clean it up I'm sure. I'm just wondering if you'd come have a look at it later." Her voice trailed off.

Sean glanced at the stove. "I'll come up with you."

Mandy shook her head again. "If you're in the middle of cooking it'll wait. Just come up when you're done."

Sean found himself smiling. Mandy seemed to release some of the worry from her forehead. "What are you making," she asked. "It smells good."

"Thanks," Sean blushed. "It's just spaghetti sauce," He paused, "but I like to add my own spices and chopped vegetables."

"Sounds wonderful." Mandy leaned her head to one side.

"Really? You think so? Maybe…" Sean scratched his forearms nervously.

"Maybe what?

"Maybe you'd like to have dinner with me? There's lots of spaghetti…"

Mandy smiled at Sean. "Sure. I'd love to. You know, I think I could pull together some garlic bread. I only have regular sandwich bread but I do have some fresh garlic. I'll crush a few cloves into olive oil and brush that on the bread before toasting. You'll like it. Really! Don't frown; you'll love it."

"Bellissima!" said Sean

"I'll assume that that's a good thing. I'll be back down in a few minutes." Mandy turned and glided out the door. After a few moments Sean remembered his sauce and ran back to the kitchen.

After ensuring that both the sauce and spaghetti were well underway, Sean returned to the living room. He folded his bed into a couch and was suddenly embarrassed by the collection of dust underneath. He pulled the couch forward, concealing the dusty floor, and so that the seat was now adjacent to the low table in front of the TV. Sean sat on one end of the couch and then slid himself along its length. He looked the blank screen of the TV the whole distance, checking for a good clear view.

"Nice," he congratulated himself. He stood up and then frowned, "No, no, no, she's not coming to watch TV." He pushed the couch to its original spot and ran to the kitchen for the broom and dustpan.

Sean swept frantically, glancing at the apartment door every few seconds. He pictured Mandy arriving before he had finished. She would turn up her nose, "Ewww—I'm not eating in this dump!"

Sean gathered the dust into one place. It made a disgustingly impressive pile. In the midst of the mound of sweepings he saw a narrow slip of white paper. Sean drew it out and shook it free of dirt.

"Trouble is sure to find those who run from it," Sean read.

"I almost lost you," Sean spoke to the fortune, "I'd better keep you where I can see you." He took the slip of paper into the kitchen and stuck it back on the fridge door with a magnet. "That oughta hold you," he quipped.

He returned to the living room and the cluster of sweepings. "No Mandy yet," he said. He bent down to bush the dirt into the dustpan. "I'm sure that she'd be completely disgusted," Sean smiled, "or not."

He pictured Mandy sitting right down on the mound of dirt. "I'm a nurse," she'd say, "I've had to deal with much worse…"

Once the floor was swept, Sean washed his hands and set to straightening up the rest of the living room. He picked up a cup from the floor beside his TV chair and returned it to the kitchen, then collected a pair of magazines from the low table and returned them to the bookshelf. He repositioned the table by dragging it until it was in front of the couch. The movement seemed to dislodge a slip of paper. The scrap floated off the tabletop and onto the floor. Sean picked it up.

"Noble Peter Hastings!" Sean said aloud. He looked over at the window. He wondered if Mandy would find his apartment cold. Then the memories slid over Sean again.

They were more vivid now, even more than they had been during the car ride with Tony. The face in the mirror. His shock. The fall. Regaining consciousness in his bed. Mandy…

It had been a boy's face, young and earnest with an old-fashioned haircut, parted in the middle, so that waves went out over each ear. It was a lean face with a firm, maybe even masculine, chin, but one that had not yet had beard or razor against it. Now Sean remembered the boy's eyes too. Wide. Something in them. Trust? Maybe. A question. Maybe not as much a question as an appeal. As if the boy were asking for information, or a favour. "Noble Peter Hastings," Sean said again to himself. He took the slip of paper, walked to the kitchen and stuck it to the fridge under the same magnet as the Chinese cookie fortune. Back out in the living room, Sean doubled checked the radiator setting. Then he was back in the kitchen to wash two sets of cutlery out of the jumble of items in the sink. By the time Mandy knocked on his door, the low table in front of the couch was not only clean, but bore two immaculate forks, and a pair each of dinner knives, and shiny spoons, resting on clean sheets of paper towel. Another two sheets were folded like napkins beside the cutlery.

Sean answered the door quickly. "Welcome to Chez Sean!" He beamed at Mandy.

She laughed. "Thanks, but shouldn't this restaurant of yours have an Italian name?"

Sean, "I guess. What do you recommend?"

Mandy, "Oh I don't know. I don't know much Italian."

"Well how about, Antonio's?" said Sean.

"Sound's good to me." Mandy was holding a covered tray. "I'm pleased with the way these turned out. You should have one while they are still warm from the oven." Mandy lifted the edge of the tea cloth, and held the tray up to Sean's face.

Sean took a slice and bit into it right away. "Exquisite." he said as soon as he had cleared his mouth of crumbs.

"Thanks!" said Mandy, "but how is the bread?" She held Sean's eyes for a minute but then burst out laughing. Sean laughed too.

"Everything is almost ready," Sean said, "Why don't you have a seat and I'll bring your food to you?"

"Oh I like the service here!" said Mandy, "but let's put this tray in the oven so it'll stay warm."

"Good idea! Follow me."

Mandy followed Sean into the kitchen without a glance into the living room that he had spent a hectic ten minutes cleaning.

"Here you go," Sean held the oven open for Mandy. She put the tray in and straightened up. Her eyes fell on the fridge door.

"Oh," Mandy exclaimed, "a selection of take-out menus!"

Sean, feeling his face grow red pulled a couple of fliers from underneath the fridge magnets. "I don't use these all the time..."

"Of course not," said Mandy, "but we all need a break from cooking once in a while." She took the papers from Sean's hand and replaced them under the fridge magnets. "Hey! You save those fortune cookie sayings too!" Mandy reached for the slips of paper that were held up by a single magnet. Sean caught her hand and gave it a gentle squeeze.

"Sometimes I do—most are just silly though. They are really just good for a laugh. Why don't you go make yourself comfortable on the couch? I've kinda set the table for us."

"Ok. Sounds nice." Mandy seemed a bit puzzled at Sean's reluctance to let her look at his kitchen but she allowed him to direct her back to his living room. Sean uncovered the pot of spaghetti and began spooning the noodles onto each of two plates he had set side by side on the kitchen counter. He layered on the sauce and then sprinkled Parmesan on each in a circle. Suddenly Mandy's agitated voice came from the next room.

"Oh. Oh. I had no idea. I'm sorry. Didn't Sean tell you?…"

Mandy backed into the kitchen. She looked startled and flushed. She gave Sean a look that seemed to be almost a reprimand.

"You didn't tell him someone was coming over for dinner! I'm not upset that he's here and I'm sure that he's a wonderful guy; I'd be happy to meet him, under slightly less casual circumstances of course—but shouldn't you have told him that you guys weren't going to be alone."

"What?" asked Sean.

"Your boyfriend," said Mandy. "I guess you two were … but he's not dressed."

"My boyfriend?"

"I think he's very cute by the way. You've got good taste, Sean." Mandy smiled at him. There was something different about her smile this time. She seemed a bit relieved and a bit disappointed at the same time. "But as open-minded as I am, I really would be more comfortable if he put on at least a pair of shorts and a T-shirt." Mandy looked at the two plates Sean held in his hands. "Shall I serve myself?" She brushed past Sean and approached the cupboards. "Where do you keep the plates? Let me guess: right here above the sink." Mandy pulled open a cupboard door.

Sean, confused, but still carrying the two plates of spaghetti, sauce, and cheese, stepped towards the living room.

"Wait!" said Mandy. Sean turned to face her. "You forgot the garlic bread." She reached into the oven, grabbed a pair of slices from the tray, and balanced one on each of the plates in Sean's hand. "There you go." Sean hesitated. Mandy continued: "Run along before everything gets cold." She shooed Sean out of his kitchen.

Sean stepped into the living room. Mandy called after him. "Don't worry I'll serve myself. I'm sure it won't take more than a minute—and it'll give your little friend time to pull up his shorts!"

Mandy really knew how to carry a joke, Sean said to himself. The naked boyfriend thing really wasn't very funny but it was remarkable how Mandy could keep a straight face while talking about it. Sean moved cautiously toward the couch. The last thing he wanted Mandy to think was that he could not carry a couple of plates without dropping them.

Sean gingerly placed the food down on the low table and settled into the couch. He heard Mandy open and close the oven. "Boy she's proud of her garlic bread," thought Sean. He had found her bread a bit dry, as if she not brushed on enough oil or left it to toast too long, or both. "But," thought Sean again, "Dinner with Mandy! This was a dream come true—Thank goodness the apartment is relatively clean." Sean reclined, trying to relax. He looked around the room. The TV was dusted. The food looked great on the little table. The bookshelf was neat and ... there was naked boy in the chair by the TV. Sean jumped up out of his seat. His foot caught a leg of the low table and upended it, releasing a mass of noodles, sauce, cheese, cutlery, soggy paper towels and two overly crisp slices of garlic bread into the air. Sean watched, his mouth open, as his carefully prepared dinner cascaded across the freshly swept living room floor. Sean groaned. Then he looked up at the boy. The boy was staring back at Sean. He looked embarrassed.

"The boy in the mirror!" shouted Sean "Mandy it's the same boy that I…" but before Sean could finish his sentence the boy was gone.

Chapter Seven

Expired, Like Me

Noble:

I Purging swear I didn't mean it. It embarrassed me when it happened. I was ashamed. The thought of it made me blush. Ok. I couldn't blush since I didn't really have any blood flow. But I would have blushed if I could have. It was stupid to be caught out in the open like that, but I plead ignorance. I didn't know that I was rolled up enough for my Stringer to see me. And how could I have known that my Stringer's girlfriend was able to see me. She was a Voyant.

I flashed my Stringer's girlfriend. Threaded pipe and washers on full display and I didn't figure that both of them could see me till the Stringer dumped his dinner and the girlfriend ran into the room and looked right at me too.

When I figured that I was on display I headed out of there as quickly as I could. I may have been only a Dead'er but I had my dignity. Or should have had some. I didn't have to be sitting out in the open like that. Any Dead'er I knew claimed to be capable of appearing or not. And most with sense and decency appeared only from the neck up. It was not an accident that most Stringers saw only a disembodied head when their Dead'ers chose to appear, or were summoned. It's because we Dead'er were all Purging naked. If we needed to show up with a body we could blur out most of our torso and lower parts so that we appeared to be coated in mist or wearing a sheet or some-thing. Whatever energy or force kept us Dead'ers existing extended to our bodies, thoughts, and some of our memories but didn't extend to our clothes. Even if I had somehow been a Dead'er who got to keep his clothes, mine would have rotted away decades ago. I heard female Lye'vers complaining all the time that they had nothing to wear. They should be forced to be a

51

Dead'er for a couple days. Then they would have to switch to complaining that there was nothing they could wear.

When I left my Stringer's apartment I descended to the building's basement. I didn't want to go too far. I just needed some time to collect myself and to figure out the next step. Maybe Pedro could help.

Pedro laughed when I told him.

"Enough!" Now I was angry as well as embarrassed. "I'm not rolled up enough to listen to you laugh all night," I said.

"This is true," said Pedro. "Look Noble, it will be easiest if they can hear you. Just screech a bit and see if they react. If they can't hear you will have to spell things out. Write in the dust or something like that—something light and dead."

"Like rice?" I asked.

"Exactly. And hurry. Sometimes Voyants can only see you for a while. They fade down too."

"But not Stringers?"

"Voyants come and go, but once a Stringer always a Stringer … I think," said Pedro. "But go now, quick, before you forget everything."

"Thanks Pedro," I said.

"No, you silly, Purging ghost. Soon I will have to thank you."

The sound of Pedro's thoughts left me. I felt truly alone. I drifted back up the heating ducts into Sean's kitchen and then out into his living room. It was empty and the noodle and sauce mess was still all over the floor. I thought of writing in it but then decided not to. The whole thing looked too much like blood. I didn't want to give my Stringer the wrong impression about the kind of Dead'er I was.

I checked Sean's bathroom but he wasn't in there either. I slipped back into the duct and drifted up another branch that led up past Sean's ceiling and over to Mandy's apartment. I emerged in her kitchen. There were Sean and Mandy, huddled on their knees in the middle of the floor. Mandy's kitchen was smaller than Sean's and with the two of them crowding the floor it was near impossible for me to see what they were looking at. I kept invisible and spun over them to get a good look.

"Oh, did you feel that? Like gust of cold air," said Mandy. She shuddered and Sean put an arm around her. What a slick Lye'ver he was. "That can't be natural?" Mandy asked.

I thought of giving them another chilling bypass—just to see what Sean would do next but then I saw that they were reading something on the floor.

"M-A-R-Y-N-" read Sean.

"No! No! No!" I screeched but they did not react. Sean was making out letters spelt in rice on the linoleum.

"A-S-H-C-" continued Sean.

I looped by them as quickly as I could. Only Mandy shuddered. Sean continued to read.

"R-O-W-"

"No! No!" I drove onto the floor and began to scatter the rice grains.

"L-E- ... wow would you look at that," exclaimed Sean, "The rice is scattering on its own. Freaky. But I didn't get to the last letter. I wonder what it was."

"Oh it's easy enough to figure out," said Mandy. "It was somebody's name. Just like the name on the fortune cookie. Whatever is going on, it's about these names."

"Maybe you're right!" said Sean. He was excited. "See it's just like I told you—the boy appears when we say the name on the fortune cookie. That's what just happened in my apartment. So maybe a girl appears when we say this name!"

"Let's say both names!" said Mandy, "then they can be together."

"Noble Peter Hastings." said Sean. He turned to Mandy, "Come on say it with me."

They looked at each other: "Noble Peter Hastings!—Noble Peter Hastings!—Noble Peter Hastings!"

I never felt so powerful in the hundred years since I became a Dead'er. I slid down unto the floor in a flash and began to rearrange the grains of rice. I was in a mad rush. "Read it Sean! Read it Sean!" I screeched.

Mandy turned to Sean. "I figured out the other name, the last letter was probably a Y: Mary, Nash, Crowley. That must be it."

"Sounds like it," said Sean, "Let's try it."

"No! Don't!" I screeched with every bit of my being. "No!"

"Mary Nash Crowley. Mary Nash Crowley."

Mandy and Sean looked around.

"Nothing," said Sean, scanning the kitchen. "No girl." He sounded disappointed as if he had not only expected a girl Dead'er to show up, but also that she would show up naked, like I had.

I manifested an arm.

"Look!" said Mandy.

Sean looked down. It was clear to me that both of them could see my arm but that only Sean could read the message I had spelt in the rice gains.

"DO NOT SAY MARY'S NAME."

"Uh oh." said Sean.

"That makes no sense," said Mandy, "Why would a ghost or whatever spell out a name and then tell us not to say it."

"Yeah. That makes no sense..." added Sean. I could see the thoughts forming on his forehead. "Unless there is something else we are supposed to do with the name."

"You could be right," said Mandy.

The two of them stood up and faced each other. Sean looked at Mandy as if he had never seen her before.

"You know," continued Mandy, who was definitely not staring at Sean as if she had not seen him before, "I could go to the research library tomorrow and look up these names. I have classes till three but the library is open till five I think."

"That's a great idea," Sean was grinning. "We could meet up tomorrow evening and take a look at what you find out."

I've watched Lye'vers for decades: dozens of Lye'vers who've lived in this building that I haunt; hundreds of Lye'vers, if I include the Lye'vers I used to watch when I was stronger and I had a haunt that was blocks and blocks across. Maybe I've even seen a thousand Lye'vers since I've been dead. So even though I was fifteen when I died and I never kissed anybody but my mother, I knew what Sean wanted when he looked at Mandy like that.

"I'll come by tomorrow night. It'll probably be late; I've got studying to do. Is that OK?"

"Oh yes," said Sean, "yes, yes, yes ... I mean that it's ok."

Mandy giggled. "Good to know that I'll be welcome." She stood up and looked around her kitchen. "Wow, lots of excitement this evening! Can I get you some tea?"

"Oh yes," said Sean. "yes, yes."

Mandy laughed and opened the cupboard where I had stuck the dead flies. In one smooth motion she reached down with her right hand and tore off a sheet of paper towel, brought the hand with the paper towel back up to the cupboard, scooped up the dead flies, cobweb and spider, scrunched the paper towel and its contents into a ball and pitched all into the open trash bin. With her left hand she brought out a pair of mugs.

"I think I'll pass on the tea," said Sean, eyeing the trash bin.

"Ok. Suit yourself," said Mandy, returning one cup to the cupboard.

"And I've got a living room to clean," stammered Sean, "and we didn't actually get to eat. I'm going to go home and make myself a peanut butter sandwich."

"See you tomorrow then," said Mandy, "you can let yourself out."

Sean left the kitchen and was most of the way to the door when Mandy called after him, "And don't forget the garlic bread in your oven. It'll be too dry tomorrow."

"Tomorrow?" mumbled Sean. He closed the door to apt 3B behind him.

After her tea, Mandy swept her kitchen floor. The rice and my message to her, unread, ended up in the trash next to the paper towel with the crushed spider. I checked but the spider wasn't a Dead'er.

"They got the right idea," I told Pedro.

"Yes they do. But the tough part's still to come." Pedro sounded discouraged which didn't make any sense: my Stringer read a message I wrote—I don't know why I hadn't thought of rice before—and my Stringer's girlfriends was a Voyant. We were closer than we'd ever been to getting my Stringer to do what Pedro needed. Sometimes discouragement doesn't make much sense; it is nevertheless what you have to deal with.

"You should have written in the tomato sauce."

Pedro was right about that. I needed to get messages to Sean anyhow I could. I really didn't have many options since Sean couldn't hear me. I didn't like the idea of writing in tomato sauce however. All that red. I didn't want Sean to think I was some creepy ghost. I was just a Dead'er but I still had some self-respect.

"Find name of seventeen-year-old boy drowned two years ago, New Year's Day, el Rio resort, Playa Verde, Mexico."

"Wow that's pretty specific," said Sean to himself. He wrote the message on the inside flap of a cereal box. He was excited. The flour had done the trick. He had tried leaving things on the floor overnight: salt, sugar, spices, and finally flour. Sean thought he had seen a letter or two in the spices but he had not had much pepper and had used chives and oregano as well. Whatever was written had been difficult to read. The flour worked best. So did, he had discovered, leaving the powder out overnight. Nothing happened during the day or while he was at work. The massages always appeared at night.

Sean ripped off another flap of the cereal box. Mandy would not be back from her hospital shift until late so he left her a note: "Another message received. I'll be up late."

About midnight Mandy knocked on his door.

"Sean! You up?" She knocked again, "Sean?"

"Yah coming…" Sean pulled on the pair of pants he had left hanging over the chair. "Just a sec!" He ran to the bathroom, splashed some water on his face, towelled off and then ran his fingers through his hair.

"Oh, look at you," said Mandy when he opened the door. "There is no need to talk about this tonight. I know you've got to work early in the morning." Despite her words Sean could tell that she eager to talk.

"No it's ok," said Sean. "Why don't I make you some tea?"

Mandy followed Sean into the kitchen. Just inside the doorway he pointed her where to walk so that she wouldn't tread on the message in the flour.

He stepped over the message himself and reached into the cupboard for the box of tea bags.

"I don't see anything. It's odd how you can see these things that I can't." Mandy leaned tiredly against the wall. "What does it say?"

Sean pulled a teabag from the box. "Is chamomile ok? I think that's good for bedtime. Isn't it?"

Mandy laughed. "The message is about chamomile tea?"

"No. No." Sean felt his face grow warm. "The message is about a drowning kid. See here…" Sean pointed at the message. "Uh oh."

"What's wrong?"

"The message is gone." Sean scratched his forearms.

"Do you remember it?"

"Oh, I wrote it down. Here." Sean took the flap of cardboard off the counter and handed it to Mandy. She took it and studied it for a minute.

"You know…" She looked up at Sean. "The last message was a dead end. I couldn't find anything about a Noble Hastings or about a Mary Crowley in any of the historical registers I looked at."

"If they were actual people there would be records of them, right?"

"Not necessarily," replied Mandy, "Not everyone leaves a record behind them. Some people never do anything of note; they are never in the newspapers or they never even purchase property, that sort of thing. There might be birth records, baptismal records, maybe even a marriage license, but those are hard to find unless you know exactly where to look. For birth records you might need to know what year. You need to know what church for baptismal records. Same for marriages and deaths, without a year or exact location it's going to be impossible to find out anything about the people involved."

"What about on the Internet?"

Mandy shook her head. "Most historical records are not online. They are on microfilm or even still on paper somewhere."

"Oh," sighed Sean.

Mandy held up the flap of cardboard, "This looks much more promising. We have an event, a date, and a place. I could look at old newspapers."

"Mandy look, the message is changing…"

"I don't see anything…"

Sean dropped to his knees and began to move his finger just above the spilled flour. "See right there!"

"I can see the flour moving—like someone is blowing on it or something, but it's not spelling out anything."

"A-S-K-H-E-R-T-O-C-H-E-C-K-T-H-E-O-B-I-T-U" read Sean.

"Check the Obituary Records! Of course! Yes I will. Tell it that I will! With the date it gave us in the last message the boy should be easy to find."

Sean began to write in the flour "Y-E-S—S-H-E—W-"

"Look there," said Mandy, "the flour is moving on its own again."

"I-C-A-N-H-E-A-R-Y-O-U … oh" said Sean. "I guess I don't need to write our answers."

"Well it's about time we got some answers then!" said Mandy. She cleared her throat: "Who are you?"

"N-O-B-L-E-P-E-T-E-R-H-A-S-T-I-N-G-S-A-T-Y-O-U-R-S-E-R-V-I-C-E-M-A-N-D-Y" read Sean.

"Oh I like my spirits polite," Mandy smiled. "So Noble, Peter, Hastings why did you contact us?"

"F-I-N-D-D-R-O-W-N-E-D-B-O-Y"

"But he's already drowned," said Mandy, "what can we do now about it now?"

"F-I-N-D-P-A-R-E-N-T-S"

"Are you the drowned boy?" asked Sean

"Of course not," answered Mandy. "He knows his own name!"

"S-H-E-I-S-S-M-A-R-T-E-R-T-H-A-N-Y-O-U" read Sean. He grit his teeth. "Very funny."

"What are you?" asked Mandy.

"D-E-A-D-E-R" read Sean.

"I don't like this," said Mandy.

"S-O-R-R-Y-I-D-I-D-N-O-T-C-H-O-O-S-E-T-O-D-I-E" read Sean.

"I hadn't thought of it that way," said Mandy softly. "So Mr. Ghost, why don't you just go find the boy's parents on your own."

"M-Y-N-A-M-E-I-S-N-O-B-L-E" read Sean.

"Sorry," said Mandy.

"Jeeze, Mandy, you're apologizing to a ghost," said Sean.

"T-H-A-N-K-Y-O-U-M-A-N-D-Y"

"See," said Mandy, "Noble has feelings too."

"Yes, but why doesn't he do this on his own."

"L-I-B-R-A-R-Y-C-A-R-D-E-X-P-I-R-E-D—L-I-K-E-M-E"

Mandy laughed.

"That still doesn't explain it," said Sean.

"D-E-A-D-E-R-S-H-A-V-E-L-I-M-I-T-S"

"Like only being able to come out at night?" asked Sean.

"S-U-N-L-I-G-H-T-M-A-K-E-S-U-S-W-E-A-K"

"Us!" exclaimed Mandy. "So there are lots of you—of course there would be—there should be billions of dead people."

"B-I-L-L-I-O-N-S-A-R-E-D-E-A-D-B-U-T-F-E-W-A-R-E-D-E-A-D-E-R-S"

"So you can walk through walls and stuff?" asked Sean.

"S-O-M-E-T-I-M-E-S"

"Sometimes. What does that mean? When you feel like it?" demanded Sean.

"Yah. That's kinda creepy. I don't like the sound of that Noble. Sorry." said Mandy.

There was a pause before the flour stirred again.

"N-O-T-W-O-O-D"

"You mean you can't go through wood? The interior of this building is almost all wood," snapped Sean.

"Oh no," Mandy sounded stricken, "coffins are made of wood! You'd be trapped if…"

There was another long pause before Noble wrote again.

"I-T-D-O-E-S-N-O-T-H-U-R-T-T-O-F-A-D-E-D-O-W-N"

"I don't know what that means," mused Mandy, "but it sounds sad."

"Y-E-S"

Mandy straightened up. "Ok Mr. Noble, Peter, Hastings as fascinating was this has been, and even though I still have a hundred questions, I'm super tired. And as it turns out the tea someone promised me has not yet materialized. So I'm off to bed. I need to be fresh. I don't want to be dead on my feet during my practicum tomorrow!—oops!"

"F-U-N-N-Y"

"I'm glad he thought that was funny. It would be awful working with a humourless ghost."

"D-E-A-D-P-A-N"

Mandy laughed.

"Sorry about the tea," said Sean.

"Don't be; you were busy translating. You boys don't stay up all night talking. Sean has to work in the morning. Got that Noble?"

"Y-E-S-M-A-A-M"

"You think we're talking to a kid, don't you?" asked Sean.

"Intuition." Mandy turned to leave. "He's probably the same ghost we saw in your living room. I thought at the time that he looked a little young to be your boyfriend." Mandy smiled. "But who am I to judge?"

"S-O-R-R-Y"

"For what?" asked Mandy.

"I-N-D-E-N-C-E-N-C-Y"

"I've seen worse," laughed Mandy, "right here in this apartment even!"

Sean felt his face grow hot.

Mandy changed to a stern tone. She faced Sean. "I know you are going to keep asking him questions once I'm gone. Two things though. One: don't keep asking him questions all night; you'll wear him out. Don't ask me how I know that but I do. Two: write down the answers. I don't want him to have to repeat himself. No one likes to have to repeat himself, dead or alive."

"What was that second point again?" asked Sean.

"F-U-N-N-Y"

"Keep that up and you'll both be writing me messages in the flour."

"I-L-I-K-E-C-O-M-P-A-N-Y"

"Good night boys," Mandy smiled, but her eyes looked sad. Sean walked Mandy to the door and then returned to his kitchen. He drew a deep breath.

There was something odd, he felt, about speaking aloud when there was no one else to be seen in the room.

"How come I can read what you write and Mandy can't?"

"Y-O-U-A-R-E-A-S-T-R-I-N-G-E-R"

"And Mandy isn't, I guess."

"N-O-B-U-T-S-H-E-C-A-N-S-E-E-M-E"

"So only Stringers can read these messages I guess. Hey, I guess it was you that I saw in the bathroom mirror too, so how come I can't see you now."

"L-O-O-K"

Sean stood up from where he had been stooped over the spill of flour and scanned the kitchen. For a moment or two he saw nothing, then he thought of looking against the relative dark of the cupboards rather than the white of the fridge or walls. When he did so the boy's face appeared. Now that he had some sense of whom the face belonged to, Sean found it easier to distinguish its features. In fact, the more Sean thought about seeing the boy, the sharper the boy's features seemed to be. As Sean watched, Noble's neck, bare shoulder, arm and hand came into view as well.

"Pleased to meet you Noble." Sean stuck out his hand but immediately afterward felt silly for having done so. Noble smiled. The arm traced letters in the spilt flour.

"P-L-E-A-S-E-D-T-O-M-A-K-E-Y-O-U-R-A-C-Q-U-A-I-N-T-A-N-C-E-S-E-A-N"

"Likewise," said Sean and then immediately felt even more foolish.

"How old are you?" Sean asked quickly, "Twelve?"

"1-5"

"Oh. You don't look it!" said Sean

Noble continued to look at Sean but made no move to write in the flour.

"I guess that that wasn't a question." Sean looked away from the boy for a moment. "Ok. When were you born?"

"I-D-O-N-O-T-R-E-M-E-M-B-E-R"

"Well if you don't know when you were born how could you know how old you are?"

Sean took a deep breath. The letters appeared more slowly this time.

"I-R-E-M-E-M-B-E-R-D-Y-I-N-G"

"Oh, I'm sorry," said Sean. Sean looked at Noble's face. Whatever it meant to be a Dead'er, thought Sean, it didn't mean you had no feelings. Noble looked down at the flour. Sean followed the boy's gaze. Noble wrote slowly again.

"I-W-A-S-1-5-W-H-E-N-T-H-E-F-I-R-E-H-A-P-P-E-N-E-D-E-V-E-R-Y-T-H-I-N-G-B-U-R-N-E-D-S-O-Q-U-I-C-K-L-Y-T-H-A-T-W-E-D-I-D-N-O-T-K-N-O-W-W-H-I-C-H-W-A-Y-T-O-R-U-N"

"Wow," said Sean, "Where did this fire happen?"

Noble had a puzzled look for a moment.

"R-I-G-H-T-H-E-R-E"

Before Sean went to bed he ripped another flap off the cereal box. On this one he wrote: "Noble died in a fire at our address when he was fifteen. See what you can find out about it. Have a good day, Sean." Then he tiptoed up the stairs and slipped it under Mandy's door.

Chapter Eight

"Only Single Young Women of Good Character and References Need Apply"

"He's not listening."

"How do you know that?"

"I just know!" Mandy's eyes flashed in way that told Sean she was angry. He had never seen her angry before. She was beautiful.

"Well he can walk through walls and stuff. He could follow us anywhere. Even here."

"Not through wooden walls. He told us that and anyway it's broad daylight."

"There's not much wood in this place." They were seated at a café table. Large glass doors separated them from the street. It was Mandy's idea to come to the café. She said that it was nicer than being in either of their stuffy little apartments. Sean had been wary of coming. He had a sort of fear of cafés. He pictured himself knocking over dainty teacups or saying things that would make everyone laugh. Now that he was in the café he saw that he need not have worried. The other customers looked like ordinary people. They were all casually dressed and, from what he could over hear, the conversations around him were not about literature or opera. The tea was even served in study looking glass mugs. "Still we shouldn't take any chances. He's invisible after all." Sean continued.

"You don't trust him, do you?" Mandy looked up from her tea. The anger was gone.

"Mandy, he's a ghost or something. Why should we trust him?"

"This may sound strange Sean, but just because he's dead, a Dead'er I mean, doesn't mean that he's not..." her voice trailed off.

"… not human?" Sean was about to laugh but he saw that Mandy was serious.

"Yes, that's what I was going to say. But that's not the right thing. Trustworthy is maybe a better way of putting it." Mandy frowned, "Most living people aren't very trustworthy." Mandy paused, "You want know what I really think?"

"What?" asked Sean.

"I think that he's just a boy who wants our help."

"He can go anywhere he wants…"

"But not though wood and he's probably got other limitations he hasn't told us about. I'm sure about that." Mandy reached into her bag and pulled out her notebook. "His memory is bad for one. He's got the details of his death screwed up. There's never been a fire at our address that I found any reference to. I did some searching, land registry, insurance certificates, newspaper archives. Our building was opened as a residence for single women in the 1940s."

Mandy flipped through some photocopied sheets. "Only single young women of good character and references need apply." She winked at Sean, "I wonder if I'd qualify."

Sean thought Mandy might be teasing him, but he was not sure.

She continued, "It was converted to rental apartments in the 1970s. That's when separate kitchens and bathrooms were added."

"That explains why the rooms are so odd."

"There were communal kitchen facilities in the basement, and showers and toilets on every floor. The records of all renovation and additions are at city hall, building permits were necessary—as are records of every major structural repair, for fire, flood, etc."

"And there was no record of any fire?"

"None. And I checked the records for the whole block. No fires. Some flooding, burst pipes and backed up storm drains, even some damage during a windstorm, but no fatalities."

"So he lied to me about the fire."

"Or he was confused but the location," said Mandy.

"Or he was lying," said Sean.

"I'm giving him the benefit of the doubt," Mandy said firmly. "The other story, however, checks out. Here." Mandy produced a photocopy of a newspaper clipping.

Sean read the headline aloud: "Mexican vacation ends in tragedy for local family as 17 year old drowns on New Year's Day." Sean silently read the rest of the article and then passed the sheet back to Mandy. "Well that's a great start."

"More than a great start. It gives the name of the couple and the fact that they live in Kitsilano."

"So it should be easy to look them up."

"Dead easy—five more minutes searching on the Internet and I'll be looking at a picture of their house. I don't know how people did research before they invented search engines."

Mandy tilted her head upward and then tossed her hair back over one shoulder. Sean decided that this was her self-satisfied look.

"Do you want to contact them this evening?" asked Sean. "We could look up their address on my phone and go over."

"We're not ready Sean. We now know *who* we are supposed to find but we don't know *why* yet. And if you think about it we've not actually done what Noble asked us to do."

"What's that?"

"We were supposed to find the name of the boy that drowned."

"Oh you're right," said Sean.

Mandy looked directly into Sean's eyes. "I usually am Sean. Please don't forget it." She held the serious look a moment or two longer before breaking into smile. "You're so easy to play with." Sean shrugged in response.

"Are we going to try and find the name of the boy tonight? I have Internet on my phone."

Mandy shook her head, "Nope, tonight I have too much studying to do."

"I guess the mystery can wait. The drowned boy has been dead for years, another night or two won't hurt." Sean sipped his tea. "We can get to it when you have time."

"We'll get to it when you have time, i.e. tonight. You don't have anything better to do, do you?"

"Maybe I do," said Sean hastily.

"Watching TV doesn't count." Mandy gave Sean the direct stare again but this time did not add a smile. "Also see if you can find out anything more from Noble about the drowned boy—and what we're supposed to do with his name once we get it."

"Aye-aye captain." Sean saluted.

Mandy did not smile. She reached into her knapsack and pulled out a book, "I've got my studying to do now." She waved Sean away with one hand, dismissively.

"Bye then." Sean got up and left the table.

"I'll be anxious to hear what you find out," Mandy called after him. "I'll drop by tonight for tea."

Sean barely managed to contain his grin till he was outside the café.

Even as she walked up the hallway, Mandy could see that the door to Sean's apartment was wide open. Her first thought was that Sean had knocked himself unconscious again—somehow managing to leave the door ajar as he had the first time. She dismissed that thought but then began to suspect that Sean might be purposefully repeating the circumstances of their first meeting. Sean could be in bed or in the bathroom waiting for her to enter his apartment. If he were, Mandy promised herself, she would leave whether or not he were clothed. "And I'll never speak to him again!" But it would be a pity to have to do that, thought Mandy. She knew herself well enough to recognize that she had grown to like his earnestness. Mandy knew too, however, that she had to draw clear boundaries. She had met enough men in her young life to know that many of them were willing, and unfortunately often too eager, to push an acquaintanceship forward into uncomfortable territory. Mandy sighed. If she did not draw clear boundaries with Sean, she might soon find herself dealing with unwanted advances, or worse.

She looked into Sean's apartment. It was a mess. Ripped magazine pages were strewn everywhere. The small table and chair had been turned over. Mandy heard the sound of someone moving about the kitchen. She also perceived the distinct crackling sound made by footsteps on finely broken glass. She made her way across the living room and cautiously poked her head into kitchen.

"Snakes 'n heck!" said Mandy, "What happened here?"

The kitchen floor was littered with bits of broken plates, shards of glass, and kitchen utensils. Among them were several broken bottles, their contents splashed across the floor and walls, as if they had been deliberately dropped onto the mess of smashed crockery.

Sean was on his feet, but stooped over, carefully picking up the fragments of his dishware, and dropping them into a plastic bin. He was trembling.

Mandy looked up at Sean's cupboards. It was clear what had happened even if why were a mystery. The cupboard doors were all open and every shelf was broken. Someone or something had pushed down on the forward edge of each shelf so that it had broken and so that whatever it held had slid forward and tumbled onto the floor. Mandy saw that there was nothing random about the damage. Sean's kitchen had been deliberately destroyed.

"I don't get it," said Mandy. "Why would this happen?"

"Why? Why? There is no wondering why!" Sean snarled. "We didn't do what he asked or didn't do it fast enough, or whatever, or there is no reason at all. He's just evil or mean!"

"You don't think Noble did this, do you?"

Sean looked up at Mandy. She could see that Sean was like other men she had seen in similar distress. His anger was fuelled by fear.

"Oh let me see," Sean seethed, "How many ghosts have we been talking to lately? How many have been writing messages in spilled flour and sending us on crazy errands after dead people's names? And how many have been appearing in my living room and in my bathroom mirror, scaring me half to death!"

"Oh so that's what happened that night! You were frightened by Noble and slipped and fell."

"Well he's succeeded in reaching me. I don't know exactly what his message is but I'll bet it's something like get the hell out of here. And guess what I'm doing tomorrow morning. I don't care about the damn lease."

Sean straightened up. The glass under his shoes made a crunching sound.

"There's something I should have thrown out the first time I saw it." Sean walked over to his fridge door. On his way he sloshed through the splatters of tomato sauce from a smashed jar and left bloody-looking footprints across the floor.

"Here's where it all started." Sean reached for the slips of paper he had placed under the fridge magnet. His hand froze midair for a moment but then continued to descend on the paper. "That's odd."

Mandy heard the puzzlement in his voice.

"What?"

"The paper with the ghost's name on it and the fortune cookie that started all this were both under this fridge magnet—I put them there when I was cleaning the apartment." Sean pulled the magnet from the fridge door. Two pieces of paper fell into his hand. "Now look at this: the paper with the name on it has been ripped apart on both edges. Only the part that was under the magnet is left." Sean held the paper out for Mandy to see. "The fortune cookie stuff has not been ripped at all."

"That's strange."

"Yeah, but this whole thing is strange." Sean thought for a bit. "I'll bet that the fortune cookie proverb is powerful—maybe that's why he couldn't touch it."

"Maybe," Mandy, echoed, "but that doesn't seem right to me."

"Lots of things don't seem right to me." The anger was back in Sean's voice. "I get crazy messages on the beach in Mexico. I get spooky messages in your apartment. I get faces in the mirror…"

Mandy jumped, "Mexico! You got messages in Mexico? What message did you get in Mexico?"

"The name: Noble Peter Hastings. But I thought it was Noble Parch Hastings at first. But then I figured out that it was Peter. That's what I was saying when he appeared in the mirror when I was in the shower. And that's what I was saying to myself just before you came over for dinner and he showed up in my living room … Darn … I don't think I should be saying his name should I?"

"Maybe," said Mandy, "but aren't you intrigued that you got a message in Mexico about a Dead'er in Vancouver, and then a message in Vancouver about a boy who drowned in Mexico?"

"… and then a message in my kitchen telling me to mind my own business." continued Sean.

"If that's what this message is," said Mandy.

Sean looked at her, "What about your kitchen?"

Mandy felt a squeezing sensation travel through her gut.

"I'll come up with you," he said.

"When is running away ever a good choice?" asked Mandy.

She had her head down and did not see Katie put her pencil into her mouth. Katie did that when she was thinking.

"Oh I can think of lots of times," said Katie after a pause. "Bad blind dates. Out of money at a restaurant. No bus ticket when those bus police guys come by. Diarrhoea in the bedpan…"

Mandy looked up at her friend. "Three things Katie. One: The term is liquid stool. Two: that was a rhetorical question. It doesn't need an answer because everybody is supposed to know the correct answer—which, in case you haven't heard, is no! There isn't any good reason to run away."

Katie pursed her lips. Mandy reached up and took the pencil out of Katie's mouth.

"And three: don't put your pencil in your mouth when you're on the ward. That's a route for germ transfer and they'll fail you if you keep doing it."

Katie pouted, "One: you've obviously never been on a really bad blind date. And two: that's just how I think," Katie added with a lopsided smile. "And three. Oh I don't have a number three." Katie looked at Mandy and frowned, "You're always full of smart answers. I wish I were more like you."

"Really?" Mandy raised an eyebrow.

"Well only when it comes to smart stuff. In normal stuff I still want to be me."

"Normal stuff?"

"Hair, and make-up, and boys," Katie said in a voice she might have used when explaining things to a child, "Things the rest of us are interested in."

Mandy smiled.

"Can I have my pencil back now?"

If Katie managed to pass practicum, it would be a miracle. It would also be a great loss to the profession if she failed. Katie was compassionate and intuitive with patients. Unlike Mandy, Katie seemed to have difficulty retaining clinical knowledge. Memory work was a struggle for her. When it came to patient interaction however, Mandy felt like a clumsy beginner when she saw Katie at work. Katie was brilliant at handling even the most difficult patients. Fortunately for Katie's friends, her intuition was not just reserved for her patients.

"Are you thinking of running away from that strange and awkward, but good-looking boy in your building?"

"No, *he's* thinking of running away."

"Running away from you? I don't believe it. You're not pregnant or anything, are you? No, you're way too smart for that. And a bit of a prude: I'll bet you haven't even kissed him yet," Katie mocked Mandy's voice, "A nursing student shouldn't be distracted from her studies!" Katie laughed. "*He's* not running away from you. If anything, you're probably just leading him on by being a big tease."

Mandy sighed, "I'm beginning to regret that I told you anything about Sean in the first place."

"Oh you never have anything to regret, Mandy. So what's up with this, Sean?"

"He thinks someone is trying to force him out of his apartment."

"Really? Why would someone try to do that?"

"We're not sure. Sean thinks that it's someone we know—or at least someone we've met. I'm not so sure. It seems out of character for this guy to do something like that. I don't even think he'd be capable of it."

"Does this 'someone' who may or may not be forcing your boyfriend out of his apartment have a name?"

"Noble…"

"Ohhh, I like that," Katie got a faraway look in her eyes. "It's nice and old fashioned. My grandfather had a friend named Noble. They flew planes together in the war or something. My grandfather used to tell us stories but he's dead now, so of course no more stories. It's only been few years and already I'm forgetting some of them."

"You should write them down."

"I should get one of my cousins to do it—you know, at the time we didn't think that they were all that important. We only miss them now that he's dead," Katie sighed.

"We don't miss some things till they're gone."

"I guess so," Katie said, "and in a way he did write the stories down, by telling them to us. I'm like a book of my grandfather's stories. Aren't I?" Katie cocked her head to one side, "I just wish I had a better memory."

"What happened to your grandfather's friend, Noble?"

"Oh he's dead too. All my grandfather's friends died before he did. He went to a lot of funerals."

"Sometimes a long life isn't such a good thing."

There was a pause between the young women for a time. Katie spoke first.

"So why would this Noble want your boyfriend to leave his apartment?"

"I don't know. It makes no sense for him to do what he did."

"Do what?"

"Break all the dishes."

"Break all the dishes!" Katie laughed then stopped herself, "I'm sorry for laughing. It's just that breaking dishes sounds like the sort of thing an angry woman would do."

Mandy eyes widened, "It does; I hadn't thought of that."

"It's something a woman would do in the middle of an argument—people communicate in the strangest ways sometimes," said Katie in a matter-of-fact voice. "Remember that elderly man I dealt with yesterday."

"The one who was refusing to eat," said Mandy.

"Yes. His name was Gordon. He was upset because he was being moved to a elder care facility and he had no say in the matter."

"And refusing to eat was a good way to communicate that?"

"No it wasn't a *good* way to communicate but neither is breaking dishes—or running away." Katie smiled, "but people might do either when they're frightened."

"Oh," said Mandy.

"So did you actually see Noble breaking dishes?" asked Katie.

"No," said Mandy, "neither of us saw a thing."

Sean could not remember being so tired in his life. The morning at the car dealership dragged on and on. At lunchtime Sean sat at the empty table and opened his little container of sandwiches. His plastic lunch kit and the jar of peanut butter, also plastic, were among the few things the ghost had not broken.

After taking a couple bites of his sandwich he rested his head on his arms. He needed just a little rest before taking on the afternoon's washing.

"If I hadn't seen it, I might not have a believed it. Pauletta, she'd tell me I was lying. That Sean, she says, he's too skinny, but he's a good boy. Hard worker. No waste time. But should I tell her this? Look at you. Sleeping in the middle of the day. No shame."

Sean rubbed his eyes. "I'm on my lunch break."

"Lunch break? It's three o'clock!" said Tony.

"Oh!" Sean looked at his watch, "Farts in a cup," he mumbled and began to scratch his forearms. "I'm sorry. I guess I had better get back to work." He stood.

"I have a delivery to make. You come with me," said Tony.

"I'm really sorry, but I'm so tired. I really shouldn't be driving."

"No sleep? Must be this girl. She is good, no?" Tony smiled at Sean.

"No. I mean yes. The girl is nice. I did what you said; I just talked to her. And it's true: the more I talk to her the nicer she is. She's not the problem right now."

"Oh," said Tony, "you stay up all night because of boy?"

"Yes. I mean no! It's not like that. Noble wrecked everything in my kitchen and he tore up my magazines."

"This is not good," said Tony, "you come with me now. You no have to drive. You tell me everything. But you say no names. You promise?"

"I promise," said Sean, "no names."

"Good boy. First we tell Pauletta you wash no more cars today. You coming with me."

Sean hurriedly placed his half-eaten sandwich back into the plastic container and sealed the lid. Tony left the room and Sean hurried after him. Sean did not stop to put his container into his locker. Today he was not going to be tempted to eat in the car. Curiosity had pushed his hunger aside. Sean suspected that Tony knew more about the situation that Sean was in than Tony had let on during their last conversation. Maybe Tony knew how to make the whole problem just disappear. Maybe he could make Noble go away.

"That would be the perfect solution; if Tony can make Noble go away then I can stay in my apartment!" thought Sean. After a moment Sean frowned. "No, not so perfect." He remembered that even with everything that had happened in his kitchen Mandy still seemed determined to help Noble. "Without this whole business with Noble what reason will I have to see Mandy?"

"Why does it have to be so complicated?" thought Sean. "I don't want to live in a haunted place and if I leave the apartment the ghost won't follow me. That's what Tony said. But if I move out of my building, how will I see Mandy?" Sean shook his head "and if Noble was gone why would Mandy come see me?"

Chapter Nine

Out of Sight . . .

Noble:

I knew that she had been leaving messages written in rice or flour all over my haunt. I saw them when I drifted back from Gavin's grave. I should have also considered that Stringers like Sean must be pretty rare in this city. He was the first Stringer in my haunt in decades. I should have known that a thief like Mary would go after something as rare and valuable as a Stringer, even if he wasn't in her haunt.

I was waiting for Sean to come through the front door when she caught me. I didn't see or feel her approach at all. She must have come through the window behind me. Mary sieved me down quickly. She threw me out of Sean's chair and then spun Sean's table over on top of me and used it to pin me down. It's difficult to move some things—especially big things. It takes concentration and fades you down a fearsome lot. While I was still half in shock and struggling under the table, she ripped up all Sean's magazines and threw the pages around the room. I wanted to stop her but I was pressed between the wooden floor and the wooden table. Purging! I couldn't lift the table off me. By the time I managed to pull my wits together and figure that I could slide from under the table, Mary was already in the kitchen. I heard the crack that wood makes when it splits and then the sound of breaking dishes. She must have gone Purging berserk in there. I got out from under the table, but by then, the noise had stopped and she was gone. It was all over in seconds. I sped into the kitchen. It was worse than I had imagined. She broke everything. I felt awful. It was all my fault. I'm not sure how Mary found Sean but I am sure that she never would have been looking for him if it had not been for me trying to use him as my Stringer. She never would have found him, and she never would have wrecked his kitchen.

I don't what Mary thought she would gain by scaring my Stringer half to death. Maybe she thought that he would get angry and refuse to be my Stringer. Maybe she thought he would leave. Who wouldn't leave after what she did? Maybe Mary wants to be the only Dead'er in this whole city with a Stringer. Maybe she wants to be the only Dead'er in this city period.

Mary must have had her own haunt somewhere. I swore, right then, that if I ever found out where it was, I was going to go there and trick her Stringer into summoning me, and then we'd see who would end up being sieved down.

When I heard Sean coming, I was ashamed. That mess was my fault as much as if I had been strong enough to break all of those shelves myself. I was sure that Sean wasn't going to even want to talk to me again. I don't blame him. If I was a Lye'ver, and I had met up with any of Mary's attacks or stunts, I'd never want to have anything to do with Mary or any Deader ever again! If I kept away from Sean, then Mary would too. I resolved to do what any decent Dead'er would do: keep his Stringer safe.

I couldn't bring myself to slide away through the window the way Mary had done. I waited till Sean unlocked his door to let himself in, and I drifted out of his apartment and away from him. I would use doors from now on, like a decent Dead'er, and not slide through windows, or crawl through vents into places where I wasn't welcome. I waited outside the front door of the building till Mandy arrived. She looked tired, the way she often did after studying. I thought of manifesting myself to her but I didn't want to frighten her. Then again, I thought, Mandy didn't frighten easily. She didn't jump when she saw me the way Sean did. By the time I had reached a decision to show myself to Mandy, she had already walked past me into the building. I followed her. She mounted the stairs. She didn't climb as far as her own floor but went through the door that led to the second floor hallway. I was glad that she was going to Sean; he would need her support. I only hoped that she wouldn't think that I had done the damage. The thought of losing Mandy hurt more than the sense of loss for my Stringer. And Mandy was only a Voyant. I wasn't a very logical Dead'er. I hoped that I wouldn't forget Sean and Mandy like I had forgotten nearly all the others over the years. Even more, I hoped that they wouldn't forget me.

A SUBURB JUST OUTSIDE VANCOUVER, JULY 2009

"The problem with Coquitlam," Ty announced, "is that it isn't what it pretends to be, and so it can't help but fail to be what it is."

"What?" Katie asked in a voice that always seemed to slide up in pitch. She was sitting beside Ty in the back seat of Sean's car.

"Just nod as if what he says makes sense," snorted Mandy over her shoulder. "Then he won't try to explain himself. It's much less painful that way."

Sean laughed, but kept both hands on the wheel and his eyes on the road, the way he had been taught by Tony.

"What I mean," added Ty when the laughter had died down, "is that Coquitlam is just a bedroom community for Vancouver. That's what it is, and that's what it should accept being. It doesn't need to, and shouldn't waste money duplicating urban structures."

It was a Sunday morning. All four were dressed casually and in good humour. Sean had purchased the used sedan from the dealership where he worked. Of course it was one Tony had recommended. Despite having relatively high mileage it ran well. Paula had written up a purchase agreement for Sean with generous repayment terms. Tony had also seen to it that Sean only paid for parts when the car was due for its regular maintenance.

"Bedroom community or not, people need sewers, schools, skating rinks, and swimming pools where they live," said Mandy.

"Its comments like that that remind me that you're the most 'alliterate' person that I know." Ty laughed at his own pun.

Mandy ignored him, "Those aren't duplicate urban structures; they are community services."

"People like to shop and go to the dentist close to home," added Katie.

"See, Katie agrees with me," said Mandy.

They were driving on a wide boulevard past a series of sprawling retail structures and their vast parking lots. The names of the various stores and outlets towered above them on colourful signs. There were relatively few cars on the road.

Ty turned to his left, "Would you like to live out here?"

"No way!" said Katie. "It's so far from everything."

"Ha!" said Ty. "Katie knows what she likes. Despite all the shopping opportunities, this place has no urban heart."

"Maybe people don't want to be in the big city all the time," countered Mandy.

"No," said Katie, "sometimes we'd rather be at the beach—where it's quiet." She leaned forward so that her face was next to Sean's. "Is it much further? I'm not sure I can listen to these two bicker much longer."

Ty turned his attention back to Katie, "It's not bickering, Precious; it's simply a discussion."

Katie sat back and giggled, momentarily leaning her head on Ty's shoulder. "I like it when you call me that."

Mandy turned to Sean, "Yes, Sean. Are we there yet?" She asked quizzically. "I'm not sure how much more of 'that' I can take," she tipped her head towards the giggling pair in the back seat.

Sean smiled. In the rear view mirror he saw Katie stick out her tongue at Mandy.

As they drove on, the suburban shopping district transitioned to a more residential area. Then further on, the homes and lots became larger. There was a general sigh of relief and anticipation when Sean turned the car onto the regional park road.

"White Pine Beach," Sean read the sign aloud.

"Hurray," said Katie. "I thought we'd never get here."

Sean parked the car. Katie got out immediately and ran down to the water, slipping off her shoes as she crossed the sand. Ty followed her, picking up one shoe and then the other a few steps away. Katie splashed her way along the shore, every few steps stopping to turn a laughing face toward Ty, who was following, grinning, holding her shoes.

Sean helped Mandy lift a blanket and a picnic basket out of the trunk. They spread the blanket on the grass above the sandy beach area. Without discussion they both removed their shoes, and sat next to each other. Mandy sighed and ran her fingers through her hair. She had worn her hair loose. Sean decided that he liked her hair this way best.

"Thanks again Sean, you're a darling for doing this."

"My pleasure to be at your service, ma'am!" Sean smiled, but stopped when Mandy seemed serious.

"I don't just mean for the ride out here. I thought that it might be good if we reconnected too. Seems like we've been nearly strangers the last little while. I haven't even seen you at the Laundromat—just the occasional glimpse as I'm coming in or out of our building."

"I was sure you were quite busy enough with your training," Sean hesitated. He looked away from Mandy for a bit. "It's probably pretty tough for you to squeeze in social time." After a pause he added, "I've been working lots too."

Mandy looked up at Sean. "Let's not pretend that it's just work and school that's been keeping us from getting together."

"Ok," responded Sean, "But I didn't see any way around our disagreement. And I didn't want you to get hurt."

"I wasn't going to get hurt, and I don't like leaving things half done..." Mandy found that she'd raised her voice. She took a deep breath. "Sean, I saw the damage for myself. I helped you clean up, remember? I know how devastating it was, and how scared you'd be after something like that, but whatever it was it didn't hurt you. There was no reason to think that it'd hurt me either."

"You're just guessing about that. We don't even know why it attacked my place and not yours."

"True," said Mandy, "but aren't you anxious to find out what's going on?"

"You know, I didn't sleep for three nights after that happened! I would have moved but I couldn't get out of the lease. The manager still wanted to charge me rent for the balance of the term. The only reason I didn't move was that I couldn't afford to." Sean was surprised to hear the pleading note in his voice. What did he hope Mandy would say or do for him?

"It's ok to be scared," said Mandy quietly.

"What do you know about being scared?"

Sean felt himself small and frightened. He was in bed and there were angry voices permeating his bedroom wall: his parents screaming at each other. Sean opened his eyes. Mandy was looking down at her hands. Down on the beach, Ty and Katie were looking in their direction. Had he been shouting?

Sean turned to Mandy, "I'm sorry."

"Me too," she said.

They were silent for a time. Ty and Katie wandered up the beach toward them. Katie sat down next to Mandy.

Ty borrowed the car keys from Sean and returned with a Frisbee. He tossed it into Sean's lap. "Come on, let's fling this around a bit. It's the beach!" Sean got up slowly and followed Ty down to the sandy area. After a few minutes Katie joined them. Katie had a habit of giving a little scream when she caught the disk. Sean found it difficult not to smile when it happened. Watching her play made him feel better about his own abilities. She screamed louder when she let the disk drop.

The beach started to fill with people. Ty tossed the disk to one of a pair of teenagers who had been watching the three of them play. The boys joined in and Sean saw that Ty had been indulging him and Katie somewhat. In response to the skill shown by the teens, Ty began to do tricks of his own, catching the disk behind his back or by jumping in the air. Ty kicked a leg in the air and shot the disk at one of the boys from under his thigh. Katie laughed and clamped. Sean waved at Ty and walked back to where Mandy was sitting alone on the blanket.

"You don't like Frisbee?" he asked Mandy.

"Sometimes. Today I'd just like to take it easy," she replied. She smiled up at Sean. "You looked good out there."

Sean scanned her face. There was no hint of mockery.

"Do you want to go for a walk?"

"That's more my speed." Mandy got to her feet and slipped on her shoes.

They walked away from the beach, and then through a stand of trees that sat at the edge of the parking lot. A sign next to a well-worn trail suggested that it led around the small lake.

"Let's take this one," said Mandy.

Sean nodded. They walked side by side for a time. When the trail narrowed Mandy stepped aside to let Sean lead. The next time it happened, Sean allowed Mandy to go first. They spoke little. Part way through Sean looked at his watch.

"Tired of my company already?" Mandy asked, fixing Sean in a steady stare.

"For months now." Sean smiled. Mandy tried to hold an offended face but soon laughed aloud. Sean realized how much he missed that sound. The tension between them seemed to flow away.

"Actually, I was wondering if we'd be missed."

"Not likely," said Mandy. "I think Katie wouldn't mind having me out of earshot for a while longer. She's been practicing her 'I'm so cute' giggle for weeks."

"Doesn't she use it when you're around? Sounded to me like she was already at it!"

"Oh yes. Didn't you hear her in the car on the way here; she laughed at everything Ty said."

"Yeah, it made me want to turn on the radio."

Mandy smiled, "Well the deal is that if I hear her do it more than a dozen times, then I get to start imitating her. I made the rule up so that she doesn't get too annoying. I'm used to her, but you're not and I didn't her to spoil your day."

"Oh, Katie's laugh couldn't spoil my day," said Sean teasingly.

"Is that so?" asked Mandy, her eyebrows raised.

"Of course, I'm completely distracted by someone else," Sean replied, then without looking at Mandy, he took the lead on the next section of the trail. "You smooth devil," he said to himself.

When Mandy and Sean arrived back at the beach, Katie was alone on the blanket. She was lying down and had her eyes closed. They spotted Ty at a distance. He was in the middle of a game of Ultimate Frisbee. Hearing them approach Katie opened an eye.

"Feeling abandoned?" asked Mandy.

"Not a bit," said Katie. "We just ate. I thought I'd let my food settle a bit. It seems Ty doesn't ever stand still. I want to go for a swim later. Are you in?" Katie looked up at Mandy and then, when Mandy did not respond right away, she glanced at Sean. "Or perhaps you two will be wandering off together again?"

"Not till after we eat," said Mandy. She dropped onto the blanket and patted a spot beside her, indicating that Sean should sit too. "Least I could do was prepare you a decent meal," she said to Sean, "after you were nice enough to do all the driving."

"Why is it that the girls are always the ones preparing the food?" Katie rolled onto her side so that she could look at Sean without getting up.

"Not always," said Sean defensively, "I made dinner for Mandy once."

"You did what?" Katie propped herself up onto her elbows. "Mandy, you never told me this. That sounds so romantic."

Sean grinned nervously.

"No it was nothing like that," said Mandy quickly, "It was more like a working dinner. And we never actually got around to eating."

"Oh my," said Katie lasciviously. "I'm too delicate to ask what you got up to that made you forget dinner."

Sean felt his face grow rather hot.

Mandy spoke quickly, "It wasn't quite like that—although, we did—"

Sean looked at Mandy.

She paused for a moment then gave Sean a playful smile, "We got so carried away with what we were working on, that I guess we just forgot about eating."

"Oh my," said Katie again, her eyebrows raised, "and what were you working on that was so exciting?"

"There were…" started Sean.

"… some maintenance problems with the laundry machines in our apartment building—the driers to be specific." Mandy cut Sean off and continued in a flat voice. "Sean first brought the situation to my attention when we passed in the stairwell. And after I inspected a machine, I came to the same conclusion as Sean. We both approached our building manager separately, but the manager maintained that…"

"Ok, enough," Katie plugged her ears. "I don't need the whole boring story."

Mandy winked at Sean. Katie lay back down on the blanket. "Anyway, if Sean were a gentleman," Katie clipped, "he would repeat the offer of dinner. An interrupted dinner doesn't count, does it?" Katie opened a single eye and winked at Mandy. Mandy smiled back.

"Dinner means cooking," Sean said to himself, "—pots and pans I've got—they weren't broken." He formed a mental picture of his kitchen. "The dishes are new…" He pictured the set he had purchased to replace the ones smashed in the ghost's attack. "… She better be impressed." Sean frowned, "What else would I need?—I've even got salt and pepper shakers now." Sean imagined himself cooking, "Spices! I'll need a spice rack,—and a new sugar bowl for when I serve her tea—she's always asking for tea!" Sean made more mental notes, "I have to make sure I have tea, and real garlic bread, and butter, and—" Sean grimaced. "I'm going to have to get rid of all the evidence that I've been living on takeout food—I'd better give myself a few days."

He turned to Mandy, "How about Tuesday?"

"Make it Wednesday. I can take the whole evening off," said Mandy. She tilted her head towards Katie and added, "and I'll have a late start the next morning."

After they were done swimming, the group separated into changing cubicles to dry off and dress for the ride home. While towelling his feet, Sean ran the last few hours though his mind. It had been a long time since he had so much fun. The four of them had splashed about in the knee-deep water close to shore. They played tag. Sean did not have many memories of playing like that as a child. Some of his babysitters were good. He remembered playing toy cars with one of them. His early teen years were not any happier than his childhood. He had not done well at sports, so he never tried to join any athletic team. He remembered being bored most of the time. Even his summers were dull. He remembered wishing he were old enough to get a job.

The summer Sean turned sixteen was the summer he discovered that having his own money could make him feel independent and mature. He liked working. Around the same time Sean began to think about travel. He thought it would be good for him to see new places. Some of his classmates had travelled. Their parents took them places: Europe, Britain, Italy, The States, California, Florida, Mexico. Mexico. What if he had gone to Mexico with his parents? He was sure he would have been happier if his parents had taken him places. What if his parents had been able to go places without arguing? What if? How happy they might have all been? And what if he drowned? They would have missed him for sure.

Sean was surprised. Why he was thinking about drowning? Was it because he had just been playing in the lake? Because he had been afraid of swimming too far out? Because Ty had been teasing him? Or maybe it was because of the drowned boy? The boy was seventeen and had drowned while on vacation with his parents. How awful those parents must have felt. How awful they must still feel. And what did the ghost—Sean had to force himself to recall the boy's name—Noble—want with the name of the drowned boy?

Maybe Mandy was right. It would be good to get answers.

Chapter Ten

Opportunity Ignored
Is Seldom Yours Again

Lucky Numbers 87, 22, 5, 55, 13

Sean perused the magazine section of the grocery store until he found a recipe that he felt was straight forward enough that even he might easily follow it. It was one day before his dinner date with Mandy. He rejected one recipe that asked him to braise, and another that called for an overnight marinade. It was also critical that there were no unrecognized ingredients. Endives and fennel were instantly rejected. Pepper, butter, or onion, were acceptable. Rather than purchasing the magazine, Sean carefully copied the directions onto a discarded receipt he found near the checkout. Then he walked carefully through each aisle until he found all the named ingredients. Back home, Sean arranged his groceries across his inadequate kitchen counter in alphabetical order before beginning step one of the instructions. He stood by the stove while the rice cooked, repeatedly looking at his phone to mark the elapsed time. When meal was finished Sean served himself a portion and ate it. It seemed good, if he allowed for the fact that he had nothing like the pilaf before.

On his way home from work the evening of the dinner with Mandy, Sean stopped at the grocery store to purchase more of the items he had consumed the previous night, as well as a couple pastries. This night the texture of the rice seemed much improved and Sean noted, for future reference, that rice seemed to prefer not to be checked on, by lifting the pot lid, every few minutes.

As soon as he had served Mandy the mug of tea, Sean felt a sense of relief. In his head, he declared the dinner a success. He had gone well beyond the basic pasta and sauce that he had offered Mandy on their last dinner date. The rice pilaf was superb. Mandy complimented the dish and ate her serving with enthusiasm. She declined a second helping however, and Sean was not sure how to interpret this. He had wanted to eat some more, but of course, once Mandy demurred on a second helping, he knew better than to take one for himself. He would have been eating while Mandy had nothing to do but watch.

Mandy also seemed pleased by the flan tarts Sean served as dessert. He had kept them in the fridge right until the moment he was ready to serve them.

Their dinner conversation was lively. Sean spoke about his work, describing the sales manager, with whom he had a cool relationship, and the two he considered his friends, Paula and Tony, or Pauletta and Antonio as they called each other.

Mandy made Sean laugh with her imitations of Katie. She also had stories about some of the other girls in her year.

It was after he served the tea however, that their conversation slowed. Mandy cupped both her hands around the mug and thanked Sean. She took only tentative sips however and was still holding the mug long after her tea had cooled. Despite the long spaces Sean did not feel awkward. It seemed that Mandy was waiting for him to bring up some topic.

"I've been thinking about Noble," he said at last.

"Oh," said Mandy, she sounded only a little relived, "me too."

Whatever topic Mandy had been waiting for him to open, Sean saw that it was not Noble. He wondered what it could be.

"So I don't know why he wrecked my kitchen but maybe he had his reasons. We really don't know how things look from his perspective."

"Sean, I'm still not convinced that it was Noble," Mandy countered, "but the fact that we disagree doesn't have to stop us from figuring out what is going on. There's lots of stuff to explain: the writing in the flour, the message about the drowned boy, the wrecked kitchen, and why Noble picked us to talk to in the first place."

"That's the easy part!" Sean's voice had an authoritative ring to it.

Mandy wondered if this was because he'd managed to make it through hosting her for dinner without tripping over his own feet. She decided that she liked this side of him.

Sean continued, "The ghost explained, I'm a Stringer. I can perceive ghosts: it's a rare thing."

Sean's run of confidence seemed to have gone a little beyond certainty and now veered toward arrogance. She liked Sean less as a braggart, she thought to herself, but she also immediately forgave him his moment of weakness. She had seldom met anyone, who at their base was as modest, unassuming, or as earnest as Sean.

Sean seemed to be thinking of Noble still. He continued, "Maybe we should finish our research."

Mandy smiled as if she had been waiting for the suggestion, "I did. Well most of it." Mandy put down her tea and walked over to where she had left her bag. She pulled out some sheets of paper. "Here," she said, laying them out on the table.

Sean picked up his own mug and Mandy's and placed them on the floor. He looked at the papers Mandy had spread out on the table. One sheet held some names and address. The other two were computer printouts of photographs. Mandy put her finger on these first of these. The portrait was of the type usually taken of students each school each year. The background appeared to be a bookshelf, the titles, of course, indistinct. In front of them with his hand on a globe was a teenager. "This is the boy." After a couple seconds Mandy pushed the first photo aside and rotated the other sheet so that its image faced Sean. It was a picture of a distraught-looking couple, seen from the waist up. They were looking away from the camera. The woman, even seen in what was almost a profile, was puffy-eyed, as if she were crying. She clung to the man's arm. "And these are his parents," announced Mandy.

"Noble's parents?"

"No, the drowned boy's. That's his grade eleven school picture. One of the local newspapers ran these pictures with an article about the drowning. The pictures weren't difficult to find once I knew what I was looking for. I just scanned the archives of the smaller papers from the date of the drowning and for about two weeks after. There's a lag time for local newspapers because many of them are only published weekly."

"Interesting," said Sean, but that was not the word he had wanted to say. Oddly, Sean perceived that his sympathies seemed more with the parents than with the drowned boy. This surprised him since as a teenager he had often wondered what it would have been like to lose his own parents. He felt a pang of sadness. "Was he an only child?"

"Yes, I'm pretty sure he was." Mandy reflected for a moment. "There is no mention of any other children in any of the articles and that's just the sort of thing these human interest stories love to focus on."

"So what do we do with this now that we know who he is?"

"We tell Noble of course," Mandy had used her mater-of-fact voice.

"And how so you propose that we do that?" asked Sean.

"You call him the way you did last time."

"Last I called him he wrecked my kitchen."

"You don't know for sure that it was Noble that did that."

"I know for sure it was wrecked!" Sean was conscious of raising his voice. He took a few deep breaths. "Look I'm not calling him again. If you want to talk to him, you call him—from your own apartment!"

Mandy looked somewhat sheepish. "I tried that," she said, "It didn't work."

Sean decided that Mandy was even more beautiful embarrassed than angry. He thought that he could never hold any anger towards her.

"That's because you're not a Stringer," Sean said. "We Stringers can see and hear ghosts. We're like a string between their world and ours."

"Hear?"

"Supposedly. Except that for some reason I can't hear Noble." Sean shrugged apologetically, "And we can call them too … they want to be called." Pride insinuated itself back into Sean's voice. "Summoned is the word Noble used. They like to be summoned. It gives them energy or substance or something like that."

Mandy mused, "You're like a guitar string, I guess, able to be plucked at either end. Then again I'm not sure that music is a good analogy," she added. She suddenly smiled, "Actually Mr. Stringer, your kitchen has been the scene of quite a bit of discord!"

"I'm not summoning Noble." Sean clenched his jaw. The situation was serious and Mandy was behaving as if what had happened was some sort of joke or prank. Sean picked up the two mugs and stood. He held a mug in either hand and crossed his arms. "Would you like more tea? I could make us a fresh pot."

"No thanks. I think it's time for me to get going." Mandy stood too.

Sean suddenly recalled Mandy's remark to Katie about having the whole evening available but he thought it would be best not to mention it.

"Thanks for dinner, Sean," Mandy collected her bag off the floor. "Everything was wonderful. You're a great cook." She placed a hand tentatively on Sean's forearm. Sean felt himself take a deep gulp of air. He held it. Mandy quickly turned however and walked toward the apartment entranceway. Sean followed her to his door, carefully letting the air out of his chest.

"Thanks for coming. It was fun. I really enjoyed cooking," in his head Sean added, "for you." Sean looked over his shoulder at the papers Mandy had left on the table. "Let me get the papers for you." He took a step away from the door.

Mandy's hand was on his arm again. "No, Sean you keep them. Who knows, you might change your mind and figure that Noble needs your help after all. You may be the only one he can talk to." She squeezed his arm again. "Good night." Mandy stepped away from the door and turned down the hallway. Sean forced himself to not watch Mandy retreat. He closed his apartment door, and then laid his head against the door's smooth wooden panel.

The papers remained on the table for days. By the end of the week they were stained with spots of grease and tiny specks of soya sauce. One sheet even bore an imprint from the bottom of a takeout container.

On Friday night Sean watched his favourite crime drama over a plate of chow mein noodles. This time the woman detective was aided by a psychic. The psychic offered advice that the detective was initially reluctant to take but which ultimately lead to the identity of the killer. The psychic had urged the detective to pursue this particular case because the ghost of the killed girl could not rest until the killer was brought to justice. In the closing scene, as the killer was being led away in handcuffs, the translucent figure of the killed girl appeared and smiled appreciatively at the detective. The detective made a tentative wave to the girl who smiled, waved back, and then faded from view.

Immediately after the credits Sean turned off the TV. The chow mein noodles had come with a fortune cookie. This he cracked open and read: Opportunity ignored is seldom yours again. On the back again were a series of numbers: 87 22 5 55 13. He sat in silence for a moment before unfolding the couch, pulling off his shirt and jeans and slipping into bed.

The next morning, Saturday, Sean had his customary bowl of cereal. He sat in his chair and ate it, once again looking over the papers. Part way though the bowl he picked up one of the sheets of paper and folded up the bottom quarter, making a crease by running his fingers along the folded edge. He ripped the sheet along this crease. He fetched the pencil from the kitchen and wrote a couple sentences on the slip.

Sean showered, then returned to the living room to dress. He folded the papers and stuffed them into his pocket. Once out the door he went up the stairs and pushed the slip of paper under Mandy's door. Then, after jogging down to the parking lot behind his building, Sean got into his car and drove away.

Noble:

I used to tell Pedro that you didn't have to go when a Stringer summoned you. It was tough but you could ride it out and stay where you were. It was hard to resist though, I told him, because of course it rolls you up when you go. Resist. That's what I had planned to do. Resist. Ride it out. Even if this Stringer summoned me I was going to let him go and wait for the next— whenever that happened. Whenever.

I reached out to a Dead'er once who said that he couldn't find a Stringer in his haunt. He was pretty much convinced that he was just going to fade

down to nothing, become a Zonker. He was probably right. Without a Stringer every few decades you're bound to fade down a fearsome lot—maybe all
the way down like this guy dreaded. Never been there myself of course. You
can only fade down all the way once. That guy's problem was that his haunt
was in the country. Farms and such. He had been bit by a rattlesnake while
doing his chores. Rare to find a Stringer out there. Well, Stringers aren't any
more rare, it's that Lye'vers are more rare, and so few Lye'vers are Stringers
that it's pretty impossible to find someone to roll you up.

The point was that Sean's summoning was different. It was a pull, a deep
pull like the voice of your mother or someone else important to you. A voice
you find hard to resist and impossible to ignore. I felt it like a fishing hook in
my head. It was the easiest thing in the world to let myself drift over towards
Sean, rolling up as I went. It was like being woken out of sleep—from what I
remember when I used to sleep—even after the waking itself, the slow in-
crease of awareness, and strength. I even felt myself start to manifest, but of
course, I believed at the time, that couldn't happen during the daylight. When
I stopped resisting the movement was easier, smoother. I was pulled through
the blocks of my old haunt and then across the city, brilliant in the sunshine,
then through some undeveloped areas. I was sure that I passed through a few
haunts because I sensed some other Dead'ers as I went, but it was daytime;
they were sluggish and weak and could not speak to me even if I reached out
to them. I was amazed however, by my own growing energy. Sean must have
been a ridiculously strong Stringer.

I came upon Sean in a parking lot by some sort of uncultivated field.
There were a handful of trees nearby. The lot was deserted except for a single
vehicle that I guessed belonged to him. It was not very difficult to see why
Sean had chosen this place. It was far from his home, and far from anything
that could be easily broken. But for such a strong Summoner he wasn't
thinking very deeply. It was broad daylight. How did he expect me to do
anything in daylight? I couldn't manifest. What did he want me to do?

I arrived and hovered around Sean. He laid out a few sheets of paper on
the soil near him and weighed them down with stones, then Sean squatted
and used his hands to smooth a patch of earth directly in front him.

I suppose that Sean expected that I would write on the patch of soil he had
smoothed but soil is difficult for us Dead'ers. Most of it is bits of broken rock
and sand, which of course, were never alive. If something was never alive
then it cannot be dead and if it is not dead then a Dead'er cannot move it.
Minutes passed while Sean sat in front of that patch of dirt. I hovered near
him, unable to manifest in the daylight and unable to write. I had a strong
sense of anticipation but I could not figure out what it was that I was waiting
for. Perhaps what I felt was the hope that at some moment Sean would give
up and stop summoning me. My agitation grew to irritation. I wondered if

Sean might ever stop to think that he might be asking me to do something that I could not do.

My frustration grew to anger. I was angry with Sean for his pointless summoning. I was angry with myself for not being able to think of a way to communicate with him. I was more than read to cry—if a Dead'er had tears.

Then all at once, at last, Sean ceased his summoning. I was released.

Relief! It was being like let out of a tiny box into the open air. I rose up away from Sean and started the long drift back to my haunt. It was unpleasant to be so exposed in daylight, but being summoned had rolled me up greatly and I felt well capable of the trip. I could sense my Stringer behind me as I drifted away. I called to Sean knowing that he could not hear me, "See you tonight! The usual place, my haunt, your apartment!"

Then Sean did a stupid thing. Stupid. Stupid. Stupid. He summoned Mary.

I could hardly believe that he would do such a thing but I could hear his summons of that Dead'er even in plain daylight. He called her full name. He said he was summoning her. You can't hear your own summoning of course; you feel it. This summoning I heard, like a whistle or a note of music. I felt something go out from Sean and past me. It was the strongest I'd ever sensed. I was stunned for a moment, like you are when a horse or something rushes past you, and you aren't hurt but are thinking that you might be, just from the sheer rush of it all happening.

Maybe minutes passed. Maybe seconds. And then there she was. Mary. I don't know how far she had come from but she arrived like a tornado. I didn't hear her coming: I felt it. Like something about to slam into me from behind—which I guess was what she had been planning to do. I ducked her blow. I was pretty smart about it too: I slid right behind Sean. Mary slid right over us. It was like some freakishly fast wave that broke over our heads and then just as quickly melted away. Sean shivered. I spun keeping Sean between Mary and I as she came at us the second time, perhaps a bit slower but with just as much fury. She was working up broken pieces of bark, twigs, half-rotten leaves, whatever dead stuff she could pull up off the ground in her rush toward us. With the debris billowing around her, she hit Sean like a dust storm. I don't think Sean even had time to close his eyes. A second later he was coughing and sputtering, rubbing his eyelids with his hands. I couldn't sense Mary at that moment. I suppose that she had slipped behind a tree, somewhere where she could prepare another charge. Sean bent his face down, and squinting, started writing in the dirt in front of him. Sean's mouth and throat were also in motion so he must have been shouting, but I could not hear him in bright daylight. He was no longer summoning. I ducked under Sean's arm to read what he had written. I read the message just as I felt another wave of debris slam into Sean and I. Sean had written: "Why? Why? Why?" over and over again.

I wanted to shout at Sean that there was no why to evil. Bad people just are. Just like there are good Lye'vers like Mandy, there are also bad Lye'vers. And there are good and bad Dead'ers too. "Mary is just evil!" I shouted at Sean, my poor deaf Stringer. Sean put his hands over his face. It was just in time too, because Mary charged us again. This time she had worked up a dry branch that she must have found nearby. She tried to bring it down on Sean's head but he ducked and the branch caught me across the head. It knocked me down into the dirt. Sean got up and sprinted toward the car. He was inside before Mary could work the branch down on him again. It bounced off the car roof.

I thought that I was done for, that Mary was going to turn around and flatten me with the branch again. But she didn't do that. Instead she dropped the branch and sped over to where Sean had been crouched in the dirt. She read the message aloud, "Why? Why?" she crackled, mockingly. Then Mary spied the papers that Sean had left laid out in the dirt. Despite the turmoil they had remained in place, the stones still weighing down their edges. I saw Mary read them, crackle another laugh and then speed off. I waited a minute to be sure that Mary had gone, then I went over and read the papers for myself.

I heard the car door lock disengage and looked up. I was surprised that Sean had not fled after being forced to retreat from a ghost he himself had summoned. Sean opened the car door and sprinted out. He scooped his papers up off the ground, scattering the stones that had held them in place, got back into his car and sped away. I wanted to follow him back to my haunt. I had come out to this place pretty quickly and I wasn't sure that I'd find my way back just as easily. A Dead'er could fade down just trying to find his way back to his haunt. And being knocked into the ground by Mary hadn't helped my strength either. I thought about it for a bit. My memory wasn't very good and wandering around in daylight was too good a way to fade down. I decided to stay where I was till nightfall.

I thought about what I had seen on the papers. There was a name: Steven James Butler. A couple of address and some pictures. One picture showed a couple of Lye'vers. The other was a picture of a teenager. The teenager was a Dead'er. Don't ask me how I know but us Dead'ers can always tell from a picture whether someone is alive, or dead, or a Dead'er like me. Like most of the stuff about being a Dead'er I'm not sure if this is a gift or a curse. I suppose that Lye'vers might want to know if someone they loved and who had died was a Dead'er or not—because maybe we Dead'ers aren't really gone. But I can't see how it matters. So few Lye'vers are Stringers that chances are they wouldn't be able to see, hear or do anything for their Dead'ers anyway. I guess Dead'ers could see those Lye'vers and do things for them, like rearrange the furniture (provided it was made of wood). But that sort stuff really couldn't be of much use to anyone. It couldn't keep the

Lye'ver safe. It's not like bad Lye'vers have a ton of bricks balanced over their head or something, set up so that even a Dead'er could kick out the wooden support. Lye'vers are better at all those sorts of things. Sure Dead'ers can go through walls (provided we don't knock ourselves flat by walking into a wooden stud) and Dead'ers can listen to conversations (provided that it's not daytime of course) but doing those sorts of things is just creepy. It's things like that that got us Dead'ers such a bad reputation. We are not all ghosts. Some of us have self-respect. And manners. Manners dictate that you don't show up in someone's apartment uninvited.

Sure I made Sean call my name and summon me. But that was because Pedro wanted it. He's the one who really needed my Stinger. I don't believe that Stringers should work for free either. I paid my Stringer back. I got him together with that girl. They were having dinner together when they saw me and all my private parts on display in the living room. That was payment enough for rolling me up. I feel guilty about Mary's rampage in Sean's kitchen and about her attack on Sean in that parking lot in the middle of nowhere, but neither manifestation was my fault. Both times Sean had summoned her. I had even warned him not to call her name.

Come night time I was planning on letting Pedro know how things stood. I had already given up on this Stringer—but even if I hadn't he wasn't going to be of any use to either of us if he was going to be summoning Mary all the time. In fact he was pretty dangerous, to himself and to us! Pedro was going to have to find me another Stringer or better yet, he should just find another Dead'er to do his dirty work.

Chapter Eleven

Missing Fillings

Noble:

Pedro seemed agitated. It wasn't his voice; it was more than that. Something about the way he spoke. And as if his pauses and hesitations weren't disconcerting enough he seemed to be deliberately speaking without an accent.

"So what happened then?"

"She came at us a couple more times but by then Sean had figured out that she was just working up dirt and twigs and stuff. He ran and hid in his car."

"Why didn't he just send her away?"

"Send her away? How could he do that? Can he do that?"

"Think about it Noble. If you can call someone you can also tell them to go away. It's the same thing really."

I don't know why I had never thought of that. "So you think my Stringer will be as good at sending Dead'ers away as he is at summoning?"

"I don't know," said Pedro. "You'll have to find that out yourself. Maybe you could ask him to send you far, far away."

It took me a moment to figure that Pedro was joking. I didn't really expect that because he had always seemed to take anything I said about my Stringer very, very seriously. "I'm staying away from my Stringer unless he calls me." I said.

"You shouldn't blame yourself for anything you didn't do." Pedro sounded tender, but then his voice hardened, "however I am blaming you for not keeping your end of our bargain."

"Sorry. Things didn't work out like I expected. But I'm not going where I'm not wanted. I'm no ghost!"

"So how did you make Mary leave?"

"I didn't. She realized that she couldn't get at Sean in his car. I guess she could have gone in through the window or something but then she couldn't take any sticks in to hit him with. Maybe there was nothing dead in the car that she could work up. Maybe not even paper—he left the sheets outside."

"What sheets?" Pedro's accent was completely gone.

"Paper with pictures and names and addresses on them." I tried to remember exactly.

"What names? What addresses?"

If I had been braver, or cleverer or something, I would have made Pedro beg a bit more for the information. He teased me often enough. But that was a pretty big if. I was pretty much incapable of withholding anything from him. I told him as much of the addresses as I remembered. I'm sure my memory was rather incomplete.

"And the names?" said Pedro, "What about the names?"

"Steven, James…" I started.

"Steven. Steven!" echoed Pedro. "Yes, Steven."

"… Butler." I continued.

"That's me! That's me!" Pedro shouted. "Steven James … Butler. Knockers. That's my Purging name. It is. It is. Steven James Butler. I remember now."

"You didn't know your name? How could you forget that? … And how come you told me your name was Pedro—and what happened to your accent?"

"And you're sure Mary saw the addresses?"

"I'm sure. She looked at them and then took off."

"Well you'd better hurry! Unsummoned she won't be strong enough to do anything until night—but after sunset she could…"

"Do what?"

"I don't know why she hates every Dead'er but herself, but she does."

"Dead'ers don't have addresses Pedro, or should I be calling you Steven now. What do those addresses have to do with anything?"

Pedro sounded desperate, "You must go protect them."

"Protect who?"

"My parents, Noble. One of those addresses must be my parents'!"

"Pedro, I can't find any unknown place by its address. I only know my own haunt."

"Then you'd better ask your Stringer."

"But I don't want to go to him uninvited or unsummoned. I'm not a ghost."

"So you keep saying."

"So I have my self-respect."

"Even if it means my parents get hurt. Is that how you are my friend, Noble?"

Sean was on his knees in front of Mandy.

"You know," said Mandy smiling, "I've always dreamed about a handsome young man getting down on one knee in front of me."

Sean shifted so that he could put one knee up. "Glad I could make your dreams come true."

"Shut up and hold still," countered Mandy. She held an eyedropper in one hand. With the other, gloved, she was holding Sean's right eyelid open. "Can't believe that you drove all the way home with so much dirt in your eye. You're a tough kid."

"I've been downgraded from a young man to a kid I suppose. I'm crying with the disappointment."

"Crying isn't such a bad idea. It could help quite a bit actually. Now stop talking."

When Mandy finished, Sean felt like he actually had been crying. The sides of his face were wet. He excused himself to Mandy's bathroom where he ran water over his face and then dried himself off on the closest towel. He spent some time trying to adjust his hair while looking in the mirror.

"I've put tea on," said Mandy once Sean had emerged from the bathroom. "Would you like some?" When Sean nodded yes, she added, "And you can explain to me again what you did." Before Sean could answer Mandy continued, "Frankly, I'm surprised you got any supernatural reaction at all. You did this all in broad daylight. You already told me that Noble said Dead'ers couldn't really do anything in the daytime: they're too weak."

"I summoned both of them, Noble and Mary! With two of them coming at me I'm surprised that I survived the attack!"

"How do you know both of them attacked you?" Mandy challenged. "Did you actually see Noble in the attack … Did you see anybody?"

"No," said Sean. "There was too much dust and stuff coming at me. It was like being in a windstorm. Gusts blew at me again and again. It was dangerous…"

"Really," said Mandy, "and how did you get away?"

"I got into my car."

"Sounds like you barely escaped with your life—from all that, dust!"

"Was that sarcasm?" asked Sean, his brow furrowed.

"I just don't want you to get away with making it seem worse than it was. Patients sometimes exaggerate the events that led to their injuries."

"I'm not a patient!"

"Exactly," Mandy had a note of triumph in her voice, "you're not even really hurt. As far as I can tell all the damage that was done in this attack was that you got some dirt in your eyes. Not much to show for what you're calling a double ghost attack!"

"I'm lucky it was daylight then. It could have been much worse!"

"Maybe it could have been," offered Mandy.

Over tea, they reviewed all the extraordinary events that had taken place since Sean saw the face in the mirror. Sean had to admit that although much had taken place, no real physical harm had been done—"yet" he insisted.

After about half an hour's more conversation, Mandy excused herself, telling Sean that she planned to spend the afternoon studying for a test the next day. She managed, however, only about fifteen minutes of uninterrupted study before Sean knocked on her door again.

"Suppose," said Sean, not waiting for Mandy to greet him, "that the people in the picture know something about what we are dealing with."

"Suppose they do," queried Mandy, "What of it?"

"Well if we go ask them maybe we can find out."

"I thought you would never ask!" Mandy spun away from the door. She called over her shoulder, "I'll get my coat."

By the time Sean managed to choke out, "What about your test?" Mandy was standing in front of him with her jacket and book bag.

"I'll study in the car on the way," she said. She smiled warmly at Sean, "I love adventure. Don't you?" Her eyes sparkled.

Sean resolved to say yes to Mandy's ideas much more often.

The house was on a street that seemed crowded with residences. Sean parked in front of a four-story building. The structure turned out to consist of, on a second look, a series of two-story units stacked one on top of another. Each unit had its own entrance from the street. A forest of stairs, shorter ones to the lower units, and longer ones to the upper, led from the sidewalk to each front door. Mandy scanned the numbers as she went along the sidewalk. Sean trying to keep up, was moving at almost a jog. When he finally reached her mid-block, Mandy was standing still but her eyes were lifted towards the building.

"It's that one there," Mandy pointed to a door above them that was painted a vivid green. She read the numbers aloud while glancing at the paper in her hand.

"Oh I can see that it's one of the addresses you found, but I'm wondering if we should we really bother knocking on more doors." Sean sounded tired.

"I'm really sorry about those other places but there was no way to know which Allan Butler was the right one. And it's not like I could phone them up and ask, hey is this the Butler residence where you took your son on vacation and he drowned?"

Sean nodded. "But…"

"I didn't realize that you were embarrassed so easily."

Sean opened his mouth as if to protest.

"At least you have no reason to be embarrassed around me," Mandy winked at Sean, tossed her hair and began climbing the steps. Sean, his shoulders sagging, followed her.

Embarrassment never left Sean alone for long. He remembered how, as a child he went through a period of bedwetting. In grade school he tore his pants at school. In high school he made a fool of himself by asking one of the popular girls out on a date. Climbing the stairs behind Mandy, Sean grumbled to himself, "Now I'm an adult it's still no better. I fell asleep at work. I got slapped by that waitress in Mexico; everybody in the bar looked at me … And Mandy found me naked in my bathroom. It's not fair."

Sean felt his face grow hot, "What is wrong with me?"

When they reached the top of the stairs, Mandy put a hand to her hair and then adjusted her jacket collar. She turned to look at Sean. "Are you ok?" she asked. She put a soft hand on his forehead and then on his cheek.

If my heart wasn't racing before, it sure is now, thought Sean. "Yeah. I'm ok," he said. It was not really a lie, he thought. Whatever was wrong with him, it was not an illness.

"Well look sharp!" said Mandy. "We don't want them to think that we are freaks."

"Of course not," said Sean, "it's not like we talk to dead people or anything."

"Speak for yourself."

Sean could see that Mandy meant the remark as a joke but he felt his face tighten. Mandy rang the doorbell then turned to look at Sean. "Oh, I'm sorry," she said. She searched his face.

Sean opened his mouth to answer but they both turned to face the door and he said nothing. The door opened.

"Good afternoon," said Mandy. It was the woman from the photograph. Sean was sure of it. She looked older, and somehow, perhaps angrier.

"Good evening," said the woman as if to correct her. Sean glanced at his watch.

"My name is Mandy Simms, I'm currently completing post-graduate work at the school of nursing. My research focuses on the impact of public policy issues on citizens who travel abroad. I'm studying the consequences of resource allocation from government and public domain funding sources vs. private or individual resources in personal crisis management, concentrating on those who had to deal with exceptional situations—especially those where Canadian citizens were forced to negotiate foreign governmental or non-governmental bureaucracies."

Sean loved the smoothness with which Mandy delivered her speech. She had told Sean in the car how she had come up with the premise before she knew that she would have his help to make contact with the couple. Despite working out the speech in advance she had only practiced aloud for the first time as they drove that day in the car. The speech seemed much more authentic, thought Sean, now that Mandy had had opportunity to give it twice before in earnest.

After delivering the speech to Sean as he drove, Mandy asked him what he thought of it. Sean's only suggestion was that Mandy use the word bureaucracy in place of organization. It would more likely to strike sympathy in the listener, he asserted, since everyone has had a poor experience with a bureaucracy and foreign bureaucracies were always seen as worse. Mandy claimed that she liked the idea, and immediately recited the speech again, incorporating Sean's suggestion. Despite her enthusiastic delivery Sean was not sure whether or not Mandy was merely humouring him.

The speech had the desired effect. While the woman was puzzling over the meaning Mandy added, "This is my research associate, Sean Hughes. He's responsible for transcription and data collation. It's not necessary for him to be present during the interviews I conduct, but according to university policy I am not allowed to approach interviewees unaccompanied." Here Mandy leaned in and added a hint of a conspiratorial tone, "Safety considerations."

"Oh," said the woman arching an eyebrow as she looked Sean over.

"I find that it's often best if he waits in the car," said Mandy and dismissed Sean with a wave of her hand. Sean turned and began a tentative descent.

"What do you want?" asked the woman.

"I need to interview Allan Butler about his experiences dealing with the Mexican health authorities. I understand the incidents took place some time ago but we're hoping that what we learn will help other families who find themselves in similar situations."

The woman nodded in understanding, but then added, "My husband is out now, perhaps you could…"

"Oh! Then you must be Eva Butler!" Sean wondered at how Mandy sounded genuinely pleased. Mandy looked down at the clipboard she carried. Her voice changed, "The tragedy must have touched you too. I'm so sorry for your loss."

If the woman had been softened by Mandy's show of concern she did not show it, "Why didn't you call first? And isn't it policy to send a letter ahead of an actual contact."

"Through trial and error we found that a personalized initial contact leads to higher compliance rates and interview completions. In other words, when…"

The woman cut Mandy off. "I've done post graduate research myself so no need to over explain everything. But I'm quite sceptical about whether you accurately and honestly described your methodology in your research proposal. I'd be quite surprised that this sort of initial contact model made it past the ethics committee ... especially given the sensitivity of the material to be discussed and the potentially invasive nature of the interview process!"

What Sean found quite surprising was that the woman did not question that Mandy was doing research—only her methods.

"What was your name again?" the woman had a searching look.

"Mandy Simms."

"And your boyfriend down there?" Sean had already made it to the bottom of the stairs.

Mandy straightened and looked the woman in the eye. "You mean my research assistant?" she asked.

"Oh you're not fooling me for an instant," said the woman. "I did my graduate work in psychology. If that young man isn't already sleeping with you, I can guarantee that he wants to. I know what graduate school is like. I'll bet that he volunteered to be your assistant."

"His name is Sean Hughes."

"Well tell him to come in. You too. I'll tell what you need to know. When it happened my husband tried to be the strong one, but I'm the one who ended up doing all the paper work and dealing with the authorities. My Spanish was non-existent, and it was still better than his."

Mandy turned and waved to Sean. She winked at him as he came up the stairs. Things were going better than she had hoped.

"Sometimes the death of a child can destroy a marriage," said Eva. "My husband, Allan, and I talked about it even before we left Mexico with Steven's ashes. You see, marriages depend on a sense of optimism. You have to be headed towards something, moving forward. Without some goal, the marriage begins to seem pointless."

Sean settled onto the settee. He had been worried that he would have to speak. It now seemed that Eva was quite willing to talk with little prompting from Mandy.

"Some people think that a child will save a marriage. It can't, but it can give you something to work at."

"Something to sacrifice for," suggested Mandy.

Eva fixed Mandy in a brief stare before continuing; "My husband and I had a good measure of success in our careers." Eva lifted a hand to the side of her head and drew her hair behind one ear, "Raising a child nevertheless provides happy memories for parents, and hopes for greater happiness in the future. All parents recognize how the joy and love of the family dynamic more than compensate for the inconvenience of child rearing."

Sean wondered how his parents managed to miss what Eva had just insisted that all parents knew.

"With the death of a child, however, the joy and love give way to a sense of pain and loss. What's worse, is that while sharing positive parenting experiences can bring a couple together, an attempt to share grieving can drive a couple apart."

"Share sorrow and spare sorrow!" said Sean suddenly in a singsong voice.

Eva gave Mandy a tight-lipped smile; "Some have difficulty with the paradox," she said. "It's easy for one member of the couple to see the other as insufficiently emotional about the tragedy. This misunderstanding is compounded when one of the pair tries to be the strong one. Stoicism is misinterpreted as an inferior level of grieving or remembrance."

"Oh, you must have been very strong to recognize these emotional pitfalls even as you were working through your own great loss," said Mandy.

Eva straightened in her seat, "Fortunately my husband has learned to trust my judgment in a great many things." She sighed, "—but unfortunately not everything."

"Men, eh?" offered Sean.

Eva and Mandy shared a smile.

"The presence of other children can help. They can provide a focus for a parent's desire to 'do better.' A grieving parent might develop an exaggerated sense of responsibly, or an over-bearing manner. A parent may become inordinately anxious over the remaining child's safety, or try to continuously supervise his or her movements."

"Or they could leave the child completely alone while they argue," muttered Sean. He hoped Eva had not heard him.

"Parental approval is an important motivator. Psychologically speaking, it can be deeply rewarding."

"Psychologically speaking…" muttered Sean.

Mandy gave Sean a look. Sean mimed sealing his lips.

Eva continued, "Steven was an only child and Allan and I knew better than to seek an adoption or try for another pregnancy—so many couples fall into *that* trap."

"They try to replace the lost child!"

Eva looked at Mandy as if Mandy had finally managed to tie her shoes on her own.

"We had rewarding professional lives that we didn't wish to interrupt, and we didn't want to try to replace the lost child, nevertheless we also had to deal with our grief. I realized that to preserve our marriage we needed to move on—we needed to survive the tragedy."

"But you weren't—"

Mandy gave Sean another look.

"We gave away all of Steven's things, everything: clothing, toys, books, games, posters, all of it. We took down all our pictures of Steven and even of events where the three of us were together. Some went into albums, and some into boxes and then into storage. My husband and I can open them up when we want to grieve."

"If…" mumbled Sean.

"Our house was a problem too. Every room, every wall, every corner reminded us of Steven. It was where he had grown up—so we moved out of Kitsilano. Here, we don't have to walk past Steven's room every time we walk down the hall to the master bedroom. This has been a great help to our intimacy."

Mandy and Eva exchanged a look that Sean did not know how to interpret. Sean was hunched forward during Eva's story. Now he straightened up, and then perceiving that the conversation had stopped for a moment, leaned back on the settee. It was very comfortable. "Someday, I'd like to own a piece of furniture like this," he said to himself. He imagined how nice it would be sleeping across its cushions. And if this sofa turned out to have a bed inside—perfect, thought Sean.

"Don't you think so?" asked Eva.

Both Mandy and Eva were looking at him.

"I-I-I'd have to go with your opinion," stuttered Sean, "You seem to be the most qualified to answer."

"Hmm," snorted Eva, "My husband said nearly the same thing."

Mandy seemed to wink at Sean conspiratorially.

"So I opted to have our son cremated … There was no sense in prolonging the whole thing was there?"

It was obvious to Sean that despite Eva's apparent composure her pain was still very fresh, and the grieving very much on going. Everything about Eva seemed to support the image of a woman in control, her clothing, her hair, the way she sat with her legs crossed at the knees and her lower legs pressed together, calf to shin. That's feminine, thought Sean. He looked at Mandy's legs, shapely in her jeans, but she sat with her legs apart, like a man. At that moment Sean was not sure which he preferred.

"Yes, the Mexican officials were cooperative but I didn't get the impression that what happened to my son was particularly unusual. The interpreter seemed sympathetic and I'm sure she had difficult time of it. It takes a crisis for a tourist to want to interact with Mexican bureaucracy."

Sean saw that Mandy was making a show of taking notes.

"The Canadian consular officials were helpful, and so were the local police, but there really was nothing suspicious to investigate. Steven was brave, but he was also foolhardy, overconfident. He didn't know the local currents. He thought he was a strong swimmer." Eva sighed, "He *was* a strong swimmer. Do know that more strong swimmers drown than weak swimmers?"

Mandy looked up from her note pad. She nodded.

"Wow," said Sean.

Eva continued answering Mandy's questions: "Yes, we were taken to the morgue to formally identify the body, and, yes, there was an autopsy. I have the report. Do you need to see it?"

Mandy shook her head.

"The crematorium offered a private religious service with a priest. We accepted. Unfortunately our translator wasn't available for the service."

"So you didn't understand a thing?" asked Sean.

"I have some Spanish—I understood a little." Eva pursed her lips. "We had to return the next day for Steven's ashes."

Sean followed Eva's eyes. There was large urn on a shelf above a natural gas fireplace.

"I know it's silly of me to care really," Eva sounded pained. "It's just that I thought we were dealing with professionals so that sort of thing wouldn't happen."

"What do you mean?" asked Mandy.

"The urn they gave us was nice enough, I suppose. I imagine it was the sort of thing that the locals use. It was clay, brightly painted and so forth. But really inappropriate for long-term use. I mean, how would we display it? It really wouldn't be tasteful in a modern home at all."

Out of the corner of his eye, Sean saw Mandy nodding in sympathy. Something about the way she was nodding however, convinced him that she did not agree.

Eva continued. "So of course, as soon as we could, we transferred the ashes to something a little more understated." She lifted one hand out of her lap and let one finger point in the general direction of the shelf above the fireplace. "That's when I noticed. I wished I had looked in the urn earlier, while we were still at crematorium even. Then they could have—I mean that we could have made sure that..." Eva's voice trailed off.

"That what?" asked Mandy.

"Like most children, Steven had quite a sweet tooth. Not that we indulged him of course, but it was always possible for him to get candy from his friends."

"You gave him an allowance, didn't you?"

"Of course we did," Eva answered quickly. She paused. "Yes I suppose that he was able to purchase sweets on his own too." She paused again. "Then of course by the time he was a teenager we no longer reminded him that he needed to brush his teeth regularly. But that was one habit I'm sure we had engrained in him from his childhood."

"Of course you did." said Mandy. Sean looked at Mandy's eyebrows.

"Whatever the reason—although I'm sure it wasn't his diet, but because we always ate healthily at home—he some tooth decay when he was in his early teens."

"Did his teeth hurt when he was in Mexico?" Sean asked.

The two women looked at Sean.

After a pause Mandy said, "Please go on."

"Steven had some fillings. Two lower molars on the right, and another on the left. He got his wisdom teeth early. He got that from my side of the family."

"Wow," said Mandy, but without expression.

"The fillings were gold of course."

Mandy nodded.

"So when we transferred the ashes to the new urn I expected to see the remnants of the fillings in them."

"And they weren't there!" said Mandy.

"Allan, that's my husband," Eva added, looking at Sean briefly, "didn't think that the missing fillings were unusual. You see, so many of the Mexicans are poor. Perhaps someone desperately needed the money. Allan thought that the crematorium staff had taken them."

"But you disagreed?" asked Mandy.

"Yes. Well no. I thought that it was possible. But the director of the crematorium seemed very professional. He even spoke English. I didn't think that he would allow something like that to take place."

"The other possibility is that you got the wrong ashes," said Sean.

"Yes," said Eva. "That was another possible conclusion but once again, that would require the director to be unprofessional, and I think the man was highly competent."

"After all, he spoke English," said Mandy. Sean caught the subtle lift of Mandy's eyebrows this time.

"Yes, and he was dressed nicely too." added Eva. "Allan and I almost argued about it. I wanted him to ask the director to double check that we had been given the correct urn. Allan didn't want to bother the director. It was true that he did seem busy. There seemed to be several families present at the time and we gathered that it was an extraordinarily busy day for the business."

"But that was all the more reason to double check, wasn't it?"

Both women looked surprised at Sean's outburst.

Eva continued, "After the service and all that, we wanted to find our priest and tip him. Somehow, we were moved by what he said."

"But it wasn't in English," noted Mandy.

"No," said Eva, "but still." Eva paused for a moment. "There were three or four priests walking around the facility afterwards. We couldn't tell which was ours."

"After all they were all wearing the same thing—and spoke Spanish," suggested Mandy.

"Exactly," said Eva, looking at Mandy. "It's as if you were there."

"So you tipped them all?" asked Mandy.

"We tried to," responded Eva. "But two of them refused to accept the cash. I remember the day well. My memory is as clear as if it happened yesterday." Eva fell silent.

"Back to the urn and the ashes. Isn't it is also possible that the staff weren't dishonest but had simply made a mistake," suggested Mandy. "It must have been a difficult day for them, confusing perhaps, so many priests, families…"

"That's possible," said Eva. "But Allan said that ultimately it didn't matter what was in the urn: our son would live on in our hearts. And really only in our hearts. The urn and the ashes were really only symbols of what we had lost. We needed symbols of life not death. That's why we took away all reminders of Steven's death: everything he was before. For us he's just the spirit of his memory."

"That and the fancy urn over the fireplace," said Sean.

Eva looked upset. Mandy spoke quickly. "You've been so helpful—and you've shown such eloquent strength in the face of your grief. I'm almost overwhelmed."

Eva straightened up. She put a hand to her hair.

Mandy continued. "We really shouldn't take up any more of your time. If I have more questions once I've looked at the information you've given us, may I contact you?"

"Yes, of course," answered Eva. "It has been good to talk about it. Our friends seem to want to avoid the issue. I suppose that they think that they are being kind."

"They probably feel that there is not a lot that they can do," said Mandy.

"They're right in that of course—but they could listen."

Chapter Twelve

Reh Nommusnu

Per Mandy's request, Eva had provided the name of the crematorium and the director. Mandy took the information down on her clipboard.

Once back on the street, Mandy and Sean walked side by side to where Sean had left the car. It was near dusk. Sean unlocked Mandy's door before walking around the car to unlock his own. While waiting for Sean to enter the car, Mandy noticed a man sitting in a vehicle across the street from where they had parked. The man peered out at them as Sean started his car and drove off. Sean and Mandy continued in silence, Sean concentrating on the road ahead, Mandy looking over at the notes she had taken. Within a few minutes it was too dark to read. Mandy put down the clipboard and folded her arms across her chest. The road they drove on was lined with streetlamps, that, just as they passed the first few, suddenly illuminated themselves, pushing away the dark, at least from the space around each lamp. From time to time Sean looked over at Mandy. He liked how light from each streetlamp splashed onto Mandy's forehead, nose, and cheeks, leaving the area around her eyes still flooded in darkness. Her mood was indiscernible.

"I think part of her will always be sad," Mandy broke the silence.

"I guess so," said Sean.

"It's a mother's love for sure. It's something that will never let go. No wonder she's still bothered by the possible mix-up with the ashes. Of course her husband isn't as concerned; he's not a mother." Mandy folded her arms.

"We don't know if he felt the loss any less. We only heard Eva talking about it. Maybe what's his face, the father…"

"Allan Butler."

"Yeah, that guy. Maybe he felt it just as deeply. Maybe more. We don't know. We didn't meet him. We didn't talk to him." Sean tightened his grip on the wheel.

"Yes but you could tell from the story that he wasn't as affected by the loss. After all he didn't do anything about the potential mix up. That just shows..."

"Nothing! It shows nothing," Sean exclaimed. "You're jumping to conclusions. Just because he didn't..."

"Eva told us that he didn't do anything about the mix up. He shouldn't have ignored it."

"Maybe it bothered him just as much but he decided that it was more important to be practical. Someone has to be the practical one—even if both people are grieving!"

It suddenly occurred to Sean that he and Mandy were having their first real argument. It was an exciting thought. Then Sean realized that although he thought he understood what Mandy was trying to say, he really had no idea why she had chosen to start an argument. He also wondered if it would always be this way.

"I can't expect that you'd understand a Mother's loss. You've never lost a child. You have no idea about the emotional depth of the scarring that a mother must feel. It's in direct proportion to the incredible bond between and mother and a child. There is nothing stronger! Nothing! But you couldn't know that! You're not a mother!"

"Neither are you," Sean answered quietly. "Have you lost a child?"

"No!" said Mandy sharply. Sean braced himself for another outburst but instead Mandy quietly broke into tears. She leaned across the empty seat between them and put her head on his shoulder.

Sean continued driving. He was sure he had passed some sort of test, but the exact nature of the test was a mystery. After a few minutes Mandy straightened up and although they rode along in silence, Sean felt no tension between them. He could not suppress his grin.

The trouble started just as they re-entered an older section of the city. Mandy suddenly pulled her jacket closed. Sean felt the sudden blast of cold air as well. Mandy took her hands off the clipboard in her lap and reached toward the temperature controls on the dashboard. Sean checked his side and rear view mirrors. Fortunately, he thought, there were no cars nearby. He pulled the vehicle to the edge of the road.

"Mind if I turn up the heat?" asked Mandy, fiddling with the controls.

Sean turned toward Mandy. His eyes were wide, "I think that we're about to have a mani..."

It struck at Mandy first. The wooden clipboard flew out of her hand and slammed against the inside of the car windshield. There was a loud crack. Then the board flew back toward Mandy. She tried to duck and raise her hands but the board stuck her hard across the forehead. She screamed. The board struck at her twice more, each time slamming with a loud crack against the windshield before rushing at Mandy's head. By the second blow however, Mandy managed to place her forearms in front of her face. She felt the metal clip at the top edge of the board slice into her flesh. She screamed again.

"Mandy!" Sean cried out and tried to grab the clipboard. As if his voice were a signal the clipboard broke off its attack on Mandy and charged at Sean. Sean raised his fist and met the oncoming board with swinging punch that slammed the board into the steering wheel. Sean brought both hands against the board, endeavouring to hold it place against the steering wheel. The wheel twisted right and left with the motion of the board.

"Take out key! Take out the key!" shouted Sean.

"What?" Mandy shouted back. She was holding her forearms in front of her face and peering at Sean through the narrow space between them.

"Take the key out of the ignition!" Sean was flushed and sweaty with the effort of holding the board in place against the steering wheel. "Do it. It'll stop the car wheel from moving!"

Mandy saw the ignition key. Reaching for it would mean reaching toward the possessed object that had already cut her arms and forehead.

"I can't! I can't!"

"Yes you can," said Sean through gritted teeth. "It'll help me get this thing under control!"

"No. Sean! It's too dangerous." Mandy reached for the door handle. "I'm going for help."

"Don't be stupid; there's nothing anyone else can do! They'll think you're crazy if you try to explain. Just help me get this thing under control."

"I'll run around and open your door so that you can throw it outside." Mandy twisted the door handle.

"No! Don't open the door!"

Sean's warning came too late however. Mandy opened the car door. The car interior light came on. Mandy stepped out of the car and turned to look at Sean. Grasping onto the board with all four of its limbs was a shape that if it were human would have been that of a gaunt, middle-aged woman. Its trunk and thighs were covered with loose sinuous skin. Its limbs were stringy. Her finger and toenails were untrimmed. From her head extended a mass of wild, fibrous hair that seemed to radiate from a nearly translucent veiny skull. When Mandy screamed the figure turned to face her. Mandy screamed again. The creature's eyes were in deep sockets; her cheeks were dark hollows. She looked at Mandy and drew her lips away from her mouth into a maddening grimace.

"Sean!" Mandy cried, "It's a she!"

The creature looked at Mandy then back at Sean and spat out some words. Mandy couldn't hear but she saw the creature's lips move.

"Lamb, for, ant," lip read Mandy puzzled.

The creature saw the open door and released her grip on the clipboard with her hands but held it still with her feet. She began to tear at the pages. Sean covered as much of the paper as he could with his fingers, however doing so took away his ability to keep the clipboard pressed against the steering wheel. The ghost woman perceived this and bounced toward the door with the board braced between her feet.

"Close the door!" yelled Sean.

Even if Mandy had been able to force herself to do what she saw as shutting the creature up with Sean, she could not have moved fast enough to stop the creature from escaping. The creature bounded through the open door still carrying the clipboard. The ghost woman must have misjudged the opening because the clipboard struck the doorframe on its way out of the vehicle. The clipboard fell to the ground. Mandy scooped up the board up with a deftness that surprised Sean. She threw it into the car and slammed the door behind it. The ghost woman spun around and headed back into car, passing through the closed car door as if it were air.

Sean grabbed the clipboard from the seat beside him and slipped it under his feet. He placed one hand under the steering wheel and the other against the roof the car, flexing both arms to help keep his feet braced against the car floor, pinning the clipboard down. The ghost surrounded his feet. Mandy could see her pull and push and bite and claw at the board. Sean held his ground. The woman disappeared for a moment, then reappeared charging up through the floor of the car. Sean felt upwards thrust but he held the board steady. The ghost repeated the charge. This time the board shifted. Sean barely managed to keep it under his feet. He looked through the car window at Mandy. She saw that his face was sweaty and pale. Sean was tiring. The ghost woman charged again and again. Each time, in her fury, she managed to lift the board. Each charge weakened Sean's foothold.

Mandy threw the car door open. "Just let her have it, Sean. She just wants to leave with it. Let it go."

"No," said Sean, through his clenched teeth. "She's evil. I can feel it. Whatever she wants to do with this, it's something bad."

Sean looked at Mandy. There was a fine line of blood leading down from the wound in her forehead. Mandy's eyes were wide. She was panting. "Call for help then!"

"From whom?"

"The ghost boy! Noble. Call him. You said he appeared because you called him. He can probably help."

"I'm having enough trouble with one damn ghost. We don't need another!" Sean's breath was coming in pants.

"You're not fighting Noble. You're fighting some crazy woman ghost."

"Even if he decided to help us this time, he's just a boy ghost. What could he do?" Sean shook his head. "Think it through Mandy, she's a bigger ghost than him; she'd probably kill him in a fight."

"You don't know what he could do. Maybe he could … I don't know. But you have to do something quick."

Sean looked at his feet. Despite his efforts the clipboard had shifted part way from under his left foot. With the fury of the ghost's onslaught he could not reposition his feet without losing control of the board altogether. "Ok I will. I will." Sean closed his eyes. "Noble. Noble. Parch, Noble Hastings. Whatever. Come here; appear! Now!"

The ghost woman's rage intensified. As Mandy watched the woman's hands moved so quickly that they began to blur. Sean felt the clipboard lift his feet off the car floor. He stomped down.

"Say what you said in the park!" shouted Mandy.

"But that brought on the dust storm!" Sean retorted.

"Leave out Mary's name this time! You have to do something now! The board is almost loose. Try it."

Sean swallowed and closed his eyes. "I summon you, Ma. . . "

"No!" shouted Mandy. "Not Mary!"

"No, no, no. I mean, Noble Peter Hastings. I summon you: Noble Peter Hastings. Lucky numbers: 45 62 21 11 15, or 12 16."

"What?" shouted Mandy.

"I couldn't read the last two numbers on the fortune cookie paper, so I say the other possibilities just in case!"

Without releasing his grip Sean looked around the interior of the car. There was no sign of Noble.

"Do you see him anywhere?"

"No," answered Mandy. "Maybe it will take him a while to get here. I don't know. But do it again just to be sure he heard!"

"Ok. I'll do the other one." Sean took a deep breath and raised his voice. "I summon you Noble! Lucky numbers: 87 22 5 55 13." He recited the numbers from the second fortune cookie.

Sean scanned the interior of the car again. Nothing. Mandy leaned into the open car door. In a glance she took in the ghost woman's renewed fury but there was no sign of Noble. Mandy stretched her head up and with desperation looked up and down the street. Surely there was some one around who could help, she thought. But the street was deserted. She turned back to the car and suddenly felt a gust of cold air against the back of her neck. She spun around. It was Noble, but he was holding his finger against his lips as if to shush her. Mandy nodded. Noble reached out a translucent finger and pushed it through the rivulet of blood running down the side of her face. Mandy could not feel Noble's touch only a sense of cold where his finger had passed.

Noble drifted over the windshield of the car and wrote "*reh nommusnu*." Mandy tried to puzzle it out. Her lips moved. Noble pointed at Sean. Mandy understood.

Mandy tried to speak as calmly as she could. Her voice came out strangled. "Sean! Read the windshield!"

Sean looked up. "Oh! I didn't know I could do that." Sean relaxed the hand he held on the steering wheel. Suddenly the clipboard twisted up from the car floor, knocking Sean's feet to one side. It struck his shins, then the underside of the dashboard, then came down hard on his thighs.

"Owf!" Sean let his breath out. He grabbed at the clipboard. It spun from his grasp. The metal clip sliced into his knuckles. "I unsummon Mary!" he managed to shout. The clipboard wavered uncertainly in the air a moment but then struck Sean again, this time in the chest.

"Again! It's working. Send her away again!"

Sean brought one arm up underneath his face to protect it. With the other he grabbed at the spinning clipboard. The board eluded his grasp again and flew upward, striking him, clip first, under his chin.

"Get lost Mary! You bitch!" shouted Sean.

The clipboard fell to the ground. Mandy saw a flurry of white slips of paper emerge from the surface of the board, and then the ghost woman was gone.

Mandy heard Sean's breathing. He had laid his head back against the car seat, both of his eyes closed. His hands were on the steering wheel. One set of knuckles was bleeding. Mandy could also see the bloody cut under his chin and although she could not see them, Mandy was sure Sean had received cuts to his legs as well. Mandy found herself evaluating Sean's injuries as if he were just a patient and not her … what was he to her?

Mandy walked around the car to the driver's side door, opened it, and leaned in. Sean opened his arms toward her. They hugged.

"Ouch!" said Sean. He winced and ran his fingers lightly over his midsection. "I think my ribs are bruised."

Mandy heard her breath go out sharply. She had pressed her forearms against Sean. She looked down and saw that there were cuts and bruises all along the skin between her elbows and her hands. Mandy grimaced but then looked at Sean and laughed. "Looks like the ghosts won that round!"

Despite the painful looking gash on her forehead, thought Sean, Mandy's eyes were sparkling. Could she be proud of him?—But why? Had he done anything especially brave or smart? Whatever the reason, Sean decided that of all the looks he had seen on Mandy's face, this was his favourite.

Mandy walked back to the passenger side door. She opened it and exhaled as she slipped into the seat. "Thanks goodness Noble came to the rescue."

"Yeah whoever it was did some nice ghost writing. At first I thought it was you until I realized that the words were written backwards across the outside of the windshield—not even Mandy Simms could have done that. But only because she couldn't reach."

Mandy smiled but found it hard to take her eyes off the windshield. "Do you have anything to clean it up with? It's kind of creepy seeing my blood smeared there."

Sean started the car and turned on the wipers. He held down the button that released the windshield washer fluid. The blood smeared at first. Mandy looked away. Sean looked at her.

"I'll let you know when it's clean," he said.

"Thanks." Mandy looked around the inside of the car. Nobody. She peered out the side and rear windows. "Noble is gone, I think, but we didn't thank him. Don't you think we should?"

"I'm sure we will remember to next time we see him."

"Why not call him back now and talk to him?" insisted Mandy.

"How do we know it was even him?" asked Sean, "Any ghost could have written that."

"Don't be stupid Sean. How many ghosts do you know of? Besides I saw him do it."

"You saw Noble? How come I didn't?" There was an edge to Sean's voice. "I'm his Stringer. I should be the one who can see him."

"Maybe you were too busy fighting Mary? Maybe I'm getting better at being a Voyant. You told me that's what he said I was." Mandy paused for a moment. "Or maybe because I believe in him more."

"Oh I don't just believe he exists. I know he exists." Sean tapped the steering wheel with his fist.

"I know you do Sean, that's not what I meant." Mandy took a breath. "I didn't mean believe. Maybe the word is trust. I think that he's good and that he wants to help us. And I'm not sure why you can't see that."

"Look at us Mandy!" Sean raised his voice, "Someone, something is definitely trying to hurt us!"

Mandy fired back: "And whatever it was, she, it, went away after you summoned Noble!"

There was silence in the car for several moments.

Mandy continued, "You should summon Noble and, we should thank him. Isn't that what Stringers are for?"

Sean did not speak. He turned so that Mandy could not see his eyes.

"I understand if you're scared to do it after what we've just been through."

"I'm not scared!" Sean heard his own voice. He had spoken quickly, his voice strained. He took a deep breath and cleared his throat. He thought about the ghost boy before speaking: "I summon. . ."

The boy appeared instantly. He was standing, no more than an arm's length in front of Sean, the lower half of him disappearing into the car bonnet. He was smiling.

"Thank you Noble!" Mandy shouted at the windshield.

"I think he can hear you well enough," said Sean.

Noble winked at Mandy and then curled both his hands into fists. He awkwardly extended his thumbs upward.

Mandy returned the gesture, holding both her hands up toward the windshield. She nudged Sean with her elbow.

"Ah, thanks, Noble." Sean muttered.

Noble looked at Sean, still smiling, but with some worry.

"Why don't you meet us back at the apartment?" said Sean.

The boy nodded and faded from sight. Once Noble was gone, Sean started the car and pulled away from the curb. Neither he nor Mandy saw the man, dressed as if for jogging, who stepped from the shadows to watch them drive away.

They drove in silence for a time.

It was Mandy who spoke first. "Thank you, Sean."

"For what?"

"Lots of things … Giving Noble a chance to prove himself for one."

"You're welcome," said Sean. He was thinking of Tony's words however: Only a crazy man can see a ghost.

"Well, if I'm crazy then Mandy is too!" said Sean to himself.

"What?" Mandy raised an eyebrow at Sean.

"Nothing," Sean replied, keeping his eyes on the road and hiding a grin.

Chapter Thirteen

Like a Pair of Flushed Grouse

Noble:

"You're lying to me again!"

"No Noble, this is the truth. I wouldn't lie to you. Why would I want to lie to you? You're my friend."

"The truth? Really? You have been so careful to tell me the truth that I don't even know your name: Pedro? Steven? What do I even call you?"

"Steven. That's my name. I'm sure of it now…"

"You want me to be glad you're sure? Well you've lied so much that I'm not sure of anything you told me."

"I told you everything as soon as I remembered it. Honestly I did."

"Everything is as honest as your accent! And why is it back again? I should have known something was wrong when you told me your parents were here in Vancouver, while you were a poor little lost Mexican boy."

"Noble I'm telling you that I forgot nearly everything…"

"Well Pedro I'm going to do some forgetting now too—I'm going to forget you!"

"But you promised…"

"We're even! You helped me get my Stringer's attention. I found your parents. Even Steven! And so Adiós!"

"But a promise is a promise. You're not just some Purging ghost Noble. Promises mean something to you. I know it."

"I kept my promise. We're done. Mary nearly killed my Stringer on an errand for you. We're through. I'm not reaching out to you again. And don't bother reaching out to me."

"I'm sorry Noble. Sorry about Mary and your Stringer. You can make it up to your Stringer. I'm sure you can, Noble. … Noble? … Noble? Please don't go yet. You know you're stronger than you've ever been. Yes you are

Noble. I can feel it. ... Noble? ... Can't you feel it too, Noble? ... Anyway Noble I'm not forgetting my promise to you. When I get home I'm going to help you get Gavin. ... I promised—and I mean it ... Can you still hear me Noble? ..."

I course I heard him. He's the strongest Dead'er I ever met. I could hear him all the way from Mexico—if that was where he even was. How could I trust anything about him? And how could he help with contacting Gavin? He wasn't a Stringer. He was just a stupid Dead'er. Like me.

"N-O-W-T-H-A-T-M-A-N-D-Y-I-S-G-O-N-E-H-O-W-C-A-N-I-H-E-L-P-W-I-T-H-T-H-A-T"

"Nothing. You've done enough."

P-L-E-A-S-E-I-N-E-E-D-T-O-H-E-L-P

"Just like you helped with the kitchen!"

"I-T-O-L-D-Y-O-U-T-H-A-T-W-A-S-M-A-R-Y"

"Well why didn't you stop her?"

"S-H-E-C-A-M-E-I-N-T-H-E-W-I-N-D-O-W-S-H-E-I-S-S-T-R-O-N-G-E-R-T-H-A-N-M-E"

"Well I'm sick and tired of you ghosts wrecking my life."

"S-O-R-R-Y-I-W-A-S-T-R-Y-I-N-G-T-O-H-E-L-P-"

"Well I'm sick and tired of your help too."

"S-T-E-V-E-N-W-A-N-T-E-D-M-E-T-O-C-O-"

"There is another ghost too? When is he coming to wreck my apartment?"

"N-O-H-E-I-S-N-O-T-E-V-E-"

"I wish you guys would go away and leave me alone. And not creep around my apartment or Mandy's either."

"A-S-Y-O-U-W-I-S-H"

"For real? You're just going to go away just 'cause I asked?"

"O-F-C-O-U-R-S-E"

"And not show up in the shower or naked in my living room or anything like that?"

"N-O-T-U-N-L-E-S-S-S-U-M-"

"I knew there was a catch!"

"-M-O-N-E-D."

"Great. See you later kid. Or not!"

"G-O-O-D-B-Y-E"

Sean waited a moment then began sweeping up the flour. By the time he had dumped about half the flour into the trash his smile had become a grin. Then suddenly he paused. His grin faded.

"What about Mary? Will she stay away too?" Sean stood and looked down at the remaining flour on the floor. He waited some time before repeating himself. "Is Mary going to stay away?" He stared at the floor some more. Then with an annoyed sound in his throat Sean fetched more flour out of the cupboard and spread it across the floor. "Ok. Now tell me if Mary will stay away."

The flour remained undisturbed.

"Fine! I get your game!" Sean hissed, but then continued in a clear voice. "I summon you Noble!"

The boy's head appeared. He seemed to be in the middle of making an obsequious bow.

"Whatever," said Sean. "What about Mary? Will she stay away?"

"I-D-O-N-O-T-K-N-O-W" appeared in the flour.

"Well what can I do to make her stay away?" Sean asked sharply.

"S-T-O-P-C-A-L-L-I-N-G-H-E-R-N-A-M-E"

Sean was sure that Noble's expression was a smirk.

"I unsummon you Noble!" Sean said fiercely. Noble's face disappeared. Sean carefully swept up the rest of the flour and poured it all into the trash.

Noble:

When the man with the red beard waved me in off the street, it was the split. To me everything was like chopping firewood. That is because chopping fire is most work I did in my life. Every morning of every day I chopped firewood. The split is the last stoke you make with the axe. It's the stoke where the piece of firewood finally comes into two. The wood you chop is on a stump of hardwood and if you are too eager to chop, you waste sweat chopping the firewood and sending the axe down into the hardwood stump underneath too. If you know what you're doing, you do the split without wasting a damn drop of sweat. I chopped so much firewood that half the time I could get the split just right. I take the last stroke, the one that's going make that piece of firewood into two, and I get the axe moving just so it splits the wood and doesn't do no more. I could get that firewood into two and not make a mark on the hardwood stump underneath any deeper than if I swung at it with Mr. Hallman's shaving razor.

So when that man with the red beard waved me in off the street I thought it was the luckiest day of my life. Of course I was dead wrong but how could I have known differently then. Everything was singing like it was my day. Singing real as you're born. For a bright start there was a bird in our room that morning. Before my mother woke up I heard it. It'd come in the corner, from that part in the wall where the brick chimney from the fireplace in the parlour room below came up past our room on its way up to the roof.

The rest of that outside wall, except for the brick chimney, was wood. Pretty good lumber too. Hallman used to stand in the parlour and slap the wall, and brag to the Englishmen how the trees that he cut himself for the house lumber were as tall as three Nelson's columns put one on top another. That was a funny brag because I'd seen the men that did that sort of cutting. They were big men with muscles as big as your head in their sleeves! I couldn't picture Hallman in his soft jacket, with his little round belly and flour-white hands doing any of that real work. Those men made good money out in the forest. Not money like Hallman though, who could spend more on his pipe tobacco and liquor in a week than my mother would see in her pocket from a year of working for him. More money than I could ever plan on making hauling ash out of kitchens, and chopping wood for the big houses that didn't have their own boys. Even if I got big enough to take work hauling crates off the ships I couldn't bring home as much as the timber men did. I'd love the work even if I'd have to be out in camps for a fortnight or months or more. Given my circumstances, I saw that as a distinct advantage to this form of employment.

The whole point of this reminiscing was that in one place between the great thick-timbered wall in that room, and the square tower of the chimney, there was a bit of a gap. And I never told Mr. Andrew about it. So it never got fixed. Mr. Andrew came to the house for a few days, twice a year or more—fixing what needed fixing. Of course that was my deliberate oversighting. In the winter, maybe December, January, February or so, if it was very cold at night, my mother and I would grab our sleeping things off the beds, and even the coverlets, and all the pillows we had, and snug up against the brick chimney. Hallman kept a fire in parlour on the coldest nights and even though this gave my mother and I comfort, it seemed a great waste of work— my work. Chopping the wood was part of what I had to do for the house. And I didn't get any pay for it because I lived in Mr. Hallman's house. On the very cold nights Mother would lay her things out on the left side of the chimney and put her pillow against the bricks. She said this kept her head, face, and neck warm. Even a widow ought to care for her looks, was all she said about that. I was on the right side of the chimney. I'd put my feet to the warm bricks. I'd make a tent out of my covers, and pull the whole thing right up over my head if it got that cold, and I'd pretend I was in between shifts at a forest camp, making good money felling logs. And if I put my head just right and looked out of my little tent, I could see straight out the gap between the chimney and the wall. And if the sky had no clouds, I could even see a star or two. No wet ever came in that gap but I supposed that some cold must have come in that way.

As soon as I was big enough, I was chopping all the wood at the Hallman house. And I'm sure that I chopped wood for more heat than all the cold that gap ever let in on my mother and me. I'd chop a couple more pieces of wood than I knew was enough, knowing that that gap would be letting in some so cold. I never wanted that gap to get fixed.

All this to say how the bird came to be in our room early that morning. I was astonished to hear something inside that should have been outside, and it should have been heard so faint through the thick lumber walls, that were Mr. Hallman's pride. But I wasn't surprised that the bird found its way in, since there was that gap I knew about. The bird was singing away so sweet and so close by that I don't even blame me for thinking it was my lucky day. Some awful things start so nice, that even looking back, you can't blame anybody for thinking that they were going to have good things ahead, no matter how bad the rest of the stuff turned out.

First thing I did was catch the bird by throwing, fast as I could, a bed sheet over the table it was perched on. Then I gathered up the sheet from the edges inward, till the bird was balled up in the sheet in my hands. It was too damn scared to sing while this was happening. I fished the bird out of the sheet and took it up in one hand, and then took up the chamber pot in the other. I fetched them both down the back stairs and out the servants' door. My mother was up when I came back up. She had dressed and told me to wash the sleep off my skin before I got into the suit. That meant back down and out for a half bucket of water and the basin.

My mother made her way to the kitchen. She had plenty to do before the Mr. and Mrs. sat down to their breakfast. I had the room to myself to wash and dress. Dressing today was the great thing. If the birdsong hadn't told me it was a great day, the clothes would have picked up the message and delivered it. I had a new suit. And I knew that a man in a new suit could not be told no. The suit used to belong to Mr. Hallman, but, my mother told me, it didn't suit his figure anymore. I knew that that meant he could not achieve buttoning the trouser waist. Maybe even the waistcoat didn't close in front of him either. Either way he had seen fit to give to the suit to my mother as an act of charity, knowing, I'd supposed, that she could make it do for me. My mother could have just as easily opened the seams up for Mr. Hallman and he might have worn it for another good year or two, until he outgrew it again. But Mr. Hallman was having only tailored suits to wear. It would not do for him to show a home-seamed suit to his Englishmen associates.

What my mother had done was make the suit to stay on me even without the help of a belt or suspenders. It might not have looked as nice as a new tailored suit, she said, but she didn't want to cut away any of the material. We will want the extra when you grow a bit, she said. Maybe I will be opening it up all the way by the time you'll be marrying. She said that and laughed. I didn't want to frown back when she was smiling at me, but I had enough love and no need of marrying, but she knew nothing about that and the talking about marrying seemed to make her happy through and through. I kept quiet about my plans.

I liked to sit on the stool in the corner of the kitchen while I ate my breakfast. It kept me out of the way of my mother and Miss Jane. I loved to watch them fly back and forth, from the ice box, to the oven, to the stove, or right out the door to the littler dining room were Mr. and Mrs. took their morning and noon meals.

My mother or Miss Jane kept filling my bowl till I said no more. Then I had a mouthful of hot tea to wash it down. My mother asked me five times more than usual if I had had enough to eat. No one likes to hire a hungry man, she said. That didn't make much sense to me. I was thinking that a hungry man would be ready to take any kind of work that would put him out of the desperate need for food but my mother was not in habit of telling me things that didn't turn out to be truer that I thought likely when she was saying them.

I was early enough to walk down to the centre of town without any hurrying-out-of-breath. Nothing was open yet, not even the post office. When I reached the Northwest Company office however, there was already a line-up of men and boys in front of the wooden building. The line went down the street a ways. I guessed that I wasn't the only one to know that they were looking to take on new men today. And I wouldn't have guessed that there were half as many men who were willing to run the danger and hardship of a cutting timber. Money, I suppose, can make you jump into something that otherwise you'd just walk right past.

I stood in with the rest of them, trying not to look too eager. And also trying to not look like I had somewhere more important to be. More men came and stood in the line behind me and we all had a good long wait out there in the street. Since I had no pocket watch I could not have known how the time passed, other than the feeling in my stomach that told me it was maybe an hour or more since I ate my breakfast. Waiting didn't particularly suit me and I sure didn't know who it would suit.

It was an odd thing how waiting weighed on a body like real work. If it had been any other day of my accustomed life, I would have been up just after my mother, and breakfasted, and out chopping the day's worth of stove wood. By that hour when I stood there contemplating if I was going to waste the whole day standing in the street, I would have already chopped my way through a good cord of wood and had it all stacked up in the box outside the kitchen door. I could have hauled out the ash and the done the rest of my chores and been off to earn my coin doing the same for a couple more of the big houses. Instead I was hopping from one foot to the other and itching under the collar of my new suit and no work done for the whole blasted morning. Despite all the nothing I had done all morning in my head I felt as tired as if I had been at my chores!

I was thinking about the strangeness of being tired and not having done any work when I saw a pair of men in suits walk up to the porch of the Northwest Company office. They moved though the line of us waiting men as calmly as if they were stepping 'round a dog sleeping in the street. One of them took out a key and unlocked the office door and both of them stepped inside and shut that door behind them. At that point a sound and a movement went through the line of men. Nearest thing I knew to that was when a sudden wind, out of a still day, moves through a stand of hardwood in full leaf for the summer. Then we all waited, and I remembered, for the last time, that it was my lucky day. There was that bird singing in the room in the morning. And there was the new suit that I was wearing so that the hiring men would take me for a man they could train to work clearing logs down to the river, or maybe even cutting trees. They should see me like I was seventeen or even eighteen and could earn a man's pay—not a boy of fifteen only good for fetching things around the camp or peeling potatoes for the cook.

I was looking at all that in my head so I almost didn't see one of the two men who had gone in the building come back outside. It was the big red bearded one. He pointed to a tall man who was standing in the line and told him to go inside. The man did, saying "Thank you sir" and all sorts of stuff like that on his way in.

The rest of us outside waited some more. We were all looking at the door like we were hungry and we were waiting for Mr. and Mrs. to be done their dinner so we could all go in and eat.

The red bearded man came out again and this time he pointed at two men, and they went into the office behind him. Then some more time passed and he came out again and again, taking a few men in with him each time. I practiced talking slowly in my head so that I wouldn't spoil my answers when I got the chance to talk for myself.

Then the next thing I remember I was inside the store, standing in front of a big desk. The smaller man was writing things down, and the big red bearded man was asking questions like, where I was born? Did I have any dependants? Have I ever worked on a logging crew before? I was giving him straight answers. I added sir at the end of everything I said.

I didn't have to pay any special mind to what my mother said to me that morning. I already knew that straight answers were best when someone had something that you wanted, and was letting you speak for yourself before giving it to you. I thought it through like this: if a man was ready to give you something, then it's already yours. All you have to do is play it straight with him. If a man is not going to give you something then any question he asks you, is just him trying to see that you are not play straight. He's trying to find you out. If he finds you out he is going to say that you are not a man.

I think too that there are some men who don't know if they are going to give you a yes or a no. But they are not going to say yes if they figure you aren't playing straight. I figure that you make yourself a man when you play straight. Most of life you get an easy chance to play it straight.

When I was talking to the big red bearded man it was like there was this boy named Noble inside my head. This boy was thinking of things, and trying to play it straight. He was watching himself and he was watching the big red bearded man. But there was this other Noble too. The other noble was a man. The man, Noble, was talking about working for Mr. Hallman, and chopping stove wood and hauling ash all up and down the street. The big red bearded man was listening to the man named Noble. The big red bearded man was nodding and even the boy Noble was growing well sure that that the big red bearded man had a job for him.

Everything was all straight and then the smaller man who was writing looked up at me and asked, "How old are you son?"

I was frightened. I was hearing two answers fighting inside my head. And I was trying make my face look like whatever came out of my mouth was the only thing that was trying to make it out of my head.

I looked at the big red bearded man and then I looked back at the smaller man. Then there was a voice from outside yelling, "Fire!"

The shorter man who was writing dropped his pen and stood up but the big red bearded man started laughing. "We're supposed to go running out the door like a pair of flushed grouse and they'll all be out there hooting."

The smaller man sat down again but I could see on his face that he didn't think that it was time to sit. He picked up his pen and looked at big man and then at me.

"Fire!"

I could tell that the voice yelling was not telling stories. There's something about a voice when a man knows that he's telling you the real truth and that he expects you to heed. I wanted to run but the neither of the two men at the desk were moving for the door. It was a strange thing how I stopped myself from running when I knew that I needed to run. I stood where I was and I looked at the two men and fought my tongue to tell my age straight. Then there was something wrong with the air. It was like I was hauling ash but there was still fire in the coals. And then there was more noise and shouts from outside.

The smaller man stood up again and said, "I'm going to see what the damn fuss is!" but there was no need to go to the door because now all three of us could see what the damn fuss was.

There was a fire where the door was. Then there was a fire instead of a roof. Then the fire started falling on us and then the walls were made of fire too.

The big red bearded man said, "Damn, I didn't believe him. Damn."

Then the smaller man said, "Hell, that's what you didn't believe. You can see it now, can't you?"

And they were running around although there was no place any man could go that wasn't made of fire.

And then floor under me was made of flames, and then my new suit was made of flames, and I smelled ash, and smoke and burning hair and heard bubbling and crackling. And "Hell!" said one of the men and that was the last thing my living ears ever heard.

Chapter Fourteen

Something Strange to Call Fatherly

Noble:

When I was twelve I walked on one of my mother's sewing needles. It went straightaway into my foot, right between the next to biggest toe and the littler one beside it. I thought it was a hundred bee stings right in that one spot. When my mother got the needle out and the bleeding was done, I was sure that that was the worst thing that I was going to ever let come about on my body. I never went anywhere without my shoes, or my eyes on the ground for that whole time of my life. But that wasn't forever. Two summers after that I walked good and hard on one of those shell creatures that glues itself to a rock. It cut my foot open and I bled. Gavin had to make me sit down and lift my foot up to him so he could see how bad the cut was. He made me sit like that for a long time, then when the bleeding had mostly stopped on its own, he ripped a piece off the bottom of his own shirt and wrapped it round and round my foot. It was a good dry bandage because of course neither of us had been wearing any of our clothes at all in the water. That hour was pain for me, but it was sacrifice for him, because it could have been that he had only that one shirt or maybe that one and only one other. I loved him for it but I didn't think till I was marching home putting mostly none of my weight on the cut foot, that I had forgotten about that needle pushing itself in between my toes, and that that had just happened when I was twelve. There I was, limping home at fourteen, because I had forgotten about never putting my feet in the way of anything that was ready to do harm. As big as that needle hurt was, I had forgotten. I supposed that you are going to forget everything, even your name, if it's never brought to mind.

Its sounds well strange to hear myself think it, but what I thought was going to the best day of my life was the worst day of my life. It was the last day of my life. There was nothing that ever happened to me before or since like burning up in that room. It was like that needle in between my toes but on every bit of my skin. Needles in my eyes and chest and back and hands. Last thing I smelled was my own skin and hair burning and two men screaming their last words. All I saw was red and then black. And then I couldn't see or hear anything. It was just black roaring. The pain ripped every part of me to pieces. Then I thought that there was no way it could get worse. But it got worse. And I said I must be dead because this pain is the end of the world. And I thought of my mother and of Gavin, who were the only two people in the world that I knew how to love more than I loved myself. During the burning I fell over and had one quick idea to crawl somewhere but I could not move anything and I could not feel any skin to close my eyes with, or to close my mouth with, because the ripping was already deep in my throat. And then it got worse. It was too much pain for anything. Then a quick nothing. Nothing, just for a thought but no thought. Then all of a sudden I heard screaming and I felt the ripping on my skin again and smelt the burning wood, and also hair, fat, and meat burning, like they had all fallen off the roaster into the fireplace and had made a broiling ashy mess that I would have trouble to scrape off the brick. Then I could see that there was nothing but ash and bits of things around me, like nails and bolts and such, but all of it was heat-twisted to useless shapes, and I could tell that all the strength had been fired out of the metal bits.

And slowly I knew that I wasn't just burnt all over the outside, but I was burnt till I was gone, and that there was nothing that could be done for me, except scrape me out of the fireplace and into the ash bin, and haul me away for dumping far from the house.

I didn't know I could move so I stayed right where I was, thinking tears for Gavin and my mother, but mostly for Gavin because of what we were going to do after I got the logging job and had worked a couple seasons in the forest. Then it was night and I stayed right where I was, thinking my mother would come get me after she had finished serving the Mr. and Mrs. their supper. Then it was morning and she had not come for me. And then I thought my mother would come for me in the afternoon when she had her two hours to her own use—after the cold lunch had cleared off and she was not expected in the kitchen until it was time to begin preparations for supper. I waited for her, but she did not come for me all that second day or that night.

Then in the bright day men started shovelling to fill up the hole lined with ash and mess that was what had become of the fine Northwest Timber office, and the big desk, and the big red bearded man in his suit and the smaller man in his suit, who had started to learn that I was pretending at being a man, and that the fire was for real, but never got to the end of learning either thing in time to do anything about them.

They shovelled earth and stone fill, right on top of where I was, but I didn't move any and I didn't feel any of it landing on me.

The next night, without thinking too much on the process of how, I got up and went home. I was thinking the whole way of that room of over the parlour in Mr. Hallman's house that was for my mother and me to sleep in and keep our things in. And when I got to the big house I went in though the servants' door in back, which was wide open to the night air. I saw Miss Jane trimming lamps, and gave her a polite greeting but she didn't acknowledge me any. I didn't mind her lack of manners and I kept going up till I was all the way up the servants' stairs and then at the door of that room over the parlour where my mother and I slept. I went to knock a bit before walking right into the room, because that's how my mother and I made sure to give each of us our necessary privateness. I knocked and knocked on the door but it hardly made any sound. Then I was worn out from knocking on the door and leaned my head like a weary tired man against it. That's when I heard my mother weeping ever so softly inside the room. There is no sound in the world like your mother's crying to move you to madness. In the whole rest of everything I ever had to hear before or after there was only one terrible, terrible thing that moved me as even close to as much as that crying. I went to take hold of the door handle but I could not. My hand went right past the brass handle like—like the handle was just the reflection of something in a basin of water and it could not be touched because it was not the true thing but only the water's picture of it. I threw myself at that door and should have known that any right day I would have gone right though that fancy sheet of wood. But I had none of the strange things of the past two days in my head. I was crying for my mother. Then the door opened and she was in front of me. Her eyes were red and her hair was uncovered. I shouted, "I am here. I am here." But her eyes did not fix on me. She looked past me into the hallway and then slammed the door shut. I stood as astonished as if she had slapped me. And then the howling started. It took me some time to understand what was in my mother's voice. It was my father's name and then my name, run into her screams like mortar between bricks. She said that we were both taken from her and that her life was worthless and that everyone she loved would die.

Then I heard the Mrs. and Miss Jane at the bottom of the stairs behind me. And the Mrs. said, "Go to her, Jane." and I heard Miss Jane coming up the stairs. I turned and looked at her coming up to me and the door but Miss Jane went straight past me and knocked once on the door and then opened it up and went in, and I went in too. Miss Jane took my mother into a hug.

"I heard him knocking! I know I did Jane! I heard him at the door!" My mother said this to Jane crying and breathing hard the whole time, like she had just run up the stairs.

"Don't say anything so foolish," said Jane. "Mrs. will think you have lost your mind."

My mother pushed Miss Jane back a bit. "I know what I heard Jane. He had a way of knocking. Hard soft, hard soft. Only he did that of all the men in the world that I had ever heard knocking, only he did that!"

Then my mother started sobbing again. But I had begun to learn the strangeness of the situation and I was thinking of ways to let my mother know that it was me knocking. Maybe I could knock on the wall some more or maybe I could move my bed covers over to my cold night place by brick chimney. I was considering these things when Jane said something that hurt me like the fire.

"What good is he to you now? You would do better to accept that he is gone. I loved him too. Even Mr. Hallman and the Mrs. say that they loved Noble like a son. You heard them at the service. Now we all have to settle ourselves in our minds that he is dead and gone."

My mother let Jane rest her arms around her again, and I stopped searching the room for something that I could take hold of without my hand passing right by the thing. I was learning some astonishing things. There had been a service for me and Mr. Hallman had had a marvellous loss of memory to say anything about me being like a son to him and the Mrs., but I already knew how poor a memory Mr. Hallman had. If I cared that that man had two legs and two arms I would not put an axe in his hand and ask him to chop a single piece of stove wood into two. Yet he had some recollection to give about cutting the timber for his fine parlour.

After some time Miss Jane said to my mother that it was late in the night and that she should take her leave. Miss Jane left and I stood in a corner of the room and watched my mother. She lay in her bed but didn't turn the lamp down all the night.

My mother got up the next morning and put on her work apron. I stood the whole day in that room. I might have left after some time, but of course the whole room was wooden, walls, and doors, and ceiling and floor. I didn't think of leaving through the brick chimney. I was still in my accustomed thinking and bricks to me were something more solid than wood. The only one thing that I managed to move in that room the whole day was my mother's good hairbrush. She called it a tortoise shell and I had never been allowed to touch that brush in my whole life. "It's not for boy's hands or hair," my mother said.

That night my mother was lying in bed and crying again. And I was standing in the corner just looking at her and wishing she and I was able to comfort one another. Then my mother said something quietly. It was in the voice she used to whisper at me in night time. A voice that wouldn't carry any sound outside that room. "Noble," she said "I feel you here. You are here, aren't you son?"

And I thought about that brush. I did not think about knocking on the wall or door because that could sound like someone trying to come in. I wanted her to know that I was there in that room with her, just like we were accustomed, and that I could stay there forever to comfort her. I would. So I made to over to table with the brush sitting on it and I just about moved it around a bit just like I had earlier while she was down in the kitchen. Then I thought about how I never touched that brush within her knowing all my life. And what would she think if she saw that brush move now. Maybe she would not think at all about her dead son. I didn't know what strange circumstances had me here in that room watching my mother, while at the same time she could not see or hear or get any ordinary sign at all that I was there. And what strange circumstances had me unable to pick up the iron spoon or enamel cup I kept in my corner of the room, but able to move a fancy bush on my mother's table where I had no right to interfere. My mother could work herself to a bad state after seeing a brush I would never touch move at the mention of my name. There was nothing good that I could see coming from any action I might take in that room. Miss Jane was right; my mother would do best to settle in her mind that I was dead and gone.

It was early morning the next time my mother opened the door to that room. I came out too. I understood that I too needed to settle in my mind that I was dead and gone. Watching my mother in her grief, helpless, was not going to help me settle and accept what I needed to accept. I started down the servants' stairs to go out the back door but then had a quick thought to make my way into parts of that house where I had never gone. I went out of the house and round to the front yard and put myself to lean in the big front window into Mr. Hallman's study. It was a strange surprise to me to find that, in place of leaning on the window so that I could see all of Mr. Hallman's business inside his study, my head and hand passed right through the glass. It was like that window was made of water except that I could pass through it even quicker than if it were water, and without getting any wet on myself. Despite having no trouble to go through any of the squares of window glass, the pieces of wood frame managed to block my passing. I had to lift myself over the wooden sill and squeeze my shoulders small to bring myself into Mr. Hallman's study.

Mr. Hallman's study was a disappointment. The account books on his desk were closed. There were loose several sheets on the desk as well, but they seemed to be rough tallies under headings like *disbursements* and *expenditures*, all listed with dates.

The chamber where Mr. and Mrs. slept was more interesting. There were two beds separated by the distance of maybe one pace. Against one wall was a fancy table, full of drawers and with a mirror above. It was not difficult to guess that there were things belonging to Mrs. on that table. I looked those things over. There was a brush, comb and a little hand mirror all looking like each other, each one as fancy as my mother's one brush. There were also little jars that looked as if there could be nothing inside but a daub or two of some ointment. I looked at all those small fancy things for some time. It was not that they were so interesting to look at; it was that I was picturing my mother having some fancy ointment to smear on her face at night to keep her skin nice. It angered me to think of Mr. and Mrs. proclaiming to people that I was like a son to them when I was not there to add some truth for the first time to what they had said. Truth was that Mrs. did not look at me or call my name except when she wanted something brought to her. Mr. Hallman was a little better. He had seen to it that a fair number of his old shirts and whatnot came my way, so that my mother was able to make them over and seldom had to spend money to keep me clothed even when I was getting my growth. Mr. Hallman had given me the suit I was burned up to death in. That's something strange to call fatherly I supposed.

I went to the bed that I was sure was Mr. Hallman's. It looked like it regularly bore a greater burden of weight than the bed closest to the fancy table and mirror. It was clear to me that Miss Jane had not yet come in to shake out the bed linens. I found some of Mr. Hallman's hair, short and grey, on the pillow. I grasped these and brought them to the fancy table and let them fall on the Mrs.' hairbrush. Then I worked and worked at the brush till I had pushed it off the table and into the chamber pot.

Last thing I did was look in the kitchen. I watched my mother and Mrs. Jane go about their business for some time. My mother's face smoothed when she was busiest. In the in between times she looked as if her mind were far away. She stared out the window or at the wall where there was no window or picture. It was Miss Jane who brought my mother's attention back to the kitchen. She would ask my mother for help or remind my mother of something that was undone.

After the lunch was cleared, my mother took her apron off, held it in one hand and began a slow climb up the stairs to that room. I watched her go, and when she was out of sight I left that house. I never saw her again. I am sure that it has been over a hundred years but I remember the fire and Miss Jane, and Mr. Hallman, and the man with the red beard but I have forgotten my mother's name.

Chapter Fifteen

A Promise

Noble:

There was nothing fair about. I had no father when I was a Lye'ver. I stopped ghosting my mother so that I wouldn't scare her to death or worse while she was grieving my death. It was like I paid my money and I didn't get any goods. Now I was never to eat or grow or feel a touch on my skin, none of the good things that Lye'vers get and don't think about except that Lye'vers always seem to want more. And I was not calling Lye'vers wrong in that. I had been a Lye'ver. When any of those things happened to me I never acknowledged them except to go looking for more. Now there was no more of those good things. And maybe if the accounts were balanced, with not having got any of the good things, I would not have got any of the pain. But this was not so. Sean told me to go away. He hurt me in a big way. I didn't know if the hurt from Sean was like Gavin hurt or my mother hurt, or some other hurt. My memory of hurts was something I could not trust.

When Sean had called me to him it was like something in my head that I could not stop myself from hearing. He was strong but he did not choose to unsummon me with the same energy he used to call me. I took Sean's unsummoning into my head and let myself be unsummoned. Yes, it was painful, but no, he did not fade me down till I was a Zonker.

When he unsummoned Mary however, I was sure that every Dead'er in three cities felt it in their heads too. For me it was like a lightning strike behind my eyes and the thunder sounding so loud that I could not hear for a long time afterwards. I could not help but demanifest. I was stunned. Mary must have been demanifested into pieces like firewood chopped up for a small stove. I didn't know for sure, but unless Mary had a strong Stringer in her haunt she would be faded down a good lot. It would be a long time till she could manifest in Sean's apartment. Or destroy his kitchen. She would not even have the strength to pick up a toothpick.

Perhaps Sean and I were beginning to feel each other's thoughts; I found myself beginning to re-manifest just as soon as Sean even thought about summoning me.

Lye'ver time was a strange thing. When I didn't have a Stringer in my haunt I just drifted from place to place. I could slip through windows and walls and see little pieces of people's lives. I would never stay of course. I was determined not to be a ghost. Sometimes I was thinking that only a few days had passed but then I would look at a newspaper or hear something on a television and I would discover that I had been drifting for months. This was not true when Sean unsummoned me. When I have been unsummoned, weeks passed like months.

Sometimes a Dead'er's memory is of no good use. I believed Pedro when he talked about forgetting his own name. I have forgotten my mother's name. But I have not forgotten everything. I remember what happened after I left that big house. I stood outside the house by the woodshed where I was accustomed to doing all my chopping. I was comforted by the thought of my familiar work. Then the night came down around me. I had never liked going to the woodshed in the dark. I used to think unpleasant thoughts about what could be in the shed that I could not see. Even at fifteen years of age in that one thing I had been a child and not a man. There I was, outside that house in the dark night, and I was the unpleasant thing by the woodshed. There was no comfort for me anywhere on Hallman's property.

I drifted back to where the Northwest Company office had been consumed by fire. It was easy to find. I felt stronger and stronger as I approached the remains of the building. When I came upon the site of the fire I saw that men had been at work rebuilding the establishment. What was wood before was now being made over in brick. There was no glass yet in the windows, and I saw that I might enter the building though a hole the men had left for window glass. I had forgotten already that glass in no way prevented my movements. Inside the building I discovered that a wooden floor had been laid over the foundation. I could feel that there was some source of strength for me beneath the floor but I couldn't cross through the wooden planks to reach it. I came out of the building and searched for some way to go beneath it. In those explorations I discovered that neither brick nor stone could prevent my passage. Once under the building's floor I drifted through the stone, earth and debris on which the building rested.

I found the place that offered me strength. I lay on it.

I might have lain there for what may have been days or months. I do not know the day of the fire. I do not know the day I began to lie under the building. I do know that I emerged when I remembered Gavin, and I sought him out. Again, after I weakened, I returned to the building. Each time I returned, I lay in the place that fed me strength. I believed that years passed as I lay again under that building, seeking strength, for when I emerged again, the building had changed. The town had changed. I came out because I heard a voice reaching out to me, and I knew then that there were others like me. They told me what we were, and, as far as they knew, what we could do. They told me that I had not faded down like so many others had because I had lain on my own remains. They warned me not stray too far from my remains. They told me nevertheless to wander my haunt and to learn to read.

My remains were beneath Sean's building, so when Sean unsummoned me I returned to them. I was thankful that my remains were not encased in wood.

I didn't know how much time passed while I was unsummoned. I know that it wasn't days. It may have been months. I have a Dead'er's memory of the passage of time.

During this time I said to myself, over and over, that some day there would be another Stringer in my haunt. Maybe not like Sean, living above my remains and able to summon me across the city in bright sunlight. But there had been other Stringers. So even accustomed now to the strangeness of this deaf, powerful Stringer, I could hope for another. Some day.

There was also the matter of the Voyant, my Stringer's girlfriend. I held no anger toward her; it was not she who had unsummoned me. I thought, that once I had regained some strength, maybe it would not be such a ghost-like thing to manifest where she might encounter me. I wanted her to see me again, for she saw me as I was, just a boy.

Monday was Sean's favourite day at work. The dealership was least busy and Tony and Paula would often appear during his lunch hour. Paula liked to sit to the right of Sean. She told him stories about her children, occasionally squeezing Sean's arm for emphasis.

Tony, on Sean's left, frequently broke into Paula's narrative, "She talk too much," he winked at Sean, "Yes? You want more stories about the children of Pauletta?"

Paula sighed as if she were disappointed, but after Tony began to talk, she would forget herself, and often questioned Tony as eagerly as Sean.

Tony told them about his childhood and youth in Italy.

"What a time I had, but I was bad boy then. No good to be like that, yes? You listen to mother, yes." Tony indicated Paula with a nod. "Unless your mother like this one."

"Sean, you no have luck with girls?"

"Leave the boy alone, Antonio. When it is his time he'll find a good woman!"

"You like them big or small?" Tony put down his sandwich and made a gesture with his hands.

"Antonio! You're a pig!" said Paula.

"Every man thinks the same thing. Some are smart. They never say nothing about it. They just enjoy."

Sean laughed.

"Even your husband," continued Antonio, "I can tell you he never say nothing. He just enjoy!"

"My husband says plenty about what he likes." Paula scowled at Tony. "And stop corrupting the kid. Do you want him to turn out like you?"

"He should be so lucky!" Tony slapped Sean on the back. Sean coughed over a bite of his sandwich. "But you no answer question. How is she, your girlfriend?"

"Antonio, if he wanted us to know, he would tell us." Paula turned her attention to Sean. "Don't pay any attention to him."

"It is true. You no need to tell us nothing. Maybe you no like girls and you no want to say. That Pauletta," Tony pushed his thumb in the direction of Paula, "maybe she no understand." Tony patted Sean's knee. "I understand. It's good for you. As long as you love somebody."

Sean laughed but pushed Tony hand off his knee. "I like girls!"

"So why you no talk about your girlfriend?" Tony winked at Paula.

"I don't know. There nothing much to say."

"You have a girlfriend?" said Paula.

"Not really. Well yes. I don't know. This girl comes over every Wednesday for dinner."

Paula grinned, "Every week! Well then she likes you."

"I guess she does. She smiles a lot during dinner."

"But you no kiss her yet." Tony shook his head.

"What?" Paula looked puzzled. "Well how long have you had this standing dinner date?"

"About a month I guess."

"Mamma mia." Tony slapped his own forehead. "A month and no kiss! You no like girls!"

"Give him a break Antonio! He's a gentlemen." Paula patted Sean's arm. "So what do you talk about?"

Sean muttered, "I don't know. Her school, the stuff wrong with our building, her friends."

"What about you?" Paula asked, "Don't you talk about what is happening in your life?"

"Not really. I guess not. There's not much … What would I tell her?"

"Talk about what makes you special," said Paula "about whatever there is about you that's not like all the other guys she knows." Paula paused, "What do you do that she would admire?"

Sean reflected for a moment.

"That Pauletta, for once she's a-right," said Tony nodding.

Sean carried the freshly washed dinner plates to the table. He placed one in front of Mandy before attending to his own setting. Mandy looked up and smiled at him. Sean smiled back before returning to the kitchen for the cutlery.

There was one thing Mandy did that bothered Sean. She launched into her stories while he was still in the kitchen. He'd emerge with plates, cutlery, the second course, or anything he had gone to fetch and Mandy would be in the middle of some narrative. She seemed not to notice that he had not heard the beginning. He never knew how much he had missed. She always seemed so engrossed in the tale that he did not want to ask her to repeat herself. And she was beautiful when she was telling stories.

Sean returned to the table and placed a knife, fork, and spoon on top of each of the two paper napkins.

"… I know we haven't talked about it in a month but I really can't get it out of my mind. We were getting somewhere you know. I mean there was a set back or two, but nothing we couldn't handle. Don't you think so?" Mandy paused and looked at Sean.

Sean looked at Mandy. She seemed to be waiting for something. Sean nodded yes.

"Really?" said Mandy. There was a hopeful note in her voice.

"I'll be right back," said Sean. He was hoping dinner had not grown cold.

Mandy was speaking again when Sean returned from the kitchen, "… The crematorium has closed down. It hasn't been active for years but I discovered that the director is still in the business of death, so to speak, he manages a mausoleum now. It's not in the town where Steven was cremated but close by."

"What?" said Sean. He was spooning rice pilaf into Mandy's plate. He was trying his best to listen but it was tough to do that and serve without spilling.

"Oh a bit more for me please," said Mandy suddenly, "I've got a good appetite today. What a long practicum!" She had shown more interest in the dish since Sean had begun to prepare it with about half the paprika.

"Can I get you anything else before I sit down? Some more water may-be."

"Yes please!" Mandy smiled and held up her glass.

Mandy seemed to enjoy sending him back and forth to the kitchen. Could she be looking at my body while I'm walking away from her? Sean asked himself. On his way to the kitchen he turned suddenly and checked Mandy's face. Mandy met his eyes and smiled.

From the kitchen, Sean heard Mandy clear her throat, "Oh is this a new picture?"

Sean replied but Mandy did not seem to hear.

"I like it much better than those posters you had up on the windows." Mandy continued, "And it even matches the colours you picked for the sofa cushions! Who knew you had such good taste?"

"Oh I've got good taste in a few things, Ms. Simms," Sean whispered, grinning as he wiped up the water he spilt while fingering ice cubes into Mandy's glass.

Mandy had not commented on the dining set, a table and two chairs, that Sean had added to his apartment a little over a month ago. Nevertheless she did seem more enthusiastic about their dinners together. Enthusiastic yet relaxed, thought Sean, and talkative. He picked the names Katie and Ty out of the stream of words coming from the living room. How do I get to next level? Sean asked himself,

"So how does Katie find so much time to spend with Ty?" Sean called from the kitchen, "Shouldn't she be as busy as you?"

Mandy watched Seam appear in the kitchen doorway. He seemed less sure of himself than usual. "Believe me, her marks show that she has other things on her mind! If she's not careful she's going to end up on academic probation. But that's an old topic. I told you that while you were spreading the table cloth." Mandy paused, "I guess that you're too cute to have a good memory! You're a bit like Katie that way."

Sean looked at Mandy. He was almost sure he could tell when she was kidding him.

"Anyway, since we're back on that topic, maybe you could talk to Ty about it. You know, man to man. Remind him that Katie's gotta worry about her future right now. Sometimes guys pay more attention to things that come from other guys."

"Pardon me did you just say something?" Sean kept his face down towards his plate.

"Very, very funny Sean." Mandy smiled. "You're good." She held up a forkful of the pilaf. "Food's good too!"

Sean remembered to finish chewing before answering her. "Thanks. I don't know about talking to Ty though. I've only met him a few times. I don't know how he would take it…"

"Oh you're probably right about that. I was just trying to think of how I could help." Mandy sighed. "You're a good man Sean Hughes. I should be grateful for that. It's really unfair to ask for more…" Mandy's voice trailed off.

"Mandy you can ask me to do anything! I'll talk to Ty if that's what you want me to do!" Sean had the opening he had been waiting for. "I am not afraid to do it. I can be brave. Didn't you say that you were proud of me after that fight with that woman ghost?" Sean was surprised at the force in his voice.

"No, Sean I didn't say that," said Mandy.

Sean's face stiffened.

"But I was thinking it."

Sean took a deep breath and held it to give himself a moment of calm. He cleared his throat. "You know I'd do anything you want, don't you? Anything you asked."

"Really, anything? Are you sure?" Mandy used a throaty voice. "Even if it made you uncomfortable?" Mandy's face was turned toward Sean. She met his eyes.

"Sweet pea," thought Sean.

There was something in Mandy's voice or manner however, a warning maybe, a note of mischief for sure. Nevertheless, Sean doubted that he could ever deny Mandy anything she asked him for. "I mean it," he heard himself say, "I'd do anything in my power for you."

Mandy looked down and gently placed her fork beside her plate. She looked up and met Sean eyes again. Sean moistened his lips. He dropped his fork onto his plate and found that he had to rest his forearms against the table to steady them. Mandy reached out and placed her left hand on Sean's right forearm.

Sean knew he was helpless.

Mandy parted her lips slightly, then paused. "Sean," she said at last.

Sean, his heart pounding, leaned toward the young woman.

"Sean, I want you to talk to someone for me."

Until that moment, Sean thought he knew the meaning of the word despair. He took a breath, felt his heart slow to maybe only twice its normal rate. "Ty?" He exhaled.

"Noble. I want you to tell him everything we learned about the Steven, and Steven's parents, and the crematorium in Mexico."

"Damn," said Sean softly.

However Mandy kept her hand on Sean's forearm. She leaned in and gently kissed Sean on his cheek. Sean was sure that at that moment his heart stood dead still for several beats. But Mandy only smiled and picked up her fork once again.

"Damn," said Sean again.

The flour shifted quickly again. Sean was astounded by how quickly Noble was writing.

"S-T-E-V-E-N-I-S-I-N-M-E-X-I-C-O"

"Why doesn't he go talk to his parents himself."

"H-E-C-A-N-N-O-T-H-E-I-S-F-A-R-A-W-A-Y"

"Can't you guys travel?"

"T-H-E-F-U-R-T-H-E-R-W-E-G-O-F-R-O-M-R-E-M-A-I-N-S-T-H-E-W-E-A-K-E-R-W-E-A-R-E"

"Then his remains must be in Mexico!" Sean's voice rose in excitement. "So he is probably trying to get his parents to bring his actual remains home."

"T-H-A-T-M-A-K-E-S-S-E-N-S-E"

"And this Mary ghost seems to be trying to stop us from figuring this out. She probably doesn't want Steven to come home."

"A-T-T-A-C-K-I-N-G-S-T-E-V-E-N-S-P-A-R-E-N-T-S-W-O-U-L-D-L-E-T-T-H-E-M-K-N-O-W-S-O-M-E-T-H-I-N-G-I-S-W-R-O-N-G-I-N-S-T-E-A-D-M-A-R-Y-W-A-N-T-S-Y-O-U-T-O-G-I-V-E-U-P"

"She didn't want us to have the information about Steven's cremation. That's why she tried to grab the clipboard. Unfortunately the papers Mandy wrote everything on was ripped in the attack. So all that information is lost."

"M-A-N-D-Y-G-O-T-T-H-E-A-D-D-R-E-S-S-A-G-A-I-N-F-R-O-M-M-R-S-B-U-T-L-E-R"

"I didn't know she had contacted that woman again! How did you know?"

"M-A-N-D-Y-T-O-L-D-M-E"

"You've been talking to Mandy!"

"P-L-E-A-S-E-D-O-N-O-T-B-E-A-N-G-R-Y"

"Angry! Why would I be angry? It's not like I would be jealous of a ghost!"

"O-F-C-O-U-R-S-E-N-O-T-I-C-A-N-N-O-T-K-I-S-S-H-E-R-L-I-K-E-Y-O-U-C-A-N"

"Kiss her?"

"Y-O-U-H-A-V-E-N-O-T-K-I-S-S-E-D-H-E-R"

Sean was silent a moment. "So how do you talk with Mandy? She's not a Stringer, is she?"

"S-H-E-W-R-O-T-E-M-E-A-L-E-T-T-E-R"

"You have an address? Where do you live?"

For Sean there was a sudden sensation of alternating cold and then warmth. It was like walking through a drafty room and coming across a bit of warmth next to a tiny space heater. "Is Noble laughing at me?" thought Sean.

"M-Y-R-E-M-A-I-N-S-A-R-E-H-E-R-E"

"Here in my kitchen?" asked Sean.

"U-N-D-E-R-T-H-I-S-B-U-I-L-D-I-N-G"

"So she put the letter under…"

"I-N-H-E-R-A-P-A-R-T-M-E-N-T"

"What were you doing in her apartment?" Sean felt his throat tighten.

"T-H-I-S-B-U-I-L-D-I-N-G-I-S-I-N-M-Y-H-A-U-N-T"

"So you go everywhere you damn well please?"

"N-O-T-Y-O-U-R-A-P-A-R-T-M-E-N-T"

"You shouldn't be creeping around people's apartments. Suppose Mandy is in the shower when you go floating through her walls. Suppose I am in the shower!"

"I-C-A-N-N-O-T-G-O-T-H-R-O-U-G-H-T-H-E-S-E-W-A-L-L-S-T-H-E-Y-H-A-V-E-T-O-O-M-U-C-H-W-O-"

"Don't give me excuses. I don't want you to go into either of our apartments unless you are asked."

"M-A-N-D-Y-W-R-O-T-E-T-H-A-T-S-H-E-W-A-N-T-E-D-"

"I don't care. I want you to promise that you won't go looking in Mandy's apartment."

"B-U-T-T-H-A-T-W-O-U-L-D-"

"Promise that you won't!"

"M-E-A-N-T-H-A-"

"I'm your Stringer: you have to listen to me!"

"I-T-I-S-N-O-T-T-H-A-T-S-I-M-P-L-E"

"Promise!" Sean ran his foot through the spill of flour on the kitchen floor, erasing the letters Noble had written. "Promise!" Sean shouted again.

"I-P-R-O-M-I-S-E" wrote Noble.

Chapter Sixteen

Girlfriend's Orders

"That explains the look on Mary's face!"

"She had a face?" asked Sean.

"Y-E-S-B-U-T-I-T-I-S-N-O-T-P-R-E-T-T-Y"

"Well yes, she was very thin and her face was full of deep lines, deeper than just wrinkles, as if she were a couple hundred years old at least, but on top of all that she had a look of absolute fury. Anger like I've never seen." Mandy paused a moment, "Then in the second before she disappeared there was another look—despair, and terror. She was really afraid. It was almost made me pity her."

"L-O-O-K-A-T-Y-O-U-R-A-R-M-S"

Both Sean and Mandy looked at her forearms. The scars were fading but still visible.

"Oh, I know that she's evil. What did you call her, pure distilled evil?"

"I-S-A-V-E-T-H-A-T-F-O-R-H-E-A-R-S-T"

"What?" said Sean, "Who's that?"

"Probably Noble's arch enemy or something like that. But what I meant was that even though Mary's evil and was practically trying to kill us, Sean, there was something about what I saw in her at the last minute. Just before you sent her away, something different…" Mandy paused, "She seemed human."

"S-H-E-W-A-S-H-U-M-A-N-O-N-C-E"

"Of course she was. Just like you were. That's not what I meant." Mandy shook her head.

"If you're not human then what are you?" Sean's voice carried a hint of a challenge.

"Noble is still a human being Sean."

"I-A-M-N-O-T-S-O-S-U-R-E"

"Me neither," said Sean.

"Sean, you don't know what you are talking about."

"I-D-O-K-N-O-W-T-H-A-T-I-A-M-N-O-T-A-G-H-O-S-T-L-I-K-E-M-A-R-Y"

"Of course you're not," affirmed Mandy.

"What's the big difference?" snorted Sean.

"I-K-E-E-P-M-Y-P-R-O-M-I-S-E-S"

"From all appearances the crematorium kept great records. It should be possible to find the other families who had a loved one cremated on the same day as the Butlers. We might be able to do most of the work of tracking them down over the phone but chances are most of them speak Spanish."

"That's a problem?" asked Sean.

"If neither of us speaks Spanish it is," continued Mandy.

"You don't?" asked Sean.

"Nope," Mandy shook her head.

"That's fairly shocking to me. I didn't think that there was anything you couldn't do." Sean frowned, then covered his mouth with his hand and avoided looking into Mandy's eyes.

"Well I did take French and Spanish in high school and my marks were good, but those languages never stuck with me. Even with my workbook open I couldn't get the hang of all the verb forms..." Mandy looked at Sean's face. "Oh you were joking weren't you?"

Sean laughed.

"Oh you're being silly." Mandy gave a short laugh. "Well when you've stopped your guffaws I'll tell you the rest." Mandy frowned at Sean.

Sean mimed wiping a smile off his face.

"I was going to tell you about a guy in my practicum cohort who's from Mexico. He could probably help us out."

"Great!" said Sean, "what do we need help with?"

"You're hopeless!" Mandy rolled her eyes. "The best way to do this is to get the Mexican ghost to help us out as much as possible. He's probably in an urn in the family home or buried in the yard or something. If he looks around his remains he should be able to tell us where they are."

"Nice. Sounds like a plan. But what if the ashes have been scattered or something? What will we do then?"

"That's one of those situations where my nursing instructor likes to say, 'you deserve a D.-double-W.T.'"

Mandy paused and looked at Sean expectantly.

"Oh, that was my cue, wasn't it?"

"Sure was." Mandy patted Sean's forearm. "Ok. I'll give you the lead in again." Mandy cleared her throat. "That answer calls for a D.-double-W.T."

"What's a D.-double-W.T., Mandy?" asked Sean.

"Don't Waste Worry Twit." Mandy smiled at the look on Sean's face. "You're not a twit, Sean. It's just an expression. She means that you're not supposed to worry about catastrophes until they happen. It's not an efficient use of resources; you'll spend time, and energy preparing for a worst case scenario that may never happen, meanwhile you should be dealing with the immediate situation that you do have."

"Ok."

Mandy continued, "Let's assume that Steven's ashes are in one place until we have good reason to believe otherwise."

"Okie dokie."

"Our next step is to get the translator on board. How does a date Friday night sound?"

"I'm free Friday night." Sean grinned. "We've never actually been a real date, have we?"

Mandy laughed, "Not you and I, silly. For you and Hector. Hector loves to play pool. You're going to take him to the billiard place on Broadway."

"Why do you want me to take Hector on a date?" Sean's eyes were wide.

"It's not a real date. I just need you to make friends with him. Don't worry, I'll call Ty too. It'll be a great night out for you boys."

"Why have I got to make friends with this Hector guy?"

Mandy set her jaw firmly. "Because we're going to ask him to call up complete strangers and ask them about their relative's remains! That's a pretty big thing to ask of someone."

"I guess. You think he'll do it?" asked Sean.

"He'd do it for a friend," said Mandy.

"Ok," said Sean, "Aren't you his friend?"

"We're not that close but if you want," Mandy paused to lift her eyes slowly to meet Sean's, "I can start spending more time with him before and after class."

"Oh, is that a threat?" Sean grinned.

"No. Not at all. I'll enjoy getting to know him. He's seems like a really nice guy." Mandy leaned back in her chair. She tilted her head to one side and ran her fingers slowly through her hair.

"Fine, I'll do it," said Sean.

"Great," Mandy leaned back towards the table. "Oh, and I guess I should give you a heads up about Hector. I'm not really his type." Mandy smiled. "Don't worry you guys will get along just fine."

"I summon you Noble!" Sean's voice was a strained whisper. Noble's face appeared in the bathroom mirror in front of Sean. "I need you to help me make some shots. Those guys are killing me out there."

Noble manifested his arms and shoulders, then gave a shrug as if to say: "What do you want me to do."

"I want you to help me make some shots! All you have to do is the nudge the ball towards a hole or something. Nothing too obvious."

Noble shook his head: no.

"Why not? I'm your Stringer!" Sean raised his voice. "You should be doing stuff for me!"

"Hey you ok?" Ty had come into the bathroom behind Sean. "Who you talking to?"

"No one," said Sean. He turned to face Ty. "Well myself."

"Ok." Ty turned toward a urinal. "We all need little pep talk from time to time!" Ty groaned. "It feels good to drain that out! Next round's on you my friend. Oh yes, ..."

Sean turned back towards the mirror. He held his hands under the faucet to start the flow of water. "Why not?" he whispered, hoping that the sound of the water would cover his voice.

Noble reappeared. He manifested his hands and made the shape of a ball between them.

"The cue ball!" Sean said. Noble nodded yes, drew his finger across his throat and then shook his head to say no.

"Ball, dead, no," repeated Sean, puzzled.

"Ball not's dead till it's in the pocket my friend!" Ty called out. Sean heard the urinal flush and spun around. Ty was right behind him with his hands held out in front of him. "Gotta wash the hands after everything: girlfriend's orders."

Ty stepped past Sean and held his own hands under the stream of water. "Does your girlfriend make you wash every time you touch something? It's crazy. My hands feel like they are going to fall off from all the washing. But you should hear how Katie goes on and on about germs. Mandy must be even worse—you've been washing your hands since I came in here."

Sean nodded. He tore off a section of paper towel and scrunched it between his fingers. "No, Mandy doesn't bug me about hand washing."

"Lucky man," sighed Ty.

Sean threw his paper towel into the garbage.

"Oh man. I can see that your girlfriend hasn't taught you anything! You are supposed to save the paper towel to get you out of the bathroom!"

"What?" asked Sean.

"Follow me."

Ty tore off a section of paper towel and dried his hands thoroughly. Then, instead of tossing the paper into the garbage, he used it to open the bathroom door without touching the handle. He stood to one side and waved Sean through the open door. "See!" he winked at Sean. "No touching the door handle. Nurse's orders."

On their way back to the billiard table Ty slapped Sean on the back, "Maybe you should surprise your girlfriend by showing her that you know how to wash your hands." He laughed.

Sean felt his face go warm. "She's not really my girlfriend … yet."

"I know man. You've not even kissed her yet!" Ty winked at him then added, "Don't look so shocked. Girls talk about everything man. Everything. Take some advice man."

"What?" asked Sean.

"Go ahead and make a move. She must like you or she wouldn't be talking about you so much."

"I guess so," said Sean. They had arrived at the billiard table. Hector looked up at the pair as they approached. Nursing seemed an incongruous profession for this short, tough-looking young man. He had an athletic build however and moved gracefully.

"… and don't spend so much time in the bathroom rubbing your hands and talking about balls. She's bound to think that you're not really interested!" Ty laughed and winked at Hector.

Hector finished racking the balls and took up pool cue. "It is your break." He handed the wooden rod to Sean. "If you're not handling Mandy maybe you can do better with this." Hector and Ty laughed.

Ty continued, "Take your time man. Line up the shot. Think ahead, and then let her go!"

Sean bent over the table. He eyed the triangle of balls ahead of him and placed the cue ball on the table in front of them. He rolled the wooden cue nervously in his hands before pointing it directly at the cue ball. He brought his eyes down to the level of the table to ensure that the pool cue, the cue ball and the rack of balls were all in a line. He drew a deep breath and drove the pool cue forward sharply, imitating the way he had seen Hector handle the stick.

There was a satisfying crack as the stick made contact with the cue ball. But then Sean cringed as the cue ball rolled into the rack with only weak click. Several of the coloured balls rolled away from the formation a good distance, however none of them approached a pocket.

Sean stood up. He glanced apologetically at Ty but tried to avoid Hector's eyes.

"Foul … again" said Hector in a soft voice and replaced the cue ball on the table. Ty smiled encouragingly at Sean.

At lunch Tony was animated.

"Maybe you no concentrate very well," he said, "for this game you must be very relaxed and very concentrated at the same time. No thinking of girls or food. Foolish to think of anything else. The hands are working very hard. The head works also. You have to see where the first ball is going to go.

What ball it hits. Then you see where the second ball is going to go. What it hits. Where it falls. And so on. Then when you have seen all you move the stick just right amount. Just the right amount. That is the secret."

"You sound like you are very good at pool!"

"Biliardo!" said Tony. "I will show you."

"Oh yah, billiards!" said Sean. "Great!"

The rest of the day passed slowly. At five o'clock Sean pulled off his coverall and threw it into his locker. In a couple minutes he was in his car and twenty minutes later he was at the pool hall.

Tony's blue toned car was already parked out front. Its finish shone in the evening light. Sean paused to admire the sedan.

Inside he found Tony playing a solo game. Sean watched for some time. Tony held the clue lightly, never seeming to grip it with more than his fingertips. Before shooting he would point the tip of the cue at a ball and then at a pocket. Sean was astounded at the older man's accuracy. Tony, Sean noted with satisfaction, was a much better player than even Hector was.

"You come here. First you learn to put the ball right."

Tony was a mild but exacting teacher. He pointed Sean to the shot he wished him to make then did it himself. He would then replace the balls for Sean to repeat the motion. It pleased Sean when the balls went fairly close to what he had intended. It was clear to him, however, that even with instruction it would be a long time before he could play a respectable game.

After about forty-five minutes Sean excused himself to go to the bathroom. He locked himself into a stall.

"Noble! Come here! Noble!" Sean spoke in a whisper. He looked around the stall then peered into the bowl. Then he got down on his hands and knees and looked under the stall door. "Noble! Where are you?" Sean opened the stall door and steeped out into the empty bathroom. He walked over to look in the mirror at the far end of the room. "Noble! Come here now!"

Someone opened the bathroom door. Sean went back to the stall and closed the metal door behind him. He waited till he heard the sound of a flush and then hand washing. When he was sure he was alone again he emerged from the stall.

"Noble! I summon you!" Sean called out. He looked into the mirror.

Noble's face manifested in the mirror in front of him.

"Why didn't you come when I called you?" Sean hissed.

Noble appeared to be talking.

"Oh, damn," said Sean, "wait here—outa sight!"

Sean returned a moment later. In his hands he held a large cookie from a vending machine. He crushed the cookie while it was in its cellophane wrapping, then tore the wrapping open and spread the crumbs on top of a porcelain tank cover.

"Noble!" spat Sean.

"Y-O-U-C-A-L-L-E-D" appeared in the crumbs.

"Of course I did. Why else would you be here?"

"H-O-W-M-A-Y-I-B-E"

"Cut the polite crap; you're not talking to Mandy."

"O-K"

"Why won't you help me with my balls?" Sean said though gritted teeth.

A voice called out from the other side of the stall door, "Hey buddy, are you ok in there?"

"Yeah, never been better!" said Sean in an irritated voice. He flushed the toilet and then smoothed the crumbs out. "Why don't you help with the balls?" he whispered.

"Y-O-U-D-I-D-N-O-T-A-S-K"

"Well I'm asking now!" Sean angrily scraped the crumbs into his palm and then dumped them into the toilet. He flushed the toilet again and emerged from the stall. He brushed pass the other bathroom occupant and held his hands under the faucet. The other man dried his hands on some paper towel, threw the paper in the garbage and then exited the bathroom. Sean shook his head. After drying his own hands, Sean kept the paper towel in his right hand, and used it to avoid touching the door handle on his way out of the bathroom.

Sean made his way back to the table where he and Tony had been playing. Tony had already racked the balls. Sean sighed and picked up his cue.

"Some assistance right about now would be appreciated," Sean whispered into the table.

Sean was surprised when the cue ball struck the rack head on. The coloured balls scattered out to the right and left. Two of them fell into one pocket.

"You pick stripe or solid now," said Tony calmly.

Tony crossed his arms thoughtfully as if thinking about his strategy. Nothing in his manner suggested that he had spent a frustrating three quarters of an hour trying to get Sean to make any shot he had called in advance.

Sean chose stripes and sank two balls in succession.

"You work good now," said Tony evenly.

Sean's next shot had no obvious calls. He thought he saw a way to pocket a striped ball after deflecting one of the solid balls to strike it at an angle. He turned to Tony.

"I tell you again—if you see it happen in your head, you can see happen here on the table. Think the last part first. How does the ball roll into the pocket? Then how the next ball hits that one to make it roll just like that. Then how the ball before hits that one. And so you see how you must hold the stick. And how you must move it."

Sean tried to picture each ball's route. He adjusted the angle of the pool cue.

"Now you start to see," said Tony.

"Now would be a good time to help again," mumbled Sean. He drew the cue back and struck the white ball with a sharp hard rap. There was a pleasing crack when he did so, and another as the white ball struck the solid. The solid ball Sean had targeted only glanced against the striped ball however, causing the latter to roll across the table but not as quickly as Sean planned. It came to a stop well short of the pocket.

Sean exhaled, "Damn Noble, you could have given it a bit of a push."

"Ok. Not bad. That was a tough shot. You were close. No shame." Tony pressed against the table and pointed the pool cue at two of the solid balls and at two different pockets. "Now you see I want this here, and that one there. So I think it back like this." Tony traced a line back from one pocket towards the ball. "And I think which ball can come here to meet it just so," continued Tony. Tony traced lines between the balls back to the cue ball, and then drew a line in the air for the angle of the pool cue itself. Then he laid the cue stick on the table at the angle he had indicated. "This is for you. Come on. No pouting. You can do it."

Sean reached for the cue Tony had laid on the table. "No son." Tony taped Sean's wrist. "You find the way." Tony picked up his cue and stepped back from the table. "You go ahead now."

Sean tried to trace the balls back from the pocket to the cue ball the way Tony had shown him. Sean knew that he had failed however, since his final cue position was much different from Tony's. He prepared to take the shot anyway.

"Maybe you try again," said Tony patiently. "Each time there is only one chance to hit the balls. But you have many chances to prepare."

Sean sighed and straightened up. He began tracing the ball positions again, perhaps even a little more carelessly than he had before. He traced the paths he hoped the balls would take to strike one another back to the cue ball. Then before Tony could admonish him, Sean placed the wooden pool cue as close to the position Tony had placed his own earlier and struck the cue ball sharply. The first two balls behaved as Sean wanted, but the third struck the cushion well away from the pocket.

"Damn you Noble!" said Sean under his breath. He pointed the cue at the ball he had tried to sink and then at the nearest pocket. "You're going in there!" he hissed. Sean traced the path the ball would take, back from the pocket, to the ball itself, and back from there to the cue ball. When he was sure he had pictured the path correctly he laid his cue on the table at the angle he had calculated.

"That's it; isn't it?" Sean turned to where Tony stood. Tony had his arms folded across his chest.

Tony shook his head. Without saying anything he took up Sean's cue and changed the angle at which it lay.

"Fine!" said Sean. He gripped the cue and prepared to shoot.

As quick as a cat, Tony reached over the edge of the table and changed the position of the cue ball.

"Damn," said Sean, "I had that shot!"

"You find your own shot!" said Tony. "And stop asking your spettro to help you." He scooped the cue ball up off the table. "These American balls are not made of elephant bone—no ivory, just some heavy plastic—resin. Il fantasma cannot move then!"

Chapter Seventeen

"You Are the Man and You Have To Be the Practical One"

As soon as it began to get dark Mandy went from candle to candle with a lit match. Sean had been about turn on his new floor lamp but stopped when he saw how the glow from the two-dozen or so candles filled the room. "Oh, It's beautiful!" he said.

"I know," said Mandy, "it doesn't look like your apartment anymore!"

Sean looked at Mandy's eyes. They shone in the candlelight but he could not tell if she were teasing him. It also occurred to him that she had never appeared more beautiful to him than she did at that moment in the low warm light.

"All these candles are unnecessary!" said Tony.

"I know," said Sean quickly, turning to look at Tony.

"It seemed like the right thing to do!" Mandy folded her arms. "A séance should look like a séance!"

"This is not a séance!" Tony growled. "When it is a séance he is trying to call some spettro, ... some fantasma, what did you call it?"

"Ghost?" offered Sean.

"Yes. Séance, he is calling a ghost because he wants to talk to someone who is now dead. Someone he loves or hates: father, wife, lover, child—someone like that. This séance thing with candles and holding hands, is all a waste of time."

"Why?"

"Look, young girl..." Tony searched for her name, "Mandy, if a ghost wants to talk to you he will find you. You do not have to go looking." Tony sighed, "The candles are unnecessary. Why you have candles—because you think that the ghost cannot see by electric light?"

"I already told her that candles were a waste of time … and money," said Sean.

Tony grunted, "You are the man and you have to be the practical one."

"I beg your pardon!" Mandy had her hands on her hips.

"This is not practical!" Tony made an irritated gesture towards the three rows of candles Mandy had set up on the dining room table.

"The candles won't interfere, will they?" asked Sean.

"I'll put them out if you think they'll get in the way," said Mandy shyly.

"No. I am just speaking my mind. They are not a problem. Maybe they will help the ghost think we just want to talk. That would be a good thing."

"See! I know what I am doing." Mandy stuck her tongue out at Sean.

Sean pushed his face toward Mandy, "So you claim now!"

"You children," Tony sighed again. "Whatever you are going to do save it till after I am gone home!"

"We weren't going to do anything," said Mandy quickly.

Tony smiled, "See, Sean! No kiss for you yet. Not tonight—so no need to wonder. You can put all your all your concentration on this task."

"What?" said Mandy, her voice was unnecessarily loud. "What do you know about our kissing?"

"Nothing," said Tony, "nothing at all." Mandy looked relieved. Tony continued: "There is no kiss to know about!"

Mandy gave Sean an angry look.

Tony cleared his throat. "Sean you have the difficult part tonight. If you can do this…"

"I'll sleep better than I have in months." nodded Sean.

"Oh, you dream about her?" asked Tony.

"No, she's just a friend," said Sean quickly.

Tony looked back and forth from Sean to Mandy and then he laughed.

"What is so funny?" snapped Mandy,

"I was asking the young man if he dreams about the ghost!" said Tony. Mandy looked embarrassed. Tony laughed again. "I think we are ready now." Tony took a seat at the table. Mandy took the chair next to Tony.

Sean stood alone in the middle of the room. He closed his eyes and his brow furrowed. He began to mumble.

"Aloud!" said Tony, "Aloud! We need to know what is going on!"

"But I was just thinking it," Sean retorted, "I don't know how to put it into words."

"Save that strength for later! Don't show it. Use just the words now." Tony's voice was stern.

"Ok," said Sean. He continued: "I summon you now, Mary Nash-Crowley. Mary Nash-Crowley I summon you! Come here. Come here now Mary Nash-Crowley." Sean continued the summoning for several minutes.

"Maybe she's not coming," whispered Mandy.

"Shut up," hissed Tony. "She has been here before *senza invito*, without invitation, so she must come now."

"Don't tell me to shut up!" snarled Mandy in a whisper.

"*Sono spiacente*—I'm sorry," said Tony. "Please now Mandy, you must watch for her. Look everywhere—every corner of the room. You will see her first. Please look carefully."

Mandy stood and began to turn slowly around inspecting the room.

"Sit down please. Look calm—please." Tony patted the seat of the chair next to him. Mandy sat but continued to swing her gaze right and left and occasionally behind her as well.

After about twenty minutes Mandy felt a breath of cold air against the back of her neck. Then the hair on her arms stood erect. At once she spotted a faint grey form across the table from where she sat. The figure of a woman was materializing. It was behind Sean. Mandy drew her breath in sharply. Tony looked at Mandy and then followed her graze. He squinted for a few moments then with a half-smile quickly drummed his fingers on the table. Sean turned to look behind him. He saw the shape of ghost over his shoulder and took a half step to turn around and face the apparition. He did not however, take his right foot off a well-constructed wooden box on which it had been resting.

"Ah, there she is!" said Tony.

Mandy saw the woman's mouth move.

"My name is Antonio!" said Tony, sitting up straight. "I am not from this place!"

"What?" asked Mandy.

"I can hear her," said Tony slowly, "as I am sure that she can hear us!"

"Well ask her then, why she attacked us?" growled Mandy.

"You heard the question, Mary. Answer please." said Tony. He paused a moment: "She says that she does not care to be interrogated, and if you are finished with your foolish questions she will be glad to be on her way."

"Oh," said Sean, "it's working!"

"It's seems so," said Tony. "Go ahead now Sean!"

Sean squeezed his eyes closed and lifted his foot off of the box. The box had a hinged lid that swung open to one side. Sean now kicked this open with his toe. Sean then pointed his face down towards where the box sat on the floor in front of him. His mouth moved as if he were shouting but Mandy heard but no sound. She watched open-mouthed as Mary's form seemed to dissolve into a cylinder-shaped cloud. Then suddenly Mary's cloud seemed to take on the shape of a funnel, the lower portion of it flowing helplessly into the open box.

"Yes!" shouted Tony, "You've got the bitch!"

"You've done it Sean!" exclaimed Mandy.

Mandy saw Sean smile but he did not stop his incantation. Half or more of Mary's form was already inside the box. Then as Mandy watched, all of the grey disappeared quickly into the box.

"Now the lid! Close her up!" shouted Tony.

Sean deftly flipped the lid closed with his foot and then bent over and engaged the latch by hand. With a shout of relief, he replaced his foot on the box. He looked at Mandy.

She smiled at him. "You did it Sean!"

Sean pumped his fist in the air. "Yes I did! Sweet Great Pea!" he shouted, "I got a ghost in a box!"

"I'm so proud of you!" Mandy rose from the chair and headed towards Sean with her arms extended. She stopped suddenly. The box had begun to rise up off the floor. The movement did not take Sean by surprise however and he managed to keep his foot on the box.

"Damn!" said Tony, "She is strong that one!"

Sean stood for some time with one foot on the floor, the other in the air, struggling to keep the box from rising. It seemed to the others for a moment as if Sean were able to arrest the box's movements but then the container began to tilt back and forth. Sean had to fight to keep his foot on top of it.

"Let her go Sean; it's too dangerous." said Mandy. Sean looked at Mandy and took his foot off the box. The box seemed to continue to levitate for a fraction of a second but then shot down to the floor so that Sean, still regaining his balance, unintentionally brought his foot down to rest on top of the box again.

"This is strange," said Tony, "I thought she wanted to escape in the box."

There was a sudden cold stillness in the room.

"I hear something," said Tony. "She is calling somebody."

Tony's voice had lost its normal calm. Mandy grew frightened.

"What is she saying?" asked Mandy.

"I don't know," said Tony, "She is just calling … and someone answers her. He is coming."

"Who is coming?" Mandy's voice quavered.

"I don't know," said Tony, "This is not a good thing."

"Let's get rid of this thing now," said Sean. "Let's take my car; the shovels are already in the trunk."

"Shut up! She can hear us!" snapped Tony.

His warning came too late. The box flew upwards, lifting Sean's foot with its violent movement and throwing him onto his back. His head hit the wooden floor with a loud thud. Mandy winced. Her eyes followed the wooden box to the ceiling where it seemed to press itself against the plaster. She down looked at Sean. He groaned and sat up. "Where's the box?" he asked. Mandy pointed to the ceiling. "Oh." He said following Mandy's finger. "Maybe we should just nail it there," said Sean.

"No," said Tony, "Someone is coming for her."

"What can we do?" Mandy sounded frightened.

"We go ahead with the plan," said Sean. He stood up. "My head hurts!"

Mandy stood and approached Sean. "Sean you need to be careful; you probably have another concussion." Mandy was using her nurse's voice. "Let me have a look at your pupils. I need to see if…" A movement above her attracted Mandy's attention. She looked up and saw that the box had loosed itself from the ceiling. "Cover your head!" She shouted and placed her arms protectively around Sean's head.

The box flew down and came to rest on the table next to the candles. Sean moved Mandy's arms to one side so that he could see.

"What's she doing now?" Mandy was breathless. "Maybe she is tired out."

Sean stood up. "Maybe. It probably fades her down to move the box like that."

"She is the same ghost who destroyed your kitchen, no?"

"Maybe," said Sean. "A ghost is a ghost as far as I am concerned. They probably rather help each other out than trust us Lye'vers!"

"If you are talking about Noble, Sean, he has never done anything to…"

The box flew off the table and struck Sean in the stomach. His breath went out of him. Mandy screamed. Sean crumpled over at the waist. "Yeesh!" he said, "That really hurt!" The box slammed itself into the floor by Sean's feet and then flew up again, catching Sean once more in the stomach. This time it continued upward, lifting Sean as it went. Mandy saw Sean's feet leave the ground and threw her arms around his legs, pulling him downwards. Sean's body sagged down with Mandy's weight but the possessed box continued upward, cutting into Sean's abdomen. Sean screamed.

"Let go of my feet. Let go!"

"Yes, Mandy. What you are doing now does not help," said Tony. "We must think somehow how we must control this box." Tony had brought the calm back into his voice. It helped. Mandy released Sean's legs and stepped back.

"Think!" said Tony. He shook his head. "And take the soft cushions off the sofa and bring them here." Mandy hurried to do as Tony instructed. Tony remained looking up at Sean.

"This hurts!" said Sean. He used his hand to try and pry the box away from his abdomen. There was a red stain growing where one corner of the box dug into his flesh below the navel.

"It is good, always," said Tony, "to prepared for the good thing we want to happen even if we don't know yet, how we will make them true." Tony pushed the table so that it was no longer directly beneath where Sean hung from the ceiling. He was careful not to upset the candles. Then he indicated to Mandy that she should spread the cushions on the floor.

"What can we do now?" asked Mandy, "Wait for her to tire out?"

"Fade down," groaned Sean.

"What?" said Mandy.

"Ghosts don't tire out. They fade down. That's what Noble told me."

"Noble is the boy il fantasma, yes?" Tony looked up at Sean.

"Yes," answered Mandy. "He helped us last time Mary attacked!"

"Why you no call the boy ghost?" Tony barked up at Sean. "Call him now!"

Sean had difficulty breathing. His words began to come in patches. "But how do we know, he's not going, to be, on her side?"

"He helped last time we were attached," affirmed Mandy.

"But not, the time, before that," laboured Sean. "I called, them both, and they, attacked me."

"What?" gasped Mandy.

"And last time, we weren't trying, to kill her."

"You call him now," said Tony. "If you don't it will be worse when her help comes. And even if this boy is on her side…"

"He's not on her side! He helps us!" shouted Mandy. "Call Noble now Sean."

Sean swallowed and his lips moved.

Noble:

What a pack of dumb Lye'vers. Well really it's Sean who was the worst of all. He was handed the best opportunity in years, in decades, from my point of view that is, and he wasted it. I liked that Stringer with the accent. He was good. He was way ahead of Sean. He was not as strong a Stringer as Sean, I didn't know if they come any stronger than Sean, but that guy knew how to listen. Which is much more than Sean seemed able to do.

That Stringer with the accent figured out how to get Mary in a box. And he told Sean how to do it. I had never thought of it myself. It made sense once he had explained it. If a Stringer like Sean could summon you, he could also make you go somewhere you didn't want to go—like the inside of a box that you couldn't get out of.

I wanted to know what it was like to be in a box like that. Although I knew plenty about what it's like to not be able to go through or into some place I'd wanted to go, I'd never been trapped. Maybe once. I remembered that night I spent as a fresh Dead'er in the room with my mother. She was crying all night, saying my name and my father's name over and over—and I was just waiting till the morning when that heavy wooden door opened and I could be out and on my way. I remembered all that and I couldn't remember my mother's name. I thought about all that while I was looking at that little box, and wondering about being inside it.

I knew that I wasn't supposed to be in Sean's apartment. He made me promise to stay out unless I was asked in. And for the most part I did that. Sean ought to have known that I couldn't just leave my haunt. It was where I am dead. And he may not have wanted me around but Mandy sure did. I followed her up to Sean's apartment and waited behind the sofa. I did not manifest and found the corner with as much wood as possible to keep behind me. I didn't want to be in the way when Mary came charging in on a wave of summoning and vengeance. That last unsummoning much have hurt her quite a bit.

I was surprised when Mary lifted the box from inside. I would have not been able to do that even at my most rolled up. And even though Sean had been so mean to me, I didn't want to see my Stringer ground to bits. Why couldn't any of them, Sean, Mandy or the Stringer with the accent, figure out that all they had to do to be rid of Mary once and for all was to unsummon her while she was in the box? Once she was weak all they would have to do was bury her somewhere far from her remains. She'd fade down good then, maybe all the way down. I was wondering about this when Sean summoned me. It took all my strength not to manifest right away. Instead I fled out the window, manifested, hit the wood frame of the window a couple of times, hard, making sure that they looked in my direction and saw me coming in the window.

Mandy started screaming when she saw me. It wasn't a frightened scream as much as it was a scream for help. She went on about Mary being in the box and about Mary trying to kill Sean. I said it aloud. Only the Stringer with the accent could hear me but he said, "What did you say?"

I thought of taking my time before helping Sean. Maybe, I was thinking, Sean ought to apologize for telling me to stay out of my own haunt.

"Repeat it to Mandy," I told the Stringer with the accent.

Then a loud crack came from Sean's apartment door. Then another and another. Then door splintered open. A man pushed his way through the splintered. He was carrying a crowbar.

Mandy screamed.

"Mary!" the man shouted. He was a Stringer. A strong one, but not strong like Sean.

Mandy was gulping for air. "I've seen you before," She pointed at the man.

I had seen him before too but I had a Dead'er's memory and I couldn't recall where.

"Mary Nash Crowley!" the man shouted.

The box sprung away from Sean and down into the man's out stretched arms. Sean crashed to the floor and lay still. The man stuck the box under one arm and turned for the door at a run.

"We must stop him!" shouted the Stringer with the accent. He picked up a chair and held it as if it were a weapon to strike the man with.

I manifested between the man and the door. The man spun in a circle swinging the crow bar furiously back and forth in front of him. Mandy screamed again, but of course the crowbar was metal and it did nothing to me. It did however keep the Stringer with the accent from approaching the man. When the man's back was turned I pushed the box out of his grasp. It clattered to the floor and slid to a stop against the cushion under Sean's head.

"Unsummon her!" I shouted again.

The man dove for the box. The Stringer with the accent wound up as if he were about to bring the chair down on the man's head. Sean sat up, "What's going on?" he said groggily.

"Duck Sean!" shouted Mandy.

I moved out of the doorway and manifested where I could protect Sean from the blow with the wooden chair. Sean opened his eyes and saw me hovering above him.

"I unsummon you!" said Sean bleary eyed, pointing at me.

I struggled but felt myself begin to dissolve. I turned to look at the man. He ran out the ruined door with the box once again under his arm. I looked back at the room. My vision was fading.

"I would not have hit Sean!" said the Stringer with the accent.

Unable to speak, I nodded to him as the last of my essence, melted away.

Chapter Eighteen

Gavin

Noble:

I didn't know why being unsummoned returned me to a place of memory. I supposed that I should be grateful that it did. Each time Sean unsummoned me, more of my memory returned. I wondered if it worked that way for other Dead'ers, for Mary. I supposed that I could ask.

Grateful. Maybe.

It was never just the good memories that come to mind. I wondered if this was true for everyone. Maybe I was not like others, Lye'vers or Dead'ers. Maybe we were all different.

For me good memories meant the time I was a boy, before the fire took my body. My memory of my mother was good; I remembered good things about her. My memory of her as a person was not complete. I did not know her name. I could not, any longer, remember her face. I guessed that soon even the memory of her voice would leave me. What would that mean?

"Noble, maybe you have one good idea, that one," said Gavin.

We were by the shore. The great wide salty inlet lay in front of us. We faced north. I could see sunlight hitting the water, the ripples each transformed to a brilliant point. It was as if a road of stars stretched out in front of us, a ribbon made of shiny glass that we could walk on. Beyond the open water lay the north shore. The land across from us rose sharply from the water's edge. We could see, closest to the water, the strip of brown where the trees had all been cut, baring the soil to dry in the sunlight. Above that, another strip where there were patches of bright green, representing the few remaining stands of uncut trees, and tracks of mottled brown and green. Those mottled sections we knew to be recent cuts. Trees that were too small or of the wrong species to cut provided the dots of pale green, while brush from the forest floor, bark, branches, and fresh stumps were all nearer to the colour of the naked earth. The highest strip was a lively unbroken green, as if the hills had wrapped a knit hat and scarf across their tallest points. The tress on the highest land, grown on thin soil, were not large enough to warrant cutting.

Sometimes Gavin could put things in words that I didn't know I was thinking. Of course his words were different from mine. "Noble, you should listen," said Gavin. He saw that my eyes were on the shore across from us. "There are more trees than you can count. You think only of the trees close to you."

I will never forget Gavin's voice. I liked the way he paused after calling my name. Of course his mother and sister had the same accent, and his people's way of speaking from the throat. When his mother spoke to me she put in words I did not know. Gavin always told me what she meant, however, "welcome, friend," "it's smoked salmon," or "be careful."

"Noble, there'll be plenty more work, and for more men too. You just have to wait till you're grown up a bit. My brothers came home to see my mother. You know they work with the cutting, don't you Noble."

Two of Gavin's brothers had jobs cutting timber. They earned almost as much as the White men doing the same work.

"My grandfather says that the hills we can see are not the last of the earth. The hills go on to the end of the world, he said, and they are all covered in trees."

The day was warm enough that we could walk about without our coats. We jumped from rock to rock along the shore. If there was a good small flat rock in sight we'd try to make it skip across the water. I was better than Gavin at this. I could make a rock skip once or twice nearly every time I threw. Gavin couldn't get his rock to do any more than skink half the time but he had the world record between us for most skips, ten or eleven he did once. He said it was eleven jumps of course but I disputed the count. I thought what he was calling the last jump was just the splash when the rock finally gave up on its jumping. Of course I could see how he'd miscount since the jumps always got shorter and shorter as the count went up.

We liked to sink ships. We'd float off a piece of wood, that we'd make pretend was a big sailing ship. Often we'd take our time getting the ship ready. We could take several pieces of wood, and tie them all together with rush grass. If we were careful we could make it so that there was a tall mast on the ship and that the mast would be upright when we set the whole thing off to float. If we made the ship too big or made the mast too tall then next part of our play got too easy and wasn't as much fun. We'd take stones and make a bombardment of the ship. The best call was to skip a rock into the side of the ship and make it spin about like it was hit with cannon shot. I could do this if I sent off a dozen or more stones in the attempt. About half the time I put my mind to doing this. The rest of the time I shot my rocks at the ship, simple and plain. Gavin loved to throw rocks straight up in the air. They came down like rain on the ship. A ship could hardly stay afloat in that.

After a time Gavin and I would sit and just talk. That was when we would get past the talk of what was, and what we had done, and we would talk about what would be. I had big ideas.

"We could go look for Gold. Lots of men are going up the Fraser. There are hundreds of creeks that no one's panned yet. I saw plenty of men buying tents and things. Everyday men come in on the train and they buy things to hunt for gold."

I got pretty excited talking on that. I could think of all the things that I could do once I struck it rich. Gavin let me go on talking for some time.

"Noble, you know, many men talk about how easy it is to find gold—but none of the big talkers have any—if you find gold you don't so talk much about it. Most of those guys are pretty hard fellows. They talk but they don't take steady work. If gold was easy those fellows would have it."

Gavin had a point. I told him that neither of us knew anybody rich.

"Noble, your Mr. Hallman is rich. He has fancy clothes and a big house."

"Mr. Hallman doesn't count," I said.

Gavin disagreed, "He has a strong boy chop all his firewood," Gavin squeezed my right arm. "When I am rich I will have a strong boy chop all my firewood."

"Oh, some other boy!" I said. I punched Gavin in the arm but he just laughed at me.

Regardless of what Gavin said I knew that Mr. Hallman didn't get rich by working a gold claim. Whatever he had done to get all his money I've sure that it wasn't even a single day's hard work.

My best idea, according to Gavin, was to go east where there were big cities and factories.

"One good idea, that one," he often said. "Noble, maybe we just take the train."

The problem I could see is that there were plenty of men in town who had come here, the west, from those big cities in the east. They came with plans to make their fortunes. Those men never said that they never had work back where they came from, argued Gavin. They just wanted easy wealth. I had an argument to beat that one. There was no chance for us to make our own cabin out there, I said. All the land was already taken up with cities and roads.

"Noble, maybe we go on a fishing boat. Maybe we go on a whaling ship."

Gavin liked that idea since his grandfather's father was a fisherman. I didn't like the idea of being so far out to sea that you couldn't swim back to shore if you had to. The whole ship could go down and in that case you would just drown.

"That is a true one," said Gavin in his matter-of-fact voice. "This Noble, he is a good worker. Noble can chop wood like he is an axe. But Noble swim like an axe too."

I wasn't worried about the work. When Gavin and I had grown maybe another year, it was a pretty much a sure thing that someone would hire us. We were both able-bodied. We could swing an axe or push a shovel as well as anyone could expect. All we had to do is settle on the kind of work we wanted. Gavin and I talked lots about work, but work wasn't the point.

"Noble, we got to build that one where I can take the fish," said Gavin. I liked fishing enough, but Gavin said his people where fishing before anyone. He talked about how he'd do all the fishing and that's what we'd eat. I thought I could take fish as easily as Gavin, or learn to—but sometimes you just give way to someone else's idea of how things will be.

"Noble, you make the firewood." Gavin also said that I should be the one to clear the bush so that we could plant something. "Noble. You make vegetables."

Gavin had some idea in his head that my people must be farmers the way his were fishers. The only one of my people I knew was my mother, and she never said anything to me about a farm. Gavin also had the idea that I would mend clothes and broken furniture. Gavin would smoke meat for the winter.

There was plenty that Gavin and I could do. We figured that we could feed and clothe ourselves but we would need money too. We couldn't make pots or pans or boots. Even if we'd manage to set the cabin walls by ourselves, we'd need to buy nails and hinges to hold the thing together. We'd need a stove too, for heat and cooking. I got to figuring that a dream sometimes is also about the money you'd need to make it real.

Gavin and I talked about everything that we were going to do. Gavin kept a list in his head of everything we'd need: Rope and canvas for where we'd smoke the fish. A rifle for meat, or in case a bear or cougar came around to help himself to all the fish we'd have out to dry. A good lumber saw.

Gavin kept the list in his head because he had a better memory than me. Also because every time we'd talk about it, something new would get added to the list: rifle bullets, a couple good hunting knives. And I'd figure that the cost of everything just went up.

"I can't help but reckon that there's more things on that list than we are going to earn money to pay for."

Gavin would stop talking for a bit and put his arm around me. He always smelled like clothes that had been left out airing in the sun all day. I liked to put my head on his shoulder.

"Noble, you don't have to pay for what's in your head," he said.

I never had anything that I could say back to that. I would sit still for a while and just listen to him breathe.

"Noble, that one cabin is real," he'd say after a while. "I dreamed about the cabin. I saw Noble making a table from wood. Noble had an axe and a saw. I saw Gavin with many fish. I saw Noble with a rifle and Gavin cleaning a bear skin. This is all true."

We would sit like that, Gavin with his arms on me, and my head against his chest. He was warm.

"There really is a cabin, isn't there?"

"My grandfather said that dreams are the good spirits warning us of what is to come."

When the light started to come out of the sky I remembered my mother. I had to go home unless I wanted her to worry that I'd been drowned or killed. When I stirred Gavin would turn me around in his arms. Then, instead of saying goodnight, he'd put his lips against my forehead.

I told Gavin all about the new suit I got from Mr. Hallman. He knew that I was going to line up at the Northwest Timber office to get a job. That evening he would have gone down by the water to meet me. When I didn't come to meet him he would have wanted to come to the house to find me. But he would not have. Natives never came right up to the house, not even the back entrance. What he would have done was watch the house. He would have seen everybody come in and out of the Hallman house in black, my mother and Miss Jane crying too, and me the only one missing. That would have would have told him that I was one of the ones who died in the fire.

Gavin never did take a timber job or a job on a boat. He found employment working on the new buildings going up in town. After the fire there was work for plenty of men in construction. Buildings went up quickly, some in brick but the biggest ones were in stone.

Gavin was a good worker. He carried brick and lumber the way he did everything else. The men at the site got to a point where they would trust him to do what they wanted done. This was not like some of the other boys who did only what they were told to do and even then did it as if they had all day to finish that one thing.

I knew the place Gavin lived with his uncle, mother and sisters. I had never been there but Gavin had shown me where it was. I know that I could have gone in, and that they would have welcomed me. Gavin could tease me, saying that if I came home with him, I could marry his younger sister, that way he and I would always be brothers. This was not a lie, I knew. I knew too how to answer Gavin when he spoke like that. There are some that are brothers of neither birth nor marriage. I used Gavin's own words against him.

I never entered Gavin's home because he could not enter mine. This rule I kept to even when I could have come and gone unseen, unheard by anyone.

I watched Gavin work. I watched him wash his work clothes in a stream. I watched him fish. When I felt myself grow weak I returned to the building under which my remains lay. Sometimes, by the time I felt strong enough to go about in the day again, I learned that days had passed while I had been resting and regaining strength.

It was not my intention to make myself known to Gavin. When he went to sit in our accustomed place by the inlet, I stood behind him. I had discovered that I might move small things like bits of leaves, or small sticks but I never did when I was with Gavin. I did not want Gavin to wonder if he saw something move with no natural excuse.

One day I sat by the little steam when Gavin's family did their washing. Gavin pushed a shirt into the water, and thinking perhaps that it wouldn't float anywhere, turned to take up an undershirt he had laid on the bank next to him. I suppose he intended to soak them both and then wash them at the same time. The shirt was the one from which he had torn a strip to bandage my foot. I should have known that the shirt could not have gone far. It was a small stream, and there were a fair number of rocks along its length. The shirt would have easily caught on one of them. But I did not think. I did not think of my promise to myself to not make myself known to Gavin. I did not think that that shirt might be, to Gavin, only a shirt. It might not have been, as it was to me, a great sign of Gavin's concern for me, something of value that he was willing to sacrifice if it meant he could comfort me thereby. I slipped past Gavin, into the stream and pulled the shirt back towards Gavin. Gavin saw the shirt move against the current, reached into the water and pulled it to him. The movement faded me down a great deal. I rose out of the water and prepared to head to my remains. It was difficult enough standing the daylight and nearly impossible to do so and move things too. Gavin wrapped the wet shirt around his hand, and sat down, stunned, on the stream bank. Then he made my last best memory of him. "Noble?" he whispered as if afraid to say my name aloud.

"Gavin!" I said to him, "I'm here. I'll never leave you. Never." But of course he couldn't hear me. He looked about him in wonder, the stream, the brush, the rocks, the smoke pouring from the distant mill but not at me where I stood in front of him—manifested as bright as I could with every mite of my will. And of course what I said to him was a lie. Just that moment I felt myself weaken like I never had before and then I began to lose my grasp on the world. It's a hard thing to describe but it's like being torn from the world like meat in a pot being boiled off a bone. After a while you don't have meat anymore, just bits things in a stew and you cannot tell what anything was. That was the result of me trying to manifest in the daylight for that boy who I was sure loved me and wanted to have me there again.

I made for my remains as fast as I could, hoping that I would not be undone before I got there.

When I emerged again there were buildings all around that I did not recognize. I perceived that the building on which Gavin had been working was now completed and occupied by various businesses. I wandered further and further from the building under which I had lain. The further I went in search of Gavin the sooner weakness forced me to return to that building where I drew some strength. Now I found it necessary to return to that building daily. I learned to wander and search by night, finding the places where things were being built. Then I visited those places in the day, staying only long enough to search for Gavin among the working men but failing each time to find him. As a searched I noticed that sometimes, although rarely, some man, or woman, or even a child, would turn to look at my passing. If was as if they could sense my going by.

If you planned to keep the memory of who you are, then you had better plan to keep your promises.

I was not sure if it was days or months that had passed before I allowed my wandering to take me by Gavin's home. I stood all night outside the cottage. I knew that their outbuilding lay a good walk from the house. That first night I thought I saw each member of the family, but Gavin, come and go. I watched for days before I dared entered the cottage. Of course Gavin was not inside. Once I had settled myself from the astonishment of seeing what little the four of them had, I noticed that one of Gavin's sisters lay sick on a bed in a corner. Her mother, and then later in the night her sister, bathed her forehead, and spooned stew past her trembling lips. I returned night after night and watched them with sadness. One night her uncle left the cottage and returned with a woman who burned grasses and sang chants throughout the cabin. I could not understand what the woman said.

The following night the priest came. He spoke, sometimes in English, sometimes in a language that I did not understand. Near the end of his visit he placed something from a vial, water I thought, on the feverish girl's forehead. He drew some symbol in the air with his hand over the sick girl, and then repeated the gesture, turning to face each of the other living people in the cabin. He left quickly, ignoring the mother's offer of tea.

The girl died the next day. I hovered near the body that night. I was thinking that since living people could not hear me perhaps the dead would. I called to the dead girl but heard nothing in return. Around me the family kept a vigil over the corpse. In the morning I was weak with calling out but I was also determined to follow the family to the gravesite. They wrapped the girl's body in a sheet and placed her in a wagon. The woman who had burned the grasses rode in the wagon with the body, singing chants much as she had before but this time a waving cedar bough over the shrouded body. She left the wagon as it approached a church and disappeared into the uncleared brush that lined the road. I remained with the body, hoping that I would have the strength to stand in the sunlight until the burial but nevertheless I felt the weakness growing in me even as the sunlight warmed the day. The dead girl's uncle and some other men approached the wagon. With a start I noticed that one of the men had a face like Gavin's but he was older and thicker in his body. The uncle and the men unloaded the girl from the wagon and carried her into the church. I moved after them, entering the church hovering just above the body. The priest stood on a raised platform at the far end of the church. I had never been in this church and found it curiously small and plain when I compared it to the church my mother and I had attended from time to time.

The small wooden church was lit by sunlight coming in the windows. I was grateful that the partial shade inside the building lessened the continual drain on my strength. I saw then, through one of the windows, the sight that would cost me the rest of my waning energy. There was a graveyard directly adjoining the church. I had not noticed it before as the church had blocked it from view as I had approached the building while following the wagon.

I fired myself out of the window glass to glide among the crosses. Was Gavin here? There was a freshly dug pit in the cemetery, prepared for the girl I supposed. And next to it, a grave whose mound of coving soil had not fully settled, and at the head of the mound a cross that bore a name. I traced the shape of the letters with my immaterial finger and cursed that I could not read. The sun had drawn all but the last bit of strength from me. Weakened beyond anything I had ever felt, I turned my back to the church and crawled away. I made my way slowly across the town, and found my way eventually, back into the space beneath my building. Had I been capable of weeping I would have shed tears.

Then the long, truly lonely years began. From other Dead'ers I learned about Stringers and about how if one of them rehearses their memory of you or calls your name it rolls you up. I learned to read.

In all the years before Sean it was only once that I rolled up enough to again visit Gavin's grave. When I arrived there the church and the crosses were gone but I knew the spot. Nevertheless I lacked the strength to call out to Gavin. What a happy coincidence it had been then when I found both Pedro and Sean. Or it had seemed so before Pedro became Steven, and before Sean grew into a habit of unsummoning me as if I were responsible for Mary's violence, and before I discovered that Gavin's grave was silent.

Chapter Nineteen

"Don't Worry; I'm a Nurse"

After Tony left, Sean and Mandy sat at the table in silence. After some time Mandy moved to extinguish the candles but Sean stayed her hand. "I like them," Sean said, "and I'm not sure I'm up to electric light right now." Sean held an ice pack to the back of his head. There were abrasions on his face and forehead. Mandy had cleaned and bandaged the cuts on his stomach. Sean still wore the bloodied T-shirt however. He shifted his weight in the chair, winced and brought his free hand to his ribs.

"I'm pretty beat up," he smiled at Mandy. "I'm sorry too."

Mandy smiled back at him. "What for? You didn't do anything wrong. You were really brave today."

"I'm sorry for bringing you into this. You could have been seriously hurt," Sean continued.

"Yes. I'll admit that what we did today was dangerous but you didn't drag me into it. I'm here of my own choice Sean. And besides I've been pushing you to help Noble."

"Speaking of Noble," Sean sounded apologetic. "I'll admit that it's twice now he seems to have helped us out with Mary. You and Tony both say that he was trying to protect me. I have to say however, that when I opened my eyes and saw him hovering above me like that I was…" Sean hesitated.

"It's ok to say that you were afraid, Sean."

"I was scared. I'm not afraid to admit that. I was going to say, that I was afraid that he was going to attack you next…" Sean paused. "And I had no good reason to be afraid, other than, well, Noble's a ghost too and I thought he'd be on her side."

"No even all living people are on the same side. Just think of that man with the crowbar. He could have killed one of us." Mandy shuddered, then, without warning she slapped the table. Sean jumped back in his chair, his face contorted.

"Please don't do that again." He squeezed out between clenched teeth.

"I figured out where I'd seen that man before! The night when we leaving Eva's place."

"Eva's place?" asked Sean.

"Eva Butler, Steven's mother."

"Steven?" asked Sean.

"Yes, Steven James Butler. The boy Noble asked us to find."

"The night the woman ghost attacked us in the car."

"Mary. It was Mary that attacked us."

Sean nodded. "So he was probably watching the Butler place and if he's connected to Mary—who we now know is dead set against us having anything to do with Eva Butler—then it was probably him who cued Mary to attack us."

"Dead set?" said Mandy.

"Whatever his connection to Mary he probably doesn't want Steven's ashes brought here either."

"Or he doesn't want it because Mary doesn't want it," said Mandy.

"Maybe it has something to do with Mary's haunt. Steven would have a haunt here if his ashes were brought home."

"You've been talking to Noble," said Sean.

Mandy shrugged. Sean shook his head disapprovingly, but then smiled.

Mandy collected the cushions from where there were scattered across the room. She arranged them on the sofa and then ordered Sean to lie down. She sat in the upholstered chair close by. She set her watch to wake her every couple hours. Each time she woke, she placed a soft hand on Sean's shoulder and reminded him that when a concussion is suspected, the patient is never allowed to sleep for very long.

Just after midnight Sean woke to the sound of Tony's hammer. Tony had returned to the apartment with a panel of wood and tools.

"Does he have to make so much noise?" Sean sat up. "And it's the middle of the frigging night. Can't a guy get any sleep in his own apartment!"

Mandy placed her hands on each of Sean's shoulders. "Try and see if you can get back to sleep, Sean."

"Who can sleep with all this noise!" shouted Sean.

Tony stopped work when he heard Sean. He looked over at Mandy. Mandy met his eyes and nodded.

Despite his dizziness, once they had convinced Sean to cooperate, it only took a few minutes to get him down the stairs and into Tony's car. At the hospital, Mandy instructed Tony to park out front of the Emergency Admitting entrance. Mandy disappeared into the hospital and returned in a few minutes with a wheelchair. On Mandy's instructions, Sean got out of the car and into the chair. Mandy waved Tony towards the parking lot and then turned and wheeled Sean into the building.

Tony was slouched in an uncomfortable waiting room chair, flipping through an out-dated automotive magazine when Mandy returned. She let herself drop into the chair next to the older man. She let her breath out and then placed a hand on his forearm.

"It was really nice of you to drive us here," she said.

"It was nothing you would not have done for me," Tony voice was gravely. "Sean is a nice boy and you are a nice girl. It is a beautiful thing. Makes me happy to help." Tony flipped the magazine closed and placed one hand over his chest. "It does the heart good to help, no?"

Mandy smiled, "Yes it does." She paused briefly. "Thank you," she added and then continued, "They told me that Sean is going to be evaluated soon but you never know what that means in here." She smiled at Tony and then looked around the waiting area taking in at a glance the others scattered around the room. "There is no need for you to wait for us. I imagine that you're anxious to get home. You're married aren't you?"

"Yes, Mandy," he winked at her, "You don't need to worry. I'm a married man." Tony patted the hand she had placed on his forearm. "I've been married many, many, years. My wife, she cares, but I could call her now and tell her, 'I am spending the night in this room with a beautiful young woman.' and my wife would say, 'If she is beautiful why is she with you?' And then I say, 'She is beautiful and she is kind.' And my wife—you know what she would say then?" Tony paused and looked at Mandy.

"I don't know," said Mandy nearly laughing.

"My wife would say 'If she is real, then I pity her for being with you but God bless her for her charity!'"

Mandy laughed.

"My wife, she loves me, but she is no fool. Love is not blind. People say that love is blind but it is not. Love sees perfectly. My wife knows me. She's not worried."

"That's beautiful," said Mandy.

"Maybe some day you see your young man like that. It's beautiful when you do." Tony smiled at Mandy and settled further into his chair. After just a few minutes, Mandy perceived that he had fallen asleep. She extracted her hand and replaced Tony's grasp onto his own forearm.

When Mandy found Sean he had been moved from the wheelchair to a gurney. As Mandy approached she saw that a young male nurse was peering at his chart.

Mandy spoke at the man's back, "He's here for observation re a probable severe concussion. He has dizziness, irritability, mood swings, and difficulty walking. He's had blunt trauma to the head a few times in the past year, and one of the most serious was about four to five hours ago."

"This is your boyfriend, isn't it?" asked the nurse.

"I don't think you ought to presume…"

The man turned around and grinned at Mandy. "Mandy. It is me, Hector! I'm on Observation Rotation in here tonight. I saw this boy and thought! Hey, I know him. He's the one who can't play pool to save his life." Hector laughed aloud. Sean stirred. Hector continued, "Don't worry, the doctor told me…"

Sean suddenly sat up. "Is it my turn?" he asked Hector.

Mandy approached the gurney. Sean turned and saw her.

"Mandy! You're here. You didn't tell me you were coming!" Sean's voice was full of wonder.

"I'll add confusion to the list of symptoms," Hector winked at Mandy. He turned back to Sean. "Time for you to lie down, Sean."

"You're in hospital Sean," said Mandy. Sean lay down but still regarded Mandy with wide eyes.

Hector continued, "I was telling you Mandy, the doctor says that his symptoms don't warrant a CT scan or further treatment at this stage. He is, however, to avoid further trauma to the cranium, but I didn't have to tell you that. And no work this week: just rest. Is that possible?"

"Yes, I think so." Mandy nodded, "His supervisor's in the waiting room. I'll explain it to him."

"Oh, so this accident happened at work?"

Mandy shook her head. "No, in Sean's apartment."

"I wasn't an accident," said Sean suddenly. "She meant to hurt me! See!" Sean lifted his shirt. "This is where she ground the box into my stomach!"

Hector raised an eyebrow.

"It wasn't me!" said Mandy quickly.

"No it wasn't," growled Sean. "It was Mary! Oops! Don't say her name. Don't say her name! If you do she'll come."

"Mary?" said Hector.

Mandy placed a hand on Sean's shoulder, "Sean this isn't a good time to…" she began.

"Don't worry," said Sean turning to Hector. "You're not a Stringer, are you? She won't come if you say her name. You're not a Stringer." He squinted at Hector and shook his head, "No you're not. I can tell. I didn't know how I can tell, but I can tell." Sean nodded in self-satisfied way. "Tony is a Stringer. I could tell. That's why I told him about Noble."

Hector turned to Mandy, "Is this Mary another girl? Did she beat him up? If this is assault we should do a police report on his injuries."

"Police? The police?" Sean laughed, "The police can't touch Mary! No one can touch her! She can walk through walls—except if they're wood. She's a real bitch!"

"Watch your language Sean!" said Mandy tapping his arm.

"Sorry!" said Sean. "I won't call her again. No, I won't say Mary Nash-Crowley! Oops I said it! Now she'll come. I'm stupid. She'll wreck everything. She wants to hit me," Sean looked ashamed for a moment.

"Should I call security?" Hector asked.

"No, no, no. No need. No good. I'll stop her." Sean raised his voice, "I unsummon you Mary. Don't come here Mary! See now, she won't come." Sean seemed to relax in the pillow. "It doesn't matter how loud I say it. It's something else that I do. I don't know exactly what it is. Tony knows. You could ask him! Yes ask him." Sean laughed, "But his answer will probably be in Italian!" Sean laughed some more.

Mandy looked a Hector. "He's really confused. Sorry you had to listen to all that."

"Don't worry," said Hector. "I'm a nurse. I've heard worse."

Sean sat up again. "Now that you're both here," he said, looking back and forth between Hector and Mandy, "Mandy can tell you our plan for the finding the family with Steven's ashes."

"What plan?" said Hector.

"Oh and I'll bet you that Tony is a better pool player than you!" Sean lay back down. "I'm so tired. I think I'll nap a bit."

"Good idea!" exclaimed Mandy. There was a sheet folded at the foot of the gurney. Mandy shook out the sheet and used it to cover Sean.

Sean murmured then turned on his side, pulling the sheet around his shoulders.

Mandy turned to Hector. "Sorry again," she said. "I think Sean was only half conscious."

"I think he'll be better after some rest."

"I agree," Mandy smiled. "He's in good hands."

"Yes he is," Hector smiled. "I've been told that my hands are very good."

Mandy raised an eyebrow. "I'm going to pretend that you meant that professionally,"

"What else would I mean when dealing with your boyfriend?" Hector grinned. "You follow me. I'm going to take Sean out of this hallway into a quiet room."

"Thanks." Mandy gripped the other end of the gurney and followed Hector's lead.

He winked, "Now, you tell me about this Italian who's better than me at pool."

Chapter Twenty

Easy Money

"No, no, not so bad," said Tony, as if unconvinced.

Hector made a clean break. Three balls sank. Hector chose stripes. The first game had been close—until Hector sunk the last four balls in quick succession. He stood back with his arms crossed while Tony racked the balls for their second game.

Tony straightened up, "You break now. I give you a chance this time, no?"

Hector laughed. "You're a lucky man, Tony. But sometimes you push your luck, and then it runs out."

Hector shot a good break, sinking a couple balls.

"I don't think Tony's luck's running out anytime soon," said Sean. He was leaning against the wall beside the table. "After all you'd have to be pretty lucky to live as long as Tony has."

Tony narrowed his eyes and pointed his pool cue at Sean; "Hector, what you think? Maybe this one skinny one run out of luck with his smart mouth, eh?"

Hector grinned, "That one's lucky; have you seen his girlfriend?" Hector sunk another ball. He walked around the table, placing his cue stick down in several places. He shook his head. "Nothing's quite right," he muttered.

"Oh what a girl I have seen him with—She's beautiful and very, very smart!" said Tony, "Smarter than this one. But girlfriend, no—this one no have girlfriend. Too scared."

"Oh, I don't have to stand here and listen to this; do I?" Sean barked, but he was smiling good-naturedly.

"No. You go get stool. Two stool: one for me, one for you. This one going to take an hour to find a shot," sighed Tony.

"Fine!" said Hector. He lowered his stick to the table and lined it up with the white ball.

Sean left the table. When he returned with the stools Tony was talking a shot.

"Did I miss anything?" asked Sean.

"No," said Tony, "But ask Hector, maybe he miss something."

Hector scowled. Sean laughed.

Tony took his shot. A ball sunk. He walked to the far side of the table.

"Maybe you two talk for a while. Me, I'm busy with Biliardo!" Tony smirked as he leaned in for another shot.

It was not clear to Sean how the second game would turn out until Hector pocketed the last of his balls while Tony still had two balls on the table.

"He's ready now," Tony said in an aside to Sean. Then he added just loud enough for Hector to hear, "but this Hector, he have luck today, eh? It's good for him that we no play for money. I no like take money from young one." Tony winked at Sean. "Hector!" Tony called out. "Maybe we take a break. You like a coffee? You win—I buy coffee."

The three men sat on stools at the snack bar. Sean held a mug of decaf, into which he had put a large quantity of milk. Hector opted for a tall dark coffee. Tony held a tiny espresso cup.

"So ever since we went there, Mandy talks non-stop about Eva: 'Imagine how bad Eva feels. We should help Eva.' She brings it up every day," whined Sean, staring into his mug.

"Yeah, that sounds like Mandy. She likes to help people. She's kinda crazy with it though," said Hector.

Sean nodded vigorously in agreement.

"So this Eva—she's very sure—these ashes aren't her son?" Tony frowned.

"Yes, it seems that Eva is absolutely convinced that her son's ashes were switched accidently with the ashes of someone who was cremated the same day, at the same crematorium in Mexico."

"She's sure about the switch?" asked Hector.

"Yes, yes!" said Sean impatiently. "She has all this paper work about it."

"It's terrible, yes?" said Tony. "Your girl no talk about anything else?"

"Not since she found out," signed Sean.

"Too bad for you," commiserated Tony. "You no have girlfriend till she think about you. Now she think about this woman and her son—She no think about you."

"Yup, no girlfriend for me," Sean's shoulders sank.

"I wish I could help bro," said Hector. "I mean it." He placed a hand on Sean's shoulder.

Tony looked at Hector, "You could make phone call."

"Who would I phone? Eva? I could apologize on behalf of Mexicans," Hector gave a little laugh. "But what good would that do?"

"No call Eva," said Tony, "You speak Spanish, yes?"

Hector nodded, "Of course."

"You call family in Mexico. You explain everything. Then you go Mexico, talk with the family again and you switch ashes."

"Switch ashes?"

"Yes," said Tony, "you bring ashes from co—"

"Coquitlam!" said Sean quickly.

"Coquitlam?" Hector repeated.

"Ok, from Coquitlam, you take ashes to Mexico. From Mexico you bring ashes to Coquitlam." Tony slapped Hector on the back. "You fix everything, yes?"

"Me?" said Hector.

"You make Eva happy. This make Mandy happy. Mandy make this skinny boy happy. You no want everybody happy?"

"Sure I do," said Hector, "but I'm not going to Mexico with a bundle of ashes."

Sean looked into his coffee. Tony looked at Hector.

"Hmm," said Tony. "You no want to go to Mexico, you no go to Mexico. Maybe we just play Biliardo now, yes?"

"Yeah. Let's play," Hector hopped off his stool.

Tony broke but didn't sink any balls.

"Too bad," said Hector leaning in for a shot. "I think I'll play solids this game—and it'll be the two in the corner—"

Tony picked the cue ball up off the table. "Maybe we play for something this time," smiled Tony. He took some cash out of his pocket and placed it on the edge of the table.

"That looks like close to a hundred dollars." Hector frowned, "I don't mind taking your money, Tony, but I'm just a student; I can't match your wager." He looked at Sean. "Can you cover the wager? It's easy money. I'll split it with you."

Sean shrugged no.

"Ok," said Tony, "no problem. No wager; it's still ok. You win you take the money. No problem."

"I don't like that," said Hector.

"Well offer something then," said Sean.

"What do you want?" Hector look at Tony. "You want me to wager to wash your fancy car for a week, a month, no, a year!" Hector grinned at Sean, then he looked at the cash, "Doesn't matter I got this."

"Then promise to go to Mexico if you lose!" laughed Sean.

"Sure," laughed Hector. He turned to Tony, "'¡Ay, Caramba!' That's some easy tourist Spanish for you. That's what you should say when you lose your cash."

"You promise?" asked Tony with some irritation in his voice.

Hector laughed some more. "Easy old man, I promise!"

"Ok, he promise," Tony nodded at Sean who was racking the balls. "My break, yes?"

Tony broke. Hector leaned on his cue stick waiting for his turn. He was still leaning on his cue stick when Tony sunk the last ball. Hector shook his head.

"Hustled. I got hustled. Damn."

Tony laughed, "It's not so bad. I show you some when you come back."

"Come back?" Hector looked at Sean and then back at Tony. "You meant it about Mexico. Damn!"

Tony scooped the cash off the pool table. "No worry I pay for plane. You take this now."

"¡Ay, Caramba!" said Sean looking at Tony.

Hector counted the cash, "¡Dios!"

"Soon we deal with il fantasma," said Tony "soon."

Chapter Twenty-One

Grandpa's Ashes

"Your friend with the wrong ashes, Eva, why doesn't she call Mexico herself?" Hector was sitting next to Mandy at Sean's table, Sean's newly installed phone between them. Sean himself was reclined on the couch behind them.

"We told you; she doesn't speak Spanish," said Sean.

"But," said Hector, turning to look at Sean, "why isn't she here? I imagine that she has details about the mix-up. Little details that might seem unimportant but that nevertheless could be significant during the conversation."

"Everything is here," said Mandy patting the clipboard, "and remember that it's a very painful situation for Eva. We're talking about the remains of her only child."

"Yes, that's it," said Sean. Mandy looked at him quickly, narrowing her eyes.

Hector nodded, "True, that would be difficult for her to deal with calmly."

"When I told Eva that you would handle this for her," continued Mandy, "she was very, very grateful. You know, she even cried—just the thought that she will be finally be getting her son's remains—"

"Ok. Ok," said Hector. "Enough of the sad story. I will do my best."

Hector dialled the number Mandy pointed to on the clipboard. The phone rang twice then someone picked up. "Esto Héctor Hernández-Castillo…"

"I can't believe that you roped me into doing this!" said Ty. He was in the back of Tony's car next to Mandy. Sean was in the front passenger seat. Tony was behind the wheel.

"It's your own fault," said Mandy, "You were the one bragging about all the things you used to do when you were a kid growing up in … where was it again?"

"Abbotsford, and you knew that already!"

"Yes I remember now: not really either suburb or a city, one of those places that isn't what it pretends to be and so can't help but fail to be what it is."

Ty raised his voice, "There's a lot of good things that can be said about…"

"Shut-up, both of you," hissed Tony, "You'll make everybody look at us. You pick up the bag and close up your mouth."

Tony double-checked his own belongings. "Ready now?"

"Yes sir!" said Ty, saluting.

"Mamma mia," said Tony, "I have to work with this child?"

"I'm sorry," said Mandy, "Sean or I could go with you instead of Ty if that would make you feel better."

"No, no, no." Tony shook his head. "If she is home it is no good then. She has already seen your face. This way is better. If she answers door we say, wrong house—no problem. All she will see is good looking repair man, and this boy too," Tony pointed over his shoulder at Ty.

"Very funny," said Ty.

"Ok. We go now." Tony looked Sean, "You sit in the driver's seat, and put the girl beside you. If you see anyone come to the house, you blow the horn and drive away. Good?"

"Yes," said Sean.

"Shouldn't we wait and pick you up?" asked Mandy.

"No, we'll walk out the back. If you leave, go around the block, and in about ten minutes pick us up at the end of the street."

"Ok."

"Good luck," breathed Mandy.

"Let's go," said Ty, "Give us fifteen minutes."

Mandy looked at her watch. It was 9:05. They had watched Allan Butler leave his townhouse, dressed in sweat pants at seven o'clock. He had returned about forty-five minutes later. He left again at 8:30, this time in a suit and carrying a leather case. Eva left about ten minutes after her husband. She had on a light jacket, and was carrying a shoulder bag. Tony had insisted that they wait a few minutes in case either of the couple returned. Forgotten keys, lunches, etc. were always a possibility, he said.

Mandy and Sean watched the two men walk up the staircase to the Butler's door. Tony led the way. Both had bags and wore coveralls from the car dealership. Tony and Mandy had removed the sewn on patches with the car dealership's logo. At the door Ty turned and faced the street, Tony steeped behind him and fished a long thin tool from his bag. In a few seconds he had the door open. He and Ty went through and closed the door behind them.

Sean checked his watch. "They'll have thirty seconds or less to disable the alarm." He scratched his forearms. "If they can't disable it, they'll be coming down those stairs quite quickly."

Mandy held her breath. Almost a minute passed. She exhaled. "I didn't hear anything. Tony must have managed to take care of the alarm."

Suddenly a high-pitched mechanical shriek sounded from the townhouse.

"Oh-oh." said Sean. He started the car. "I'll drive around the block and meet them where they said!"

"Don't go anywhere. They'll be out soon."

Tony came running out of the building and down the stairs first. He displayed a flexibility and speed in his movements that seemed at odds with the quiet dignity with which he normally moved. Ty was moving just as quickly. However after descending just a few steps, Ty grabbed the handrail with his free hand, and stopped his descent. He turned and bounded back up the stairs to the door. He pulled the door shut and then spun to continue running down to the street.

Tony heard the door slam, swore, turned, and pushed his way past Ty, back up the stairs. He re-opened the door. Ty stopped and looked back up at Tony with a puzzled expression. "Go!" said Tony and pointed down the stairs.

"Why did you do that?" asked Ty, staring at the open door as Tony passed him.

"You can stay here and think about the door if you want. I'm leaving in the car before the police come!" shouted Tony over his shoulder.

Ty paused for a moment or two longer and then turned and fled down the stairs after Tony.

In the car Mandy and Sean were waiting with grim faces. They could not help smiling however when Tony open the rear door and plopped himself into the back seat of the car, grinning like a schoolboy who had just been released for summer vacation.

"Oh, that was not so bad," he said, "I've not done that in a long time."

"You've done break-ins before?" asked Sean with his eyebrows raised.

"Maybe once or twice. I cannot remember." Tony laughed.

The other rear door swung open and Ty jumped into the car. "Go. Go. Go!" he shouted.

"We go now," said Tony, "but take your time."

Sean carefully pulled the car away from the curve and headed down the street.

"So will we have to come back and try again?" asked Mandy.

"No need," said Tony. "It was not difficult. The big urn was just where you said, above the fireplace."

"But the alarm went off!" said Mandy.

"True, but it did not take long to pour out the ashes," said Tony, "The boy is quick with his hands."

"That's what Katie says!" laughed Mandy. "That's his girlfriend," she added for Tony's benefit.

Ty grinned and reached into the bag next to him on the car seat. He lifted up a plastic bag. It was full and heavy. "See. I have your grandpa's ashes right here."

"Grandpa?" Sean looked at Mandy.

"The boy is good to work with," said Tony, "only he was a bit foolish about the door."

"Yah! Why did you close the door?" asked Ty.

"What will they think?" said Tony, "when they come home. Hmm? The thieves come in but the alarm, it frightens them away. But then they take time to close door? What kind of thieves? Maybe they are polite thieves!"

"Oh," said Ty.

"It is not a problem, you are new to this, yes?" asked Tony.

"I guess so," said Ty, "I'll be better next time!"

"Next time?" echoed Mandy.

"It is not a good way of life," said Tony.

After they were well clear of the subdivision where the Butler's lived, the tension in the car seemed to dissipate.

Ty picked up his usual refrain about life outside the city centre. "These burbs are home to so many families but how many families are really loyal to the suburb they live in? There is no sense of homestead or of real belonging in a suburb. If every house looks like every other house, then why would you consider your house something special?"

"I have no idea," said Mandy in a flat voice.

"You know what's missing? A sense of history, family history. You might feel that a place is part of who you are if your grandparents or great grandparents lived there. But how can you feel part of a place if it's just where your parents moved for the third time because they want to liquidate the equity they built up with their city home."

"Maybe people grow to love a place," said Tony thoughtfully.

"It's not about love; it's about loyalty … belonging!" countered Ty, "You *love* where you go on vacation but you *belong* where you live!"

"Hmm," snorted Tony, "is the boy always like this?" he asked.

"Unfortunately yes," sighed Mandy.

"I hear you Ty!" said Sean.

Ty reached forward and put a hand on Sean's shoulder. "You've been in that townhouse we just broke into, haven't you?" he asked.

"Yup," said Sean, "I went with Mandy. We asked the woman all about…" Mandy gave Sean a sharp glance. Sean let his sentence trail off to silence.

"Yes," said Mandy "I took Sean to see my aunt. I was trying to convince her one last time to do what Grandpa wanted done with his remains."

"See!" Ty's voice rose, "that's exactly my point! If your aunt had a decent sense belonging or connection to her home or even to her community she wouldn't have needed to keep her father's ashes."

"What?" said Mandy.

"The ashes gave her home a sense of history, of homestead. That's why she kept them in her living room. The ashes helped make the place a real home for her. Her home was also her father's home. I'm going to write a book about this."

Mandy spoke in a childlike voice: "Does that mean you'll stop talking about it?" She asked.

"I'll probably have to talk about it even more!" said Ty excitedly. "I'll be interviewed on talk shows across North America. My theory will explain everything: teen alienation and delinquency, petty crime, youth gangs, depression and dissatisfaction among working adults."

"Domestic violence and divorce?" volunteered Sean.

"Yes. That stuff too," answered Ty without pausing. "North American society has suffered since the creation of the suburb. A suburb is nothing more than a refugee camp from the city!"

"A refugee camp!" exclaimed Tony.

Ty turned towards Tony, "Yes, a refugee camp. But the inhabitants don't know that they are dispossessed!" Ty sat back and folded his hands across his chest. "It's all so obvious I'm surprised that no one else is saying it."

"I think you are the only one saying this," said Tony carefully.

"Thank you," responded Ty. Tony shrugged. They drove on in silence for a few minutes before Ty spoke again. "You know, Sean, I was about to ask you about that townhouse earlier."

"What about it?"

"Do you know it was missing?"

"No, what?" said Sean.

"Grandpa's ashes!" Ty held up the bag and laughed.

Chapter Twenty-Two

"First My Friends,
I Need to Explain Something to You"

"Why did you lie to Ty?"

"What was I supposed to tell him?" Mandy's eyes flashed. "We have to exchange one ghost's remains in Coquitlam for another's in Mexico?"

"Uh oh." Sean scratched his forearms.

"Why 'Uh oh?' He totally believed us. That's why he went on and on about family and belonging. He thinks I'm going to dump these ashes into Burrard inlet—just the way grandpa wanted."

"No, no, no. It's not your grandpa I'm worried about. You can dump his ashes anywhere you want." Sean looked at the bag on the table with a worried expression.

"It's not really my grandpa Sean." Mandy giggled. Sean narrowed his eyes. Mandy stopped laughing. "So what are you worried about?"

"So whose ashes are those?" Sean pointed at them.

"Well they're…" Mandy's voice trailed off.

"See the problem! They are not Steven Butler's. His must be in Mexico because that's where his haunt is."

"According to Noble at least," Mandy cocked her head.

"Now who's mistrusting our boy ghost?"

"I'm not mistrusting him, I'm just saying that to be scientific about this we ought to accept only what we have evidence for," continued Mandy.

"It's a bit late to look for scientific explanations," lectured Sean. "We've seen and been attacked by ghosts. Things that don't even have a body. Anything about that in your science textbook?"

Mandy and Sean stared at the plastic sack of ashes in silence for several moments. "We don't know if these ashes even belong to a Dead'er," said Mandy at last. "And if they do, the people who'd care to roll him or her up are probably in Mexico. We'd be doing them a favour by taking their remains home."

Noble:

Three things every Lye'ver should have wanted to know about a Dead'er. Well maybe it was not what every Lye'ver needed to know. Most Lye'vers didn't know or didn't care about us. And we really didn't care anything about them. Why would we have cared? We weren't in their world. They were not in ours.

Maybe when you first became a Dead'er you did care. You wanted to know what happened to your mother or your lover or your enemy. And maybe after a while you didn't want to know. I mean, you might have still cared, but you were only going to drive yourself nuts trying to watch them, or even stupider, trying to watch over them. Did you want to see someone you love go on to figure out how to be happy without you? I realized that if you loved someone you wanted them to be happy. But you probably do not want to see them happy. Watching them would have just been a bit of cruelty to yourself. What if they weren't happy? Then watching them would have made you feel even worse.

Ok. So what did I want ordinary Lye'vers to know about us Dead'ers. Nothing. If a Lye'ver saw anything unusual, like a wooden spoon moving itself from one end of the dinner table to the other, he or she should just go on with their life. And most likely the Lye'ver would not have seen anything unusual anyway. Most of what us Dead'ers do could not even be perceived by ordinary Lye'vers. Stringers were a different story.

A Stringer would have seen you move the wooden spoon down the table. Most Stringers would probably even have seen the hand that you had to manifest even if only slightly to be able to do it.

So the first thing any Stringer should have known. We Dead'ers could never really go away—almost. A Stringer could unsummon us—that made us go away, sort of dissipate actually. But it did not really prevent us from drifting back once we got rolled up again. Sean unsummoned me. But I just went back to my remains, a few days or weeks I would be back at full strength. But it was also true, that I would have been less lucky if I was unsummoned so far from my remains that I couldn't get back to them.

Second thing that a Stringer should have known. Dead'ers had feelings too. We didn't like to be treated poorly any more than any Lye'ver would like to be treated poorly. It looked to me like Sean was so busy seeing the ghost boy, that he couldn't see Noble the boy.

Third thing. There were plenty of Stringers and plenty of Dead'ers. Most Dead'ers were so faded down that it really didn't matter what they tried to do, even other Dead'ers could barely see or hear them. And they couldn't move a wooden match if they tried all night. Some mean ghost could sieve them down with one unmanifested hand behind her back. They were snickered, frustrated, done for, before they even got started because no one knew their names. On the other hand there were plenty of Dead'ers who had good Stringers. And they could do plenty if they had a mind to it.

"I don't think it's going to be too difficult," said Sean. They had just finished wrapping the ashes into a package to go into Hector's luggage.

"True enough," said Hector. "When I fly home I have no trouble with customs. I tell them I have gifts for my mother and my sister. They never look."

"But what about coming back?" asked Mandy.

"Ashes might look like drugs but most of the time they check for drugs with dogs that sniff at your luggage." Hector placed the package into his knapsack. "If the dogs sniff at me I'll have nothing to worry about."

"And if they find the package what will you tell them?"

"I'll think of something clever," Hector smiled, "maybe I'll just flirt with the guard."

"What if it's a male guard," asked Sean

"What if?" shrugged Hector. He winked at Mandy, "You don't think I can flirt with a man?"

Mandy saw Hector to the door. He kissed her goodbye on both cheeks. She watched him retreat down the hall then closed the door and turned to face Sean.

"Don't worry; he's good to his word," she said.

"I'm not; you're a good judge of character." Sean threw himself into the sofa. "What do we do now Ms. Simms?"

"Nothing. We've done everything we can for Noble for now."

Sean patted the sofa next to him. "Time to relax then."

"I wish I could," said Mandy, "but I have a ton of studying to catch up on."

Sean's shoulders slumped.

"But I'm sure I'll need a break and some distraction at some point."

"Dinner?" offered Sean.

"Accepted," replied Mandy.

"When?" queried Sean.

"When will it be ready?"

Sean looked at his watch. "Eight o'clock."

"Perfect."

"We've not had dinner together in a while."

"I hadn't noticed," said Mandy flatly, "have you been keeping track?"

"Not really." Sean threw his eyes up to the apartment ceiling. "It's just that I was cooking you dinner every Wednesday for a while. I didn't mind at all, but if you're not going to be using the time slot there's others who would be glad to take it."

"Others . . . I see," said Mandy, fixing Sean in a glare.

"So don't be late!" Sean found it hard to suppress his grin.

Tony had made extensive modifications to Sean's apartment. Not only did he repair the damage done by Mary, he added what could be termed ghost barriers. Underneath the wall plaster, Tony found closely spaced laths extending from floor to ceiling and beyond. Sean's parquet flooring was already edged by a wooden trim and there was more wooden moulding around the edges of his ceiling. Tony added strips of plywood everywhere he thought that there might be enough space for "il fantasma" to slip through. He provided Sean with sheets of plywood that went over his windows. When Tony was finished even the bathroom window slid open and closed easily. It had its own plywood covering that snapped easily into the wooden window frame. Sean kept the window coverings in place each night.

Mandy made sure that Sean's apartment door was closed behind her. She stepped out of sight of the peephole and stood very still for a moment, listening, As soon as she felt the slight chill, she smiled and started to walk toward the stairwell.

"You make it out of his apartment ok?" she whispered.

Noble's face manifested in front of her. He nodded, yes.

"It's probably getting more and more difficult to get in and out of there."

Noble nodded yes again.

"Oh well. He'll come around soon. I'm sure he will. I'll keep working on him." Mandy climbed the rest to the steps to her floor.

After the dishes were done, Mandy returned to the living room and settled on the sofa. Sean appeared with two mugs of tea.

"New pot?"

"Perhaps," said Sean grinning.

Mandy grasped the mug in two hands, "you know," she said to Sean after taking a deep draught of the tea, "I had some time on my hands the other day."

"Uh oh," said Sean.

"Why, uh oh?" she asked.

"Because it sounds like you want me to do something."

"Nope, well, just look at a few things. That's all you have to do … this time." Mandy reached into her bag and fished out an envelope. She took several sheets out of the envelope and spread them out across the table. They were a series of photographs. It was clear that Mandy had obtained the images from some sort of historic archive.

"Ok," said Sean "Looking should be easy enough." He studied the photographs. Each was a black and white image of men standing in front of tents, partially constructed buildings, or even finished buildings. Each photograph bore a caption: a date; name or number of a building; or a pair of street corners. Sean studied the one closest to him. The caption read, National Building 800 Dunsmuir Street. There were a group of men, some in business suits, some in work wear, standing in front of a partially completed structure. It was clear that the building would be impressive when finished.

"Interesting I suppose," said Sean after a minute or two of peering at the photographs.

"We're just getting started," said Mandy. "Look at the faces."

Sean brought one of the printed photos closer to his eyes. After a moment he stood, turned on a lamp and sat down again to study images more closely. The men, despite the old-fashioned clothing and hairstyles, seem very real, as if they were people you might easily meet in the present, if you, say, visited their place of work, or wandered the streets of the city.

"They look surprisingly real, as if they could be alive today," said Sean.

"You have to get past that I think. These are all over a hundred years old. Everybody in them is dead."

"Wow," said Sean, studying the faces. "That's a lot of dead people." He picked up a different photo. "The people are all dead but some of these buildings are still around, aren't they?"

"Exactly," said Mandy. "Most of these buildings are still around. Take a look at this one." She handed Sean a photograph.

"I guess that those are guys who built that place."

"Yup," said Mandy, "Check that guy out!" Mandy pointed her finger a man with an oversized moustache. "He was the financier. Next to him, on the right, is the owner. And on the far side of the owner is the architect."

"Happy looking bunch!" remarked Sean.

"I don't think that the point was to smile in photographs back then. But do you recognize the building?" asked Mandy.

"That's our apartment building! Isn't it?" cried Sean.

"So it is," said Mandy, "Just look at the address at the bottom of the photo."

"It's really changed. All that's gone," Sean pointed at some ornate tile work near the front entrance to the building.

"Actually it was probably just covered over. After I found these photos, I had a look at our building; some brick facing is there now—more durable probably. And there were other changes." Mandy placed another photo in front of Sean. This photo showed the completed building. An elaborate cornice ran across the top edge of the building's façade. "All that plaster moulding is gone."

"But the basic design is the same."

"Now look at this picture." Mandy handed Sean another image. It was a newly completed building. Once again, a group of men, all in business suits, stood in front the structure.

"They look proud."

"They probably were. That building was the pride of the city when it was completed. Now, what you have to do, is figure out if the architect in this photo was the same as the architect of our building."

Sean held the two photographs next to each other. "Well there are lots of similarities," he said after some time.

"Look at the faces, Sean!" said Mandy.

Sean scanned the men in the photos. "These same two guys are in both! So..."

"That's the owner and the architect! The same pair is responsible for maybe a half dozen buildings that I've been able to identify so far."

Sean shrugged, "So that's nice but..."

"You're right. It's not much use knowing that. It wasn't what I was after anyway. I just got side tracked. This stuff is fascinating once you get into it."

"Really," said Sean raising an eyebrow.

"Can the sarcasm," said Mandy, "I just wanted to give you an idea of how difficult and interesting all this stuff is. Don't you think?" Sean was silent, "Anyway. I will get to the point. Here. Look at this." Mandy, with a bit of a flourish, placed a photo in front of Sean. "I had this one printed with the highest resolution I could get. You ought to understand that the first one I saw was a lot more grainy. Even so I think I picked him out..."

"Who? That architect guy?" Sean bent over the photo and peered from face to face. The photo was of a wooden two-story building. The front door of the building was some distance above street level, but there was some sort of platform in front of it, so that there was room for several men to stand by the door. There were only two men on the platform however, a heavyset man, with a magnificent beard, and a shorter slimmer man carrying a satchel. Sean studied the two men. Both wore the same sort of old-fashioned suits he had seen in the other photographs. Sean compared their faces to those of the suited men in the other photographs he had examined closely. "I don't think either of these guys is that architect guy," Sean announced.

"Keep looking," urged Mandy. "And there's more than those two guys in the picture."

Sean looked again. "Oh," he said. He had not noticed the row of rag tag men in a rough queue in front of the platform.

"Check out the description," suggested Mandy. "I copied it out on the back of the picture."

Sean turned the sheet over and read: "Offices of the Northwest Timber Company, 7 a.m. the thirteenth of June 1886, moments before the Great Fire destroyed the building and killed many of the men shown, including R. H. Alexander, manager, and W. Collins, clerk."

"Kind of sad I guess," said Sean, "Of course all of these men would be dead now anyway."

"Almost," answered Mandy.

"Almost?" Sean frowned.

"Check out the faces again."

Sean squinted at the photo. Among the rumpled men in the queue below the platform was a boyish face in an over-sized suit. "Our ghost ... Noble!" Sean shouted, "That's him isn't it?" Sean looked at Mandy.

"I'm pretty sure it is," said Mandy, "It all fits too." Mandy placed a finger on the photo in front of Sean, and another on the picture of their apartment building. "These buildings occupied the same site. There was no record of any fire at this address because the Great Fire destroyed nearly the whole city. The archives didn't specify which buildings were destroyed because just about all of them were."

"Oh wow," said Sean, "that happened right here. Poor kid..." Sean scrunched his forehead, stared at Noble a little longer, then began flipping through the other photos: "Is the woman ghost in any of these ... you know, M—"

"Don't say her name," cautioned Mandy. "And no she's not. I looked."

Tony insisted on making three more of the boxes. When he showed up at Sean's door with an armload of his "ghost boxes" and his tool kit, Sean raised an eyebrow. "I understand that you think Mary might show up uninvited, but what are the other two boxes for?"

"It's good to be prepared," the older man responded. "You never know. Me, I carry an umbrella. Better to carry an umbrella a few days in the sun than wish you had an umbrella in the day of the rain."

Sean spoke to Tony, but his words were for Mandy, "We're not putting Noble in a box; he's on our side!"

"Yes, you have explained. May I see the pictures of the boy, Mandy?" Tony placed the wooden boxes on the floor and sat at the table. He kept his tool kit close to his right hand.

"I have lots of pictures, but there is only one of Noble. It's not very good resolution but you can definitely see that it's him."

Mandy produced the envelope, flipped through some sheets and laid one in front of Tony. Tony peered at the photo, then fished a pair of glasses out of his jacket pocket and put them on. "Ah there he is indeed! I wonder what he thinks of this."

"When we showed it to him—" began Mandy.

"I can ask him myself," said Tony. He cleared his throat. "Noble! Noble! Come here please."

Sean looked at Mandy. She shrugged. There was a knock at the door.

"Well let him in!" said Tony impatiently.

Sean went to his apartment door. "Who is it?" he called.

"The boy is answering you. You just cannot hear! Open the door."

Sean pulled the door open a crack and peered out into the hallway. "Who's there?" he called. There was the sound of laughter behind him. Sean turned and saw that Noble had manifested across the table from Tony. Sean could see that they were both laughing, although only Tony could be heard. Sean shut the door hard.

"Come on Sean; let's put on some tea. I'm sure Hector will be here soon."

Sean shrugged and allowed Mandy to pull him into the kitchen. A moment or two later, Tony's voice rang out. "Sean could you roll up Noble a bit? He's a bit difficult to see and hear. Or maybe I'm just old." Tony laughed, then after a paused he added, "Noble says that it's not age—after all neither of you can hear him!" Tony chuckled some more, "That's very true Noble, very true."

"Noble Peter Hastings! Noble Peter Hastings!" said Sean through clenched teeth.

Mandy was correct. The water had scarcely begun to boil when there was another knock on the door. Sean walked out of his kitchen. Tony and Noble were having an animated conversation.

"And why did she use the dog's blood?" puzzled Tony. Noble's nearly translucent hands described a figure in the air. Noble's mouth moved. "Oh," said Tony, "of course the blood would still be warm…"

"Could you disappear for a bit, Noble? Hector's at the door," asked Sean.

Tony turned to Sean, "Why don't you just unsummon him?"

Noble's face turned sour.

"Unsummoning is not the same as making a Dead'er invisible. Dead'ers can become invisible at will, while unsummoning actually hurts," said Sean in a hard tone. Noble nodded in agreement, said a few words to Tony and disappeared.

"Unsummoning also puts a Dead'er out of action for a bit. And I'm counting on Noble to help us figure out what's going on," continued Sean.

The knock at the door became more insistent. "Coming," called Sean.

It was Hector at the door, looking lively and even more tanned than usual. He had a knapsack over one shoulder.

"It was a beautiful trip," said Hector once he had entered and placed his bag on the floor. "First few days I visited my home town. Ah, mother's cooking! Then I set out to do your errand. I brought some of my family with me. They insisted, and it was a good idea. My little sister is beautiful; she is like you Mandy. And who can resist when a beautiful girl asks you to do something? I explained everything to my little sister, and she spoke to the families. She was so charming. It was very easy to exchange the ashes. I believe that I have ashes of your friend's boy here." Hector patted the knapsack.

"That's great Hector! Thank you so much."

"Can we see the ashes?" asked Sean.

Hector looked sheepish. "First my friends, I need to explain something to you."

Chapter Twenty-Three

"Even You Noble?"

Noble:

Hector unwrapped the cake and placed it in the middle of Sean's dining room table.

"A cake!" said Mandy, "What are we going to do with a cake?"

Hector threw his arms up, "I didn't have much choice! Any kind of powder they would stop me. Even if not drugs, they would ask so many questions. I had to do something no one would suspect!"

Remains are remains I thought to myself. Inside a Mexican fruitcake or not, if those are Steven's ashes, then he was here, finally. It was Sean, surprisingly, who pointed out the problem.

"We can't put a cake in the Butler's urn! Now we are in a real mess. They'll eventually notice that the urn is empty and we don't have ashes to put back in it before they do."

"It's not empty," said Tony. The others looked at him. "That boy, Th—, Th—?"

"Ty," said Mandy.

"Yes, the boy who talks big. He put sand in the urn. So they will not miss their son's ashes."

Mandy frowned, "Well that doesn't solve the problem of how we get these ashes to the Butlers."

Hector looked shocked, "I thought you had me change the ashes as a favour to a friend. Now you are telling me that they don't know you've taken their son's ashes away?"

"Not exactly," Mandy said in an apologetic voice. "Like I told you it wasn't their son that they had in their urn. So it wasn't his remains that you returned to Mexico—there had been a mix-up."

Hector waved a warning finger at Mandy, "Yes, at the crematorium. I know; I made all those phone calls. But now it seems like you stole the ashes to make the switch. Why?"

"We weren't sure that the Butlers would let us make the switch," argued Mandy.

"Then why do you care?"

"Because we need to bring the son home!" said Tony. He turned to me, "Now Noble, you can introduce us to your friend Steven. But maybe first you pick up this box and put it on the table so our friend Hector can see that you are here!"

I was not about to manifest and pick up a box and call out to Steven or anything else with Hector present. One thing I had learned in years of being a Dead'er is that most Lye'vers would rather not know that we exist. They like the world that they can see best of all. Our world of moving dead things and manifestations only frightens them. They would not like to know how many haunts they pass through every day. Even if most Dead'ers are too feeble to manifest a finger, or move a dust ball, they still watch, wait and hope. Maybe someday a Stringer will chance to read their name off a tombstone, or on back of an old photograph. Maybe someday a relative or friend will mention a deceased one, and a Stringer, hearing the name, will picture the deceased or echo their name, and that Dead'er will roll up for a while. This is what we Dead'ers wait for. This is why we try not to let ourselves fade down all the way. Because when we roll up it's like, well, being alive.

"Come on, you, Noble. Pick up this box." Tony pushed at one of his boxes with his foot.

I don't know what Tony was thinking but he wasn't my Stringer. I didn't have to do what he said.

"Sean, you make the boy ghost pick up this box. It will show Hector that you know what you are doing!" Tony turned to Sean.

"Ok," said Sean.

It was like Tony had some control over Sean, as if he were Sean's father or something. Mr. Hallman used to do that to me. He would say things for me to do that I didn't have to do. But he said them as if he expected me to do them just because he asked in that certain way. I hated it then too.

I felt the attention of the Lye'vers in the room turn on me. It rolled me up but sieved me down at the same time. I went to the box and picked it up and put it on the table in front of Tony.

Hector pointed that the box, cursed and then crossed himself. "What are you doing? Is this devil-something?"

"No," said Mandy. "Noble is not evil at all. He's a good kid."

"A kid!" questioned Hector.

"Yes, it's just a boy." Tony turned back to Sean. "Make him show himself."

Sean turned his attention to me. I manifested against my will. In seconds I was clearly visible, even to Hector who was no Stringer or even a Voyant. I hadn't known that this was possible. My whole body showed, even the parts I normally kept hidden, out of modesty. It was horrible. I hated Tony for doing this. I hated Sean for shaming me and my shame was not Hector's fault, but I hated him too because he could see me naked and I could not cover myself.

"Maybe that's enough visibility. Hector now knows what we are dealing with," said Mandy. "You can let Noble go now Sean."

"No. Put him in the box. It will be safer for him there when we call the other ghosts." Tony folded his arms across his chest, "Much safer for the boy, Sean."

"Why would they want to hurt Noble?" Mandy looked from Sean to Tony.

"Remember what happened to your kitchen! Remember how the woman ghost hurt you. They might hurt the boy this time." Tony shot a glance at Mandy, "They might hurt your girlfriend this time too. So put the boy in the box where he will be safe. Then you send the girlfriend to her apartment. She will be safe. They cannot cross the wood to get her."

"Sean don't do that to him!" Mandy cried but Sean had not even hesitated before doing what Tony asked. I felt myself slide into the dark box. I was afraid, not of the dark but of the unknown. I had never been confined before. I had no stories like some of the others had, of waiting till the coffin rotted before they could reach out to others. Or of being buried in a sewn canvas bag, worse than wood because there were no seams through which the Dead'er could try to escape or through which the Dead'er, even if he could not escape, could perceive some traces of the world beyond. I could not tell who closed and latched the lid of the box: I could hear and see nothing.

When Mary was confined there must have been some tiny gap or space in the wood of her box: something that would have allowed her to perceive Sean, and so focus an attack on him. I searched, and searched and searched. There was no such gap in my box.

"Come out where I can see you. Please. Please."

It was Mandy's voice. I must have been outside the box. I was ... I was not sure where I was for several moments.

"Noble. Noble."

I could hear her and there was no strength for me in her name-calling but I was feeling some strength gather in me nevertheless. I must have been close to my remains: I was under my building. I knew my way through the space and ducts. I was by her side in seconds. I manifested. We were in the laundry room. The box was broken at one end and a hammer lay nearby.

"I couldn't work the latch," said Mandy apologetically. "Anyway, thank goodness you are ok."

I nodded.

"I'm sorry Sean did that to you. I took box out of the room with me when they made me leave. I'm really glad I did now." Mandy looked at me.

"What are Sean and that other Stringer up to?"

"I'm sorry, Noble, I can't read your lips. Just nod if you understand me."

I nodded.

"I think Sean is in trouble. I heard him yell in pain and then furniture breaking or something. I think that the Dead'er that we brought back from Mexico attacked him."

"That's not possible!" I said, "Steven needs Sean's help to get to his parents place."

"I can't understand what you are saying Noble! Look. I want you to go into Sean's apartment and find out what is going on. I can't get in; the door is locked."

"But the other Stringer boarded everything up, even the windows."

"I know you're thinking that you can't get in, but you can use the heating ducts." Mandy pointed at the opening in the ceiling. "You told me that you can come here from Sean's kitchen!"

What Mandy didn't understand was that I had promised Sean that I would not "ghost" into his apartment. I only used the door—even when summoned. I was not a Purging ghost like Mary!

"Please Noble! Please," said Mandy. "We helped you; now help us."

I was gone before Mandy finished her sentence. I knew the heating ducts. In an old building with so much wood, the ducts where are good way to get around. I was up in Sean's apartment in an instant.

Something had gone terribly wrong. All three of the Lye'vers were in trouble. Sean was pinned underneath one of his own dining room chairs. The chair had been laid on its back across Sean's chest. I could not see the Dead'er holding him there, but it whoever it was, he was very strong. Sean threw his weight from left to right but the chair was not moving. Every few moments Sean gripped each side of the chair and pushed upwards as if he were bench pressing weights. Neither of his actions moved the chair the least bit. There was a look of despair in Sean's eyes. He was yelling desperately, trying to unsummon Steven James Butler, but his unsummoning had no effect. The Dead'er who had him pinned was crushing him.

The other Stringer, Tony, was trapped under the overturned dining room table. His head and chest were free of the table but his head was rolled to one side and he looked unconscious. Hector's cake lay on the wooden floor nearby. In Tony's hand was some kind of tool. It looked like a large nail gun.

Hector's immobilization astonished me most. His shirt and pants were spread out against the wall, as if stuck there by a great blast of wind. He was imprisoned by his clothing. I was stunned to see this. Every Dead'er I had met who was strong enough to move objects, moved them as if by hand.

I thought that we Dead'ers could only move things as we did when we were alive, with our hands, feet, elbows, mouth, with any body part, but only with our body, shaped and sized as it was at the moment of our death.

Now I saw that such a limitation was only because of our lack of strength and will. A single Dead'er held Hector against wall and its ability to do so was not limited by any physical dimensions. I sensed too, that the same Dead'er that had imprisoned Hector was furiously searching the room. There was something it wanted as desperately as if its existence depended on it.

Dead'er who had Sean pinned beneath the chair, spoke to me. "Join us brother," he said.

I recognized that voice: It was Pedro or Steven—or neither.

"Your Stringer tried to sieve us down into those Purging boxes." His voice told me where to look. It was as clear as if he had pointed. That was something else I had not known we Dead'ers could do.

Two of the wooden boxes were on floor next to the overturned table and Tony's unconscious form.

"He would have succeeded too if he had known our names!" said the Dead'er.

"Aren't you Steven?" I said aloud.

Both Dead'ers laughed. It was a cruel sound.

I shouted at him, "Who are you then and where is Steven?"

"Your Steven's remains are still in Mexico, somewhere."

"But I saw Steven's picture," I protested, "I'm sure that he's a Dead'er."

"Then, yes, he must be a Dead'er! Wherever his remains are!" Both Dead'ers laughed again.

I thought for a moment, "Tell me your names then. I want to know who you are. I want to be powerful like you."

The Dead'er holding Sean spoke again. "You can be. I can show you how to be strong but we need you to take care of this Summoner first." His voice indicated Sean. "He's dangerous. And take care of that Stringer too." He pointed his voice to mean Tony. "He's not dangerous to us but he won't help us. We need Stringers who will help! Mary's Stringer will do nicely once we get her out of the way. You want us to get rid of Mary for you; don't you?"

"How will you do that? You can't hurt another Dead'er!"

"There's a lot we can do that you don't know." The Dead'er looked into me like he could read my thoughts. "We can help you find Gavin!"

"Is he a Dead'er? Can you reach out to him. Is he...?"

"Enough questions! We need you to take care of these two. We cannot sieve them down for much longer! Prove your loyalty and we will help you." He reached into my thoughts and answered my question, "No we cannot kill Lye'vers directly but there ways to set things in motion that will do it for us."

When he reached into my thoughts it was as if he opened a tiny hole into me, and peered in at what I was thinking, but to look into me he had to open himself as well. I perceived his thoughts like a picture visible only during the moment that lightning strikes.

I turned my attention to the other Dead'er, the one who had not spoken. I saw now that he was the true threat. He was an old and terribly powerful being. He knew no fear of Dead'ers like me, and concealed none of his thoughts from me. He could not speak because had no modern language, and had probably seen dozens of languages come and go. He understood, nevertheless, all that we were thinking. He needed no Stringer to be what he was. All he needed was to be summoned in this new place from his physical remains and Sean had already done this.

His remains where here in the roiling room, baked into the cake along with those of the Dead'er I had thought was Steven or Pedro.

The Dead'er who called himself Pedro had persuaded someone to move both their ashes into the cache that Hector had gone to retrieve. I had been deceived. It was my fault that these two evil beings where now in my city, and worse, in my haunt.

Dead'er who held Sean read my thoughts again, "I should thank you and your Summoner for bringing us here. Thanks to you, we are in this young city with so few Dead'ers that there are almost none who could interfere with us. Most here are too weak to perceive us. Few are as powerful as you and Mary. You are thinking of Mary now. Now you see that Mary perceived my deception and tried to warn you but you believe that she is inarticulate, and half-mad. You've never listened to anything she's tried to tell you. However, I cannot sense her presence anymore. Perhaps your Summoner has already destroyed her."

I thought of Sean. The Dead'er read my thoughts again and I read his. I saw that while I held no threat for either of them, they were terrified of Sean. They needed Sean's power summon to them out of their remains but were now afraid that his power could destroy them as well. Despite the calm with which the Dead'er spoke to me his terror of Sean was driving him to a fury.

It was the fury of the older powerful Dead'er that terrified me. He was searching the room for an escape. He knew that if he managed to escape this trap it would be easy to catch Sean unawares. His terror and frustration were growing as he pushed again and again against the walls of the apartment but met only the wooden barriers.

I thought of Tony. He had known somehow what to expect. Had Mary told him? He had brought three boxes. One to destroy each of these evil ghosts and the third—to destroy me!

The talkative Dead'er continued, "Now you see why you must help us: this Summoner will destroy you too."

"Where are the matches?" The Dead'er asked me in thought. He had hit upon a way to destroy Sean. He would hold Sean down while the wood frame building burnt to the ground.

I thought of anything I could to keep my mind from wandering to Sean's kitchen. If the apartment burned not only Sean and Tony, neither of whom I trusted, would die, but so would Hector. Others in the building could die too, including Mandy.

I pointed to Hector with my thoughts. "Release him. I'll need him to get the matches." I felt the ancient Dead'er who held Sean send a wave of mistrust outwards, but I filled my thoughts with the sights and sounds of death by fire. Such a thing I knew from my own experience. In the burning, I replaced my own self-image with that of Sean. The older Dead'er brought this into his thoughts. Hector tumbled to the floor.

I partially manifested in front of Hector and pointed to the kitchen entrance. Hector ignored me and rushed to Tony. He pushed open Tony's eyelids and peered into his pupils. He took Tony's pulse.

"Make him get the matches!" commanded the Dead'er.

"He will!" I shouted back. "But he cannot see me."

The silent Dead'er poured something into me. I felt a greater power, and something new as well. It was control. I manifested in front of Sean. Then I let my image waver and grow indistinct.

"Roll me up," I mouthed as clearly as I could.

Sean mumbled something. I heard only the final few syllables, "or 12-16…"

New strength filled me. What in my memory was like it? The sudden shock of cold water as Gavin and I jumped in the ocean inlet in May. Stepping on the needle. Seeing Gavin's grave.

I allowed my image to become more distinct. I spoke, and Sean, watching my face seemed to understand me. "Tell Hector to get the first aid kit from the bathroom, and bring the matches too!"

Sean repeated my commands to Hector. Hector jumped at the mention of the medicines and ran through the kitchen to the bathroom.

"Why are you wasting time?" shouted the Dead'er. In response I flooded my mind with more images of the fire. This time I showed Tony, conscious and therefore suffering, writhing in the flames. The older, silent Dead'er sent me a message of acceptance. He greatly approved of cruelty. He fed on pain. His memories flashed open to me. There was a brief image of a chest cut open, and joy in violence.

Hector ran back with the first aid kit. He had already unlatched the kit and now held it open in one hand. He also had the box of matches. He knelt by Tony, unscrewed a vial and held it under Tony's nose. Tony stirred. His head shook. Hector placed his hand under Tony's head and sat back on his haunches.

I moved onto the upended table, manifested a bit more and pressed the table down on to Tony. Tony groaned. His eyes widened. He saw that it was I grinding him beneath the table and shook his head.

"Make this stop!" Hector said to Sean.

"Tell him to strike the matches and I will," I said aloud. The other Dead'ers laughed.

I filled my mind with thoughts of hate for Tony and for Sean. My lips moved silently. Tony looked at my mouth questioningly. There was a knock at the door. The knock was followed by the sound of Mandy's voice.

"Sean are you ok?"

"Don't let her come in!" said Tony. "Keep the door closed! We must keep these creatures in here."

"We're not going anywhere while that Summoner exists!" While holding the table down I reached across the room and pulled the matches from Hector's grasp. I struck the wooden matchsticks against the underside of the table. There was a brilliant flash of light as the matches all lit at once. I pressed the burning pieces of wood against the matchbox and then let the whole ball of flame drop down onto the underside of the table. The table began to burn beautifully.

The Older Dead'er shone joyously at the sight of the flame. Hector saw that I was not about to release Tony and ran to Sean and tried to pull the chair off him. The Dead'er holding Sean responded to Hector's charge by picking up the chair dashing it against Hector's head. Hector groaned and crumpled to the ground. I saw blood. Both Dead'ers laughed. Sean, who had been struggling to breath under the chair, drew in a deep breath.

I discharged all the strength I had been saving into my manifestation. I appeared as solid as I had ever been able to. "Tell her to go down to the laundry room!" I screamed down at Tony.

"Noble, is that your voice! I heard you. I heard you," Mandy shouted through the door.

"Then Purging do it! I screamed back!" I turned my attention to Tony, "Tell Sean to do it now!"

Sean's hoarse voice sounded, "Do what Noble? I can hear you too."

"Unsummon us all." I said.

"I can't; I don't know their names! I can't do anything," cried Sean.

"Yes you can. Unsummon us all. All of us!"

"Even you Noble?"

I looked at Sean. "You have no choice." I swung the burning table off Tony and slammed it down onto the cake. With all my strength I ground the cake flat between the wooden table and the floor. The Dead'ers could not retreat into their remains.

The Dead'ers screamed at me. They dove into me, ripping and tearing at my thoughts. It was as if they wished to leave me as senseless as Mary had become. I thought of Gavin.

Sean opened his mouth. "I unsummon you all! I unsummon…"

I heard no more. I couldn't hear anymore…

Chapter Twenty-Four

"It's About Time!"

The building manager scuffed at the charred sections of the parquet flooring. The corners of his mouth were turned down.

"It was a grease fire," said Sean. "I need to be much more careful when I'm—frying—I think," his voice trailed off.

"Grease fire?" snorted the manager. There were scorch marks across one of the walls and soot marks on the ceiling. The manager scratched at one of the dark streaks. "You cook here, in the living room?"

"Umm," Sean looked at Tony.

"Look at this. Is pretty bad," said Tony.

"I'll say," said the manager. He flicked some soot from underneath a fingernail. "Maybe we can get away with just repainting this wall—the ceiling too: should be ok with a bit of sanding and some paint—but the floor," he shook his head. "You can't even get this stuff anymore. That kind of woodwork costs a fortune."

"Is really bad," said Tony.

"True enough. I'm thinking maybe eight, nine hours on the sanding, and painting—plus materials of course. That's just the walls and ceiling. The floor—I don't know. Sanding, filling. And then laying the carpet." The manager scratched at his underarm. "It's going to be an expensive month for you Hughes."

"But you no look here yet," said Tony. He was standing near the entrance to the kitchen.

"Did I miss something?" the manager laughed. "I hope you can pick up extra shifts at that dealership, Hughes. The labour alone is probably going to be a couple months' rent."

"You look at this, now," said Tony.

They followed Tony's outstretched finger.

"Oh," said Sean.

"So?" said the manager.

"I check the batteries; she's dead," said Tony. The three men stared at the smoke detector.

"Hmm," said the manager, breaking the silence. "I'll get on that right away. I'll have new batteries in there by this time tomorrow."

"No good, change battery after the fire," smiled Tony. "Maybe Sean, you make phone call now."

"Oh," said the manager nervously.

"Maybe this young man, no pay for labour. I show him how to paint walls, ceiling. I fix floor."

"You'll lay the carpet?"

"No carpet," said Tony, "I fix floor."

"This stuff is expensive!" said the manager.

"No problem, for me," said Tony "You pay."

The manager looked at the smoke detector. He swore under his breath.

Once they began the repairs Tony estimated that it would take he and Sean at least a month to restore the apartment. Mandy helped as much as her schedule permitted. Sean welcomed her presence, especially as she seemed to enjoy holding things in position for him, like the sheets of plywood Tony insisted that they add to some of the walls, or the small geometric strips of wood for the floor. Sean liked the satisfaction of nailing things into place. When Mandy wasn't present Sean had to hold things with his left hand. This was difficult. His palm and forearm were still bandaged. Two of his ribs had also been cracked in the attack.

Even Hector came by to help a few times. He was initially reluctant to re-enter Sean's apartment. For him, the events of that evening were even more terrifying than they were for Sean and Tony—who had understood, while Hector had not, that the two ghosts had wanted to kill them. He had heard and seen none of the threats. Hector had seen an apparition of a boy appear and disappear at Sean's command. Then Mandy was told to leave and took one of the wooden boxes with her. As soon as she was gone Tony opened the other two boxes and Sean spoke to the cake! Then there was a strange cold moment before the dining table upended and crushed Tony unconscious beneath its weight. A possessed chair had levitated and struck Sean and then pinned him to the ground. Hector tried to run to Tony but before he could reach the man, he was seized by something pulling at his clothes. The best description he could give the others was that it was like being inside a giant washing machine on its spin cycle. He was pressed flat to the wall by his own clothing, unable to move and shivering with cold.

Hector was not sure how long his torture lasted. He only knew that as soon as he was released he fell to the floor. He heard Sean shouting to get a first aid kit and matches from the bathroom. Hector got the kit and used ammonia salts to revive Tony. Perhaps not the best thing he might have done with an unconscious patient, but Hector did not think he would be able to remove Tony from danger without Tony helping to move himself.

Hector tried to move the table off of Tony but found himself unable to even shift the weight. He heard Mandy asking to be let back into the apartment, and then he heard Tony, having regained consciousness, begging him not to open the door.

Hector did not question why Sean had sent him for the matches but was shocked when something that felt like a cold invisible hand grabbed the matches from his grip. The matches flew over to the overturned table, lit themselves on fire and then ignited the table too. Hector thought that if he could free Sean then together they could get Tony to safety. Hector charged at the possessed chair that held Sean, but the chair ducked out of his way and spun and struck him across the forehead. Hector felt himself grow dizzy and he lost his balance. He fell to the floor. From there he saw the burning table levitate off Tony then slam itself down in the middle of the living room.

Everyone was now free thought Hector. Now we can escape. Hector stood up and ran for the apartment door but Tony grabbed his ankle so that Hector tripped and fell again. "Not yet! Not yet! Go Sean. Go!" Tony cried. Sean chanted something unintelligible. Hector's skin tingled. There was a feeling as if some twisted knot or terrible bubble of tension in the room abruptly burst. Then warmth suddenly flooded in and banished the cold dread that had gripped Hector. Hector got to his feet but this time ran to Sean's couch. He pulled open the folding bed and tugged the sheets free. Hector threw the sheets and then himself onto the burning table. To his surprise Tony joined him in trying to smother the flames. Sean stayed where he was and continued chanting something under his breath.

It was almost ten minutes before they opened the door to admit Mandy. By that time the fire was out but opening the door had caused smoke to stream out into the hallway where it alarmed the neighbours.

After apartment door had been propped open, Tony unfastened the wooden boards that had been secured over the glass windows, and unlatched them to let in fresh air. "I'm afraid that everything you own is going to smell of smoke," he said to Sean.

Sean spoke quietly to Mandy and when the firemen arrived almost twenty minutes later Sean was chanting again, barely pausing the acknowledge the fireman's admonition to make sure, that in the future, he always had a working fire extinguisher on hand in his kitchen.

Tony insisted that they rid themselves of the balance of the cake and ashes as quickly as possible. "It seems that Sean's unsummoning worked but maybe it's not good to take chances." They discussed burying the remains of the cake in one of the wooden boxes but Tony pointed out that anything buried maybe dug up again. After Sean consulted the tide tables, they agreed to dispose of the material the very next Sunday afternoon.

They took Tony's car. He parked near the seawall and together they walked out onto the waterside platform. There were a number of benches situated so that they looked out across the water to the North Shore of Burrard Inlet. Sean placed the box on one of the benches and then sat next to it. Tony and Mandy joined him. They did not speak for a few minutes. Mandy held Sean's hand. When it was clear that the crest of the high tide had passed and that the water had begun to flow out of the inlet, Sean let go of Mandy, picked up the box and rose from the bench. He stood for a while at the edge of the platform. The water at his feet looked deep and cold. Bits of seaweed and foam were running out to sea with the turning tide.

Mandy sighed, "Evil or not. It's hard to accept that you're probably ending another creature's existence."

"They are not like us," said Tony.

"But they were at one time," replied Mandy, "and if they could hate then they could also love."

Sean opened the lid of the box and shook its contents out into the inlet. Ash and bits of half-burnt cake fell out of the box and dissipated in the salt water. Mandy stood and joined Sean. She hooked her arm into his. They looked towards the open ocean, where the current was sure to take the debris.

After some time Mandy turned and looked behind her to where Tony sat on the bench. He met her gaze and fixed a thoughtful look on her. "Maybe it would be good for you to meet my wife," he said.

"I think I'd like that," replied Mandy. She returned to looking at the water, resting her head against Sean's shoulder. "One thing I still don't understand," she asked, turning to face Tony again. "How did you know that you would need three boxes? In fact why did you bring any boxes at all? We didn't know that Hector was bringing two Dead'ers from Mexico, and that they were dangerous and evil. We were only expecting another boy like Noble."

"Mary," said Tony, "She was screeching out hysterical warnings about the two fantasma from Mexico. Neither of you heard of course, because both of you were essentially deaf when it comes to fantasma."

"And why the third box?"

"Was for the boy fantasma." He paused, and addressed Sean. "It is better you have no dealings with these things. You can see how much trouble they bring you. What did I tell first time about ghosts? Only a crazy man sees ghost. If you want to be crazy you see ghost too! If you no want to be crazy don't look for no ghost."

"But Noble…" began Mandy.

"The best thing is now that boy ghost is gone, you forget him. You are nice girl, Mandy. You are a nice boy, Sean. You have each other. You need nothing else. Nothing. And ghost is nothing but trouble." Tony fell silent. After a time Sean and Mandy rejoined him on bench. The couple sat close together, but left some space on the bench between themselves and the older man.

When the evening grew cool. Tony and Sean looked at each other, nodded and stood up. Mandy joined them. The three of them walked back to the parked car without speaking. Somewhere on the drive home, Mandy lifted her head from Sean's chest and raised her face to his. They kissed briefly, smiled at each other and then kissed again. Tony, seeing them in the rear view mirror, laughed aloud. "It's about time!" he said.

"I know," said Sean. "I've been waiting a good long time for this."

"Next time," countered Mandy, "don't wait so long before making your move!"

When they reached their apartment building Mandy exited first. Sean watched her climb the few steps to their front door. Sean lingered at the car. Once she was out of hearing, he leaned down to the car driver's window to speak to Tony. "Don't worry. You'll hear no more about ghosts from me."

Tony nodded approvingly. He drove off and just before turning the corner he blew the horn and waved out the open car window.

Sean waved back with his bandaged hand.

Noble:

As soon as Sean's unsummoning went out I made for the heating duct. I perceived that the talking Dead'er, the one who had been pretending to be Pedro or Steven, was completely caught in the outward wave of unsummoning. He may have tried to flee but he would have found nowhere that he could go. The Stringer, Tony, had done a good job of sealing Sean's apartment. The other Dead'er the old, evil one, perceived me race away, and surely would have thought that I was trying to escape, but I also sensed a swell of futility soak through him. He did not expect to survive. While holding Hector captive, he had been probing the apartment for an escape and had found none. I suppose he knew nothing about central heating. In that last moment he despaired. I sensed this and sensed too that his despair freed the younger Dead'er who had been enthralled.

I only remember approaching the heating duct. The effort to reach it ate up the last of my will and strength. Then there was nothing more, not blackness, not darkness. Nothing.

I was with my mother and with Gavin. We faced each other cross-legged on some clean plain surface. We ate, together, from a large bowl on the ground in front of us. We laughed at what each other said, not caring that our mouths were full of food, because it was such great joy to fill our stomachs.

I could not see, and did not care, what was beyond us: walls or trees or mountains, maybe even others: I did not know.

Gavin spoke about going to see his father's people. He would travel by canoe for they lived on an inlet up the coast, four days of paddling away.

I said that I would go with Gavin, and that I would help him with the journey and that I would bring some gift with me.

We all laughed because I had never been in a canoe. And the others said that I would be more of a hindrance than a help! But then Gavin said that he would teach me everything I needed to know. My mother said that she was happy that I was going and that she would help me make the gift. My mother placed a hand on both of our shoulders.

Then there was blackness; I was in a place with no thought of time or no understanding who I was. Then I was merely in the dark; time passed and I knew I was a being. Then, at last, I knew where I was—and knew too that I wanted to go back to where I had just been. I did not know if that place with my mother and Gavin was only made of memory and imagination—or if it was some real place and time. I think it was what a Lye'ver would call heaven. I could ask what is real for Dead'er—and never find anyone to answer. Nevertheless that place and time were now gone and I was in the dank space beneath my building. No doubt I was with my remains for I could feel that I had survived a terrible, desperate unsummoning. Now, I was being rolled up. Somewhere, above, a Stringer was calling me by name and, more powerful than his uttering of my name, he was calling me by his knowledge of me. This Stringer had pulled me back from where I had been, and had pulled me once again into my remains, and now summoned me up out of them.

I lifted myself up off my remains and drifted upward. I perceived new knowledge in me. I could move my essence in a way that bore no relation to the form of the boy that I had seen myself occupy in the dream or memory I had just been woken from. I flowed through the gravel and rock under the foundation of the building and then up through the concrete and into its basement. The paneled walls were opaque to me but I probed them till I found an opening a little wider than a boy's fist. It was covered by a metal grate. I migrated through the grate and selected from the network of branching metal tubes one that led to the upper levels of this structure. I noted how the metal tubes formed a pathway of tunnels throughout the building that bypassed the alarming wooden barriers of the floors and walls. This building could be a prison for a Dead'er. I followed the path that led to the voice of the Stringer.

I emerged into a room I recognized as Sean's kitchen. I remember writing to him in flour on its floor.

I manifested, "You called me?"

Sean and Mandy stood on either side of me. It was clear that they had been waiting for me to emerge from the heating duct. I turned to Mandy.

"Yes, Noble we did." Mandy looked into my eyes. I was happy that she could hear me. Maybe, I thought, her powers might grow into those of a Stringer. I could have then, a Stringer I could trust. I perceived that Sean, moving behind me, had deftly slid a wooden plug into the duct opening from which I had emerged. I dissolved my manifestation and shot out of the kitchen and into Sean's living room. As I feared, the door was closed and windows were boarded. I re-manifested in front of Sean. I wanted to look him in the face as he unsummoned me.

"He mistrusts you Sean!" said Mandy. "Maybe you shouldn't cover his exit."

Sean reopened the duct. "You are free to leave if you wish Noble, but I won't be having this duct open all the time. I've decided to be more cautious with my safety … with everything that's happened."

Memories came to me that made me ashamed. Everything bad that had happened to Sean was my fault: Mary's attacks, the battle in the apartment, the fire, Sean's injuries. None of these things would have happened if I had left Sean alone. It was my need for a Stringer than had led me to trust the voice I thought was Pedro.

"I'm sorry," I said.

"We don't blame you, Noble." Mandy's voice came from behind me. "You couldn't have known what you were dealing with … or about evil. You are really just a boy."

"And I don't mind being a Stringer actually. It kinda makes me feel powerful." said Sean, "and I appreciate your help with Mandy." He went to her and kissed her, actually kissed her!

"We got something to show you," said Mandy. "Have a look on the dining room table."

I disappeared from the kitchen, where I had been between Sean and Mandy, and re-manifested instantly, hovering over the Sean's new dining room table.

"It's going to take a while for me to get used to his new powers," said Sean.

"Or your own, Mr. Summoner," added Mandy.

They joined me at the table where Mandy had laid out a series of photographs. I could tell it was Mandy who had touched the photos most recently. A trace of all the Lye'vers who had touched the photos came off the papers to me like an odour. Mandy's traces were the strongest of all the ones on the sheets. I could also tell that Sean had only handled one of the photos. I picked that picture up and studied it.

"Oh that's freaky," said Mandy.

I re-manifested myself as if I were a Lye'ver: a figure standing next to the table, with the photo in one hand. I added a special touch this time, smoothing the edge of my form, except that of my head and hands—which I kept distinct, so that even though I might still appear nearly solid to a Lye'ver, it would seem also that I was wearing clothing.

"Much better," said Mandy. "By the way Noble, we weren't sure at first that you had survived. When you told me to go to the laundry room I figured that you were going come down the duct to meet me. But what came out of the duct was nothing like any form I'd seen you in. It was some sort of coalesced mist. It flowed out of the duct almost like a liquid. I'd never seen anything like it. I caught as much as of it as I could in the wooden box—The one I had broken open earlier to get you out of. Then I ran up the steps to the front door and opened the box on the ground next to the building. When I went up to the apartment, I told Sean about what I had done, and he started to try to roll you up."

"Well I'm back!" I smiled.

"Yes you are," Mandy laughed. "It was an anxious month for us."

"A month…" I buried my surprise and turned my attention to the photo. I read the caption: South shore Burrard Inlet 1882. The photo was taken at some distance from the shoreline. The images of the people in the photo were correspondingly small and indistinct. On the shoreline itself, a stocky figure, most likely that of a Native woman, was hauling something from the water, probably a fishing net. Further inland, on what looked like the beginning of a road, there were a group of men that seemed to be loading or unloading barrels from a horse-drawn wagon. I scanned over several more individuals and clusters of figures. All seemed to be engaged in some sort of labour or activity—except for the group of smaller figures scattered on top of and in among the large rocks at the water's edge. These bodies were children at play. Two of them trapped my attention. I stared till I was sure. It was Gavin and I. And surely anyone in that room could have seen, Sean definitely, perhaps even Mandy, that both those figures, were Dead'ers.

Acknowledgments

I need to say thank-you to many, many people. There are hundreds in Vancouver and Toronto who have attended my performances, applauded, and said kind and generous words of praise. Thank you. Your encouragement has meant a great deal to me. I do not think I would have continued the work without it.

The people mentioned below are only a portion of the colleagues, family, friends, and students who have, with their time, effort, and talents assisted me in bringing my writing to the point where I am able to share it publically.

Ian Yuri Gardner, Gordon Albert Schmidt: you helped me find myself.

Wayde Compton, Jennifer Holland, Tess Kingston, Alyson Quinn: writers who saw to it that I knew I was a writer.

Editors, editors, editors: Paulo O'Connor, the insightful; Brent Power, the wunderkind; Peter-Brooks Sharpe, clever, clever man; and Mirela Skrijelj, the meticulous. They have helped with various manuscripts, some of which may soon see the light of publication or the stage. Any errors in this text, however, are my own fault.

Bev Cheung, for being the staging goddess. Marc Leblanc, for saying "You should write a ghost story next." Thanks to Steven Brouse, Sherwin Buydens, Debbie Cassells, Patrick Davidson, Steven R. Duncan, Vince Jiu, David Josephson, Harry James Leonard, Johnny MacGregor, Steven Miller, Matt O'Grady, Kathy Yoon-Richardson, David Sandford, Ariadne Sawyer, Pauline Veto, Owen Williams, and Nelson Wong for your suggestions and help with this project and others.

A special thanks to Shayne Niemiec and Kenny Mead for creative and design input.

Carl Blenman, and Chris Perrotte, just to name two representatives of a family that is always encouraging.

Speaking of family, my continued love and gratitude to the members of Chronicles, ACTS, CCM, Inter-A, and Rubid Theatre. You provided actors, crew, and a place to stage my dreams. And finally, CRS (&L) forever!

Thank you all.

Ghost-ary

Dead'er: What ghosts call themselves. A slang word. Residual, temporal-psychological manifestation is one of the more formal terms. But there is no consensus on the formal name. Some even use the word ghost. But many reserve that to mean the action that Dead'ers do when they wander from place to place looking for Stringers, or not.

Demanifest: To disappear or to make disappear. The opposite of manifest. See manifest.

Fading down: The tendency of a ghost to gradually lose the ability to see, hear, move, or interact with the physical world. Accelerated when a ghost is out of his/her haunt. A ghost will cease to exist if he or she fades down completely. See Zonker.

Ghost: An insult when used from one ghost to another. A more polite, but slang term is Dead'er.

Haunt: The area a ghost is able to go regularly, or to have effect. Normally limited to areas close to the ghost's physical remains.

Knockers: Great. From the idea that a ghost would be able to knock on doors—something they are rarely strong enough to do.

Lye'ver: Someone who is not dead. From the word alive. Pronounced Live-er. Most of the people in the world are in this condition. When they die, only a handful will become Dead'ers.

Manifest: To appear. A Dead'er with sufficient vigour can cause him or herself to appear to a Lye'ver that is a Stringer or a Voyant. Dead'ers can also be made to manifest against their will by Stringers who are also *Summoners*.

Purging: Swear word for ghosts. From Purgatory—meaning the world of the living—a place of torment and delight for ghosts. Ghosts do not believe in Heaven or Hell or any other after life.

Reaching out: When one ghost talks to another over a long distance. It saps their strength. Ghosts can only communicate with each other at night. The sun prevents them from having almost any effect at all.

Roll up: The opposite of fading down. Interacting with a Stringer rolls up a ghost.

Screeching: To get a rise out of living thing but annoying its main sense (hearing for dogs, sight for humans).

Sieve: To hold down a Dead'er so that he or she cannot move.

Snickered: Frustrated from reaching an objective or taking action, unable to proceed.

Stringer: A living person one who can help a ghost. Prevent them from fading down, usually by calling the ghost's name, thinking about the Dead'er, or by having an emotion towards the Dead'er. The strongest Stringers often also *Summoners*. They can almost coerce a Dead'er to appear.

Voyant: From clairvoyant. A non-Stringer who can nevertheless see or sense manifestations.

Work up: The term a ghost uses when he moves something. Normally, ghosts can, with difficulty and effort—hence the term work, move a newly dead object (like a fallen leaf) but not inorganic substances like rock or water.

Zonker: A ghost who fades down all the way.